LOST OR FOUND

Recent Titles by Graham Ison from Severn House

LOST OR FOUND

A Brock and Poole mystery

Graham Ison

This first world edition published in Great Britain 2007 by
SEVERN HOUSE PUBLISHERS LTD of
9–15 High Street, Sutton, Surrey SM1 1DF.
This first world edition published in the USA 2008 by
SEVERN HOUSE PUBLISHERS INC of
595 Madison Avenue, New York, N.Y. 10022.

British Library Cataloguing in Publication Data

Ison, Graham
  Lost or found
  1. Brock, Detective Inspector (Fictitious character) -
  Fiction 2. Poole, Detective Sergeant (Fictitious character)
  - Fiction 3. Police - England - London - Fiction 4. Missing
  persons - England - London - Fiction 5. Detective and
  mystery stories
  I. Title
  823.9'14[F]

  ISBN-13: 978-0-7278-6563-2   (cased)

All Severn House titles are printed on acid-free paper.

Typeset by Palimpsest Book Production Ltd.,
Grangemouth, Stirlingshire, Scotland.
Printed and bound in Great Britain by
MPG Books Ltd., Bodmin, Cornwall.

One

Curiously enough it was not a murder but a missing-person report that caused me to be assigned to the disappearance of Eunice Bailey.

A new enquiry was something of a relief, because we'd been coping with yet another reorganization and change of name. The boy superintendents at New Scotland Yard – that powerhouse of buzzwords – had obviously been busy. They'd decided that we were now to be called the Homicide and Serious Crime Command. I wondered just how many meetings and conferences had taken place in order to arrive at this breathtaking decision. And how many cups of coffee and fancy biscuits the Police Fund had paid for as a result. To say nothing of the overtime incurred by those lesser ranks still entitled to claim it.

The outcome of all this administrative upheaval was that I was now a part of one of four teams of investigators overseen by a detective superintendent. Above him was Detective Chief Superintendent Alan Cleaver, and even higher up, our beloved commander. The good bit, however, was that we were doing exactly the same job as before, and in the same place. *And* I had retained the services of Detective Sergeant Dave Poole, my black bag carrier.

Perhaps I should explain that. It's not the bag that's black, it's Dave Poole.

Dave is something of a character. For a start, he's married to a gorgeous white girl called Madeleine, a principal dancer with the Royal Ballet, and he has a good degree in English from London University. And that makes him very useful in a police force that, these days, is obsessed with putting everything down in writing. In quintuplicate.

'Ah, Mr Brock.' The commander entered my office – in itself unusual – waving a piece of paper. That was not unusual; the commander loves bits of paper.

'Good morning, sir,' I said rising to my feet.

The commander, unable to concentrate on two things at the same time, ignored my greeting. 'I've received a report from West End Central police station.'

'Really, sir?' Funny how the commander never calls it a nick, like the rest of us do. 'Something interesting, is it?'

'It emanates from a jeweller in the West End.' The commander peered at his piece of paper. 'It seems that a Mrs Eunice Bailey took her wedding ring there to have it enlarged. And she's not been back to collect it.'

'Is that it, sir?' I queried.

'That's all, Mr Brock. I want you to look into it.'

'But surely it's a missing-person enquiry, sir.'

'Indeed it is.' The commander spoke as though I was some-what slow at catching on, which I wasn't; but I was very quick at avoiding grief. 'It's possible that there are felonious under-tones.'

'What particular felonious undertone did you have in mind, sir?' I asked, risking a reproof for sarcasm. But I needn't have worried.

'That's for you to discover, Mr Brock.' The commander handed me the piece of paper, reluctantly, I thought. He hates parting with paper. 'The details of the jeweller are on there.' And with that, he left me to it.

I don't really know how this enquiry finished up with me. There is an entire department at New Scotland Yard that main-tains an index of missing persons. And persons go missing every day. In their hundreds. Most are fed up with their wives or husbands or children. Or their jobs or their in-laws. And there are a dozen other reasons that could cause them to take off. How on earth the commander read some felonious aspect into this particular missing person was a mystery to me. But if I knew how a commander's mind worked, I'd probably be a commander myself.

I put my head round the door of the sergeants' office and beckoned to Dave Poole. 'We're going to the West End, Dave.'

'Oh, how nice, guv. Sex club, is it?'

'No, a jeweller's.'

Hiding his disappointment, Dave put on his jacket and grabbed a vehicle logbook and a set of car keys.

'You'll never find anywhere to park a car, not since the

Mayor's reduced London's traffic congestion, Dave,' I said. 'We'll go on the Underground.'

A mistake. It was a stiflingly hot day, and I resented the convention that required senior CID officers to wear a tie and a jacket.

We walked to Westminster Tube station and eventually a train arrived.

'We'll have to change at Victoria to get a train to Green Park, guv.' Dave was jammed up against a young girl wearing shorts and the top half of a bikini, and who was avidly reading an Italian guidebook to London. Between Dave and me was a Swedish boy with a backpack that looked as though it contained all his worldly possessions, and took up the space of three other passengers.

At Victoria, we fought our way through countless itinerant musicians, a heaving mass of humanity, and sundry beggars, to the Victoria Line train for Green Park, and once again found ourselves sandwiched between tourists. God knows why these people want to come to London. I'd've thought that back-packing through Afghanistan was preferable any day.

Finally, we emerged in Piccadilly, to daylight and London's diesel-laden air.

A suave fellow in a tailcoat greeted us as we entered the impressive premises that housed the jeweller's establishment. His very demeanour and appearance indicated to my prac-tised eye that the merchandise would be highly priced.

'May I help you, sir?' The tailcoated one glanced suspi-ciously at Dave.

'We're police officers and we need to see the manager,' I said, waving my warrant card at him.

'Of course, sir.' Tailcoat seemed relieved that we weren't clients. I suppose he didn't fancy having us mixing with minor foreign royalty, rich illegal immigrants, Z-list soap stars, and footballers' wives. 'This way.'

Our leader piloted us across the thickly carpeted shop floor and up a flight of stairs, before knocking deferentially at a heavy oaken door.

The manager was, I suppose, in his mid-fifties, and was dressed in a Savile Row suit that must have cost more than I earned in a fortnight. He introduced himself as Giles Fancourt.

'I'm Detective Chief Inspector Harry Brock of Scotland Yard,' I said, having decided not to trot out Homicide and Serious Crime Command every time I introduced myself. 'And this is Detective Sergeant Poole.'

'And what can I do for you, gentlemen?' With a flourish of his hand, Fancourt indicated two expensive chairs with which his beautifully appointed office was furnished. I imagined them to be genuine antiques, but Dave later told me that they were reproduction Chippendales. He knows about things like that.

'I understand that you made a report to the police at West End Central police station regarding a Mrs Eunice Bailey, Mr Fancourt.'

'Ah yes. Mrs Bailey.' Fancourt leaned back in his high-backed leather executive chair and steepled his fingers. 'Let me see now . . . ' He shot forward and took a file from a desk drawer, and then glanced at a calendar. 'It was a month ago, Mr Brock. On the seventeenth of May to be precise.' I got the impression that Mr Fancourt was always precise. 'Mrs Bailey brought us her wedding ring. To cut a long story short, she complained that it was too tight on her finger, and enquired if we could remove it and enlarge it. One of our technicians – he's been with us for over twenty years – cut the ring from her finger and assured madam that an enlargement would not be a problem.'

'Is this technician here today?' asked Dave.

'Er, yes, of course.'

Dave glanced at me. 'D'you think we should have a word, sir?' He always called me 'sir' in the presence of civilians. Whenever he called me 'sir' in private, it meant something entirely different.

'Yes, good idea.' I glanced at Fancourt. 'Is that possible?' I asked.

'Indeed.' Fancourt pressed down a switch on his intercom. 'Celia, get hold of Higgins from the workshop for me, and ask him to come to my office.' He paused. 'Immediately.'

We waited for at least ten minutes for the man Higgins to appear. I suppose he was a valuable asset to the firm and therefore secure from interference from above. Or comments about his tardiness.

'You wanted me, Mr Fancourt?' He had wispy hair covering

an otherwise bald pate, and wore wire-framed spectacles with thick lenses.

'These gentlemen are police officers, Higgins. Tell them what you know about Mrs Bailey and her wedding ring.'

Higgins sniffed and sought inspiration from a John Constable print that adorned the wall behind the manager's head. 'Yeah, she said it was too tight, and wanted it enlarged. I had to cut it off of her finger – bit delicate that – and told her we could do the work.'

'Anything else, Mr Higgins?' asked Dave.

'Only that she asked if we could do it in a hurry. She said she never liked going around without having it on, being a married woman and that. Quite fussed about it, she was. In fact she was so touchy about it that she asked if I could do the work there and then. Well, that wasn't on, but I said I could do it in two days and I'd give her a call when it was ready. I suppose I took pity on her, mainly because she was quite a stunner. Soft touch for a pretty woman, me.'

Fancourt coughed affectedly at what he doubtless regarded as a sexist remark, but was ignored by the three of us.

'When you say she was a stunner, Mr Higgins, just what did she look like?'

'Thirty-five, she must've been. Lovely figure. And she had long blonde hair in one of them ponytails. Miniskirt and nice legs. And not short of a quid or two, neither.' Higgins chuckled and wiped his hands on his brown overall coat. 'There, how's that? Reckon I ought to be in your job.'

'Have you finished with Higgins, Chief Inspector?' asked Fancourt, obviously keen to get the technician out of his office.

'For the moment, Mr Fancourt, yes,' I said, and waited until Higgins had been dismissed from the presence. 'Your concern was that Mrs Bailey did not return to collect her ring, was it?'

'Yes. Given that she was so anxious to have the work done quickly, it seemed strange that she did not return to collect it. You see, Chief Inspector, Mrs Bailey is a valued client. On every other occasion that she has had work done, or purchased some item that we were obliged to order or have made, she has always returned promptly to collect it.'

'Presumably you were worried about the cost.'

Fancourt appeared to be affronted by this remark. 'Certainly not, Mr Brock. Our only interest is the satisfaction of our customers, and when it was brought to my attention that Mrs Bailey had not returned, I was somewhat concerned that she might have met with an accident. We attempted to contact her at the telephone number we held for her, but there was never any answer.'

'Did you leave a message?'

'No, I'm afraid not. The telephone just rang and rang. I can only assume that Mrs Bailey had not invested in an answering machine, either that or it was not switched on. In the circumstances, I thought that the only proper course of action was to inform the police.'

'Quite right,' I said, only sorry that Mrs Bailey hadn't taken her damned wedding ring into a jeweller's establishment in another constabulary area. 'Perhaps you'd let me have the number you were ringing.'

Fancourt opened a book and copied out the telephone number on to a slip of paper that bore the name of the jeweller, and a logo of some sort. 'There you are,' he said.

'I suppose there can be no mistake,' I suggested, pleased that it was not a mobile number. Mobile numbers are more difficult to trace. 'I was wondering if the number had somehow been recorded inaccurately. Even by Mrs Bailey,' I added hurriedly, as a frown descended on the manager's face.

'Certainly not,' said Fancourt sharply. 'As I said, we had her telephone number on record, and that's the one she gave this time.'

'Was it an expensive ring?' Dave asked.

'Not when set against some of the stock we hold, no.' Fancourt swept a hand across his desk. 'Four or five hundred pounds at most. Chased platinum, I believe.'

Not expensive, eh? When I married my now ex-wife Helga, I'd had to borrow fifteen quid to buy a wedding ring for her. As it turned out it was not a wise investment.

I met Helga Büchner, a twenty-one-year-old German physiotherapist, when I underwent a course of treatment at Westminster Hospital. I'd injured my shoulder after a punchup with a group of yobs in Whitehall when I was a PC. It was a whirlwind romance and we married shortly afterwards, despite advice from my mates at the nick. Particularly the women police. But perhaps they were jealous. The women police, I mean, vain bastard that I am.

And indeed they were right, because it all fell apart when Helga insisted on working after our son was born. When Robert was four she'd left him with a neighbour, and he fell in her pond and drowned. It was the start of a long period of acrimony that led to an 'open' marriage, and finally divorce.

'Thank you, Mr Fancourt. We'll let you know of any developments.'

'Do you want to take possession of the ring as evidence, Chief Inspector?'

'Evidence of what?' asked Dave.

Fancourt dithered. 'Well, isn't that what you usually do?'

Perhaps he was hoping that the police would also pay for the enlargement. I was almost tempted, just to annoy the commander.

'No, we'll leave it with you,' I said.

'Do a subscriber check on that number, Dave, and we'll take it from there,' I said, as we made our way back to our office at Curtis Green.

Curtis Green is an office block off Whitehall. Before the Metropolitan Police was conned into moving to an unsuitable, and now overflowing, glass and concrete pile in Victoria Street, it was called New Scotland Yard North. But being here has its advantages; not many people – including the police – know where it is.

'That phone number goes out to an address in Coburn Street, Holland Park, guv,' said Dave, after spending a few minutes on the telephone in the incident room. 'The subscriber's a Martin Bailey, and he lives at number fifteen.'

'Are we up and running on this one, sir?' asked Colin Wilberforce. Colin is the incident-room manager, and very good at the job he is, too. My main fear is that he's so good he may be promoted and whisked away. His impeccable administration ensures that every detail of an enquiry is carefully tabulated on the computer of which he appears to be a master. And to be on the safe side, he also records the salient points in a book. Using a pen. I like old-fashioned methods.

'Not yet, Colin, but you might as well put down the few details we have, just in case it develops. Dave'll give you the pars.' Policemen tend to talk in shorthand, and 'pars' is a contraction of 'particulars', and that encompasses just about everything capable of being written down. 'In the meantime,' I said, turning back to Dave, 'we'll sally forth and knock on the door of fifteen Coburn Street, Holland Park.'

Dave looked glum, and took a banana from his nylon excuse for a briefcase. Madeleine has told him that they're good for him – bananas, not briefcases – and who am I to argue?

The white-painted house where the Baileys lived rose three floors above a basement, and was in pristine condition.

We rang the bell and hammered on the door. There was no reply. We went to the house next door.

The woman who answered had yet to reach her thirtieth birthday, was black and gorgeous. Her colourful dress reached the ground, and was matched by a sort of turban wrapped around her head.

'Yes?' She looked at us with suspicion. I didn't blame her. Given the state of unchecked lawlessness in London, she was right to do so. Even so chic an area as Holland Park was not beyond the reach of villains of all assorted shapes and sizes.

'We're police officers, madam,' I said.

'Oh!' The woman gazed appraisingly at Dave, and Dave gazed back. As I've already mentioned, Dave is black. What I haven't mentioned is that he's six foot tall and handsome, and he too has yet to celebrate his thirtieth birthday. 'How do I know that?' she asked.

Wise woman. Dave and I produced our warrant cards, and she inspected them closely. 'Would you like to come in?' she enquired.

We stepped into the hall and waited while the woman closed the door.

'I'm Gladys Damjuma,' the woman announced, 'and I have diplomatic privilege. My husband is on the staff of our high commission.' Presumably Mrs Damjuma thought we were chasing up unpaid parking tickets.

I didn't ask which high commission; it was of no interest, and we could always find out if we needed to. That's what the Diplomatic List is for.

'It's not actually you we wanted to see,' said Dave with a disarming smile.

'It's not?' Mrs Damjuma seemed a little disappointed at that.

'We were wondering if you could tell us anything about your neighbours Mr and Mrs Bailey.'

'Oh, Martin and Eunice. Very nice people. Come and have a cup of tea.' Without waiting for a response, Mrs Damjuma opened the door of her elegant sitting room and ushered us in. Within seconds, a large black woman in a flowery apron appeared and took Mrs Damjuma's order for tea.

'Now then, what is it you want to know?' Gladys Damjuma smiled sweetly at Dave, and I began to feel left out of the conversation.

'When did you last see Mrs Bailey?' asked Dave.

'About two weeks ago, I suppose. I can't really remember. Most times we only talk if we happen to bump into each other when we're coming out or going in, but every now and then we stop for a long chat. Once or twice, Eunice has popped in for a cup of tea. We did have dinner with them one evening, though. That was about a month ago, maybe two.' Mrs Damjuma looked vague. 'Why? What's Eunice done?'

'Nothing, as far as we know.'

'Then what is it all about?'

As briefly as possible, Dave explained about the ring that Eunice Bailey had wanted enlarged, and had failed to collect. 'The jeweller was afraid that she might have forgotten about it.'

It was a masterpiece of understatement designed to allay the true reason for our interest: that someone might have topped Eunice. It was fortunate that Mrs Damjuma didn't seem at all surprised that this matter should have been followed up by a DCI from Scotland Yard.

'She's a very attractive woman, you know.'

'So we've heard,' continued Dave. 'We'd like to have a word with her husband, but there was no answer when we knocked at the Baileys' door.'

'He works, you know.'

'Really?' Dave sounded surprised. Perhaps he imagined that anyone with the money needed to live in Holland Park wouldn't have to work.

'Oh yes.' Mrs Damjuma looked up as the tea was brought in. 'Put it there,' she said tersely, waving an imperious hand at a small table near her chair. She spent a minute or two pouring tea into bone-china cups and handing them round.

'He's a very busy man. He's very often at his office until quite late at night.'

'Where is his office, Mrs Damjuma?' Dave asked.

'I don't know.'

'D'you know what he does for a living?'

'I think it's something to do with property, but I'm not really sure.' Again our hostess smiled at Dave.

'When you say he gets home quite late, how late is that?'

'Sometimes eight or nine. Even when he and Eunice invited us to dinner, he was late getting home. Eunice said it often happens. But when he did arrive, he was very interested in us, and was very keen to know what Bimbola did at the high commission.'

'Bimbola is your husband, I presume,' I said, determined not to let Dave hog the entire exchange.

'Yes, he's first secretary there.'

I wondered why Martin Bailey was so interested in Bimbola Damjuma's job, and it crossed my suspicious mind that maybe he saw a business opportunity in cultivating the first secretary. But I was straying from the reason for our visit.

'Have you seen Mr Bailey lately, Mrs Damjuma?' I asked.

'Oh yes. The day before yesterday. I was standing on the doorstep, waving goodbye to Bim, when Martin's chauffeur arrived in the Rolls-Royce. That was about nine o'clock.'

'Does Mr Bailey have a domestic staff?'

'I think he has a woman who does the cleaning in the mornings, but there's no one else that I know of. When we went in there for dinner, Eunice had done the cooking and she served it. If I had a Rolls-Royce, I'd have a butler and maids. Lots of maids.'

So, Martin Bailey was not only rich, he was mean too. A not uncommon combination. That would certainly explain why the door wasn't answered, and why Giles Fancourt got no answer when he telephoned. It looked as though Bailey was so stingy he wouldn't even lash out on an answering machine.

'Thank you for your help, Mrs Damjuma, and for the tea.' Dave and I stood up to leave.

'Do you want me to tell Martin that you're looking for him?'

'No thanks. We'll catch up with him sometime. It's not really very urgent.' However, I was under no illusion that Mrs

Damjuma would not beetle into Martin Bailey the moment she spotted him coming home. Which was a pity; I usually like to interview people without any forewarning. It tends to catch them on the hop if they're guilty of something. Not that I thought that Martin Bailey was likely to be a suspect for anything.

But in the event, we got to Bailey before Mrs Damjuma did.

Two

There was nothing else for it. If Martin Bailey worked late, then we must work even later. Dave Poole was not pleased, mainly because his ballet-dancing wife had a rare night off from swanning about in *Swan Lake* or whatever. But, as William Gilbert wrote, a policeman's lot is not a happy one.

One or two discreet lights were on in the Baileys' house when we drew into the kerb at nine o'clock. And this time we were in luck.

I rang the bell on the entryphone and an ethereal voice demanded to know who we were.

'Police,' I said.

'Hold your identification up to the CCTV camera,' said the voice. Obviously a resident who realized that crime was not confined to the poorer parts of London. If it ever was.

I hadn't noticed the camera when we'd called earlier, but now spotted it high up in the corner of the porch. I duly showed it my warrant card.

There was a buzz and several clicks, and a man of about forty-five opened the door. He was six foot tall with brown wavy hair, and was dressed in designer chinos, a tan shirt and brown loafers. All were of good quality and certainly hadn't been purchased from a high-street chain store.

'I'm Detective Chief Inspector Harry Brock of Scotland Yard, and this is Detective Sergeant Poole. Mr Martin Bailey, is it?'

'Yes. What can I do for you?'

'It's about your wife, sir,' I said.

'Really? You'd better come in.'

We followed Bailey into a spacious sitting room, predominantly white in decor, and furnished with expensive leather armchairs and a couple of chesterfields. All the trappings of wealth were there: a huge flat-screen plasma television, a state-of-the-art sound system – that was playing some sort of jazz – and several pieces of what Dave later assured me were genuine antiques.

'Do take a seat, gentlemen.' Bailey crossed to the sound system and turned it off.

'Stan Kenton?' queried Dave.

'Yes.' Bailey looked surprised. 'I'd've thought you were too young to know about him. Are you a fan of his?'

'No,' said Dave. 'I can't abide modern jazz.'

'Oh.' Bailey stood in front of us, threateningly almost. 'Tell me, why are the police taking an interest in my wife? Incidentally, would you care for a drink?'

'No, thank you, sir.' I was ill disposed to drink with anyone who was not beyond suspicion, and so far I had no grounds for thinking that Bailey was lily white. But I've been a detective for long enough to have developed an unhealthy cynicism. My current girlfriend, Gail Sutton, accuses me of being unable to see the good in anybody. I explained about Eunice Bailey's visit to the jeweller, and Mr Fancourt's concern that she had not returned to collect her wedding ring.

'Really?' Bailey expressed surprise. 'I didn't know anything about that. She never mentioned it.'

'The manager told me that he telephoned several times, but there was no answer. And it seems that your answering machine was not switched on.'

'I won't have one of those damned things in the house. If people want to get hold of me badly enough, they'll find a way.' Bailey turned to a tantalus on a side table and poured himself a large whisky. He added soda from an old-fashioned siphon – I hadn't seen one of those in ages – and finally sat down opposite us. 'She's left me, Chief Inspector,' he said, and took a sip of his Scotch. 'It was inevitable. We just didn't get on any longer.' He sounded resigned about the whole business.

'When did this happen, sir?'

'About a month ago, I suppose.' Bailey smoothed a hand over the knee of his chinos.

'D'you know where she went?'

'America, I believe. That's where she said she was going.'

'Anywhere in particular in America?'

'She didn't say. Perhaps she hadn't decided.'

'Have you heard from her since she left?'

'Not a word.'

'You've no idea where she is, then,' I said.

'No, and I'm not greatly interested. She was costing me a lot of money. Dressmaker's bills, expensive holidays that lasted for weeks.' Bailey sighed. 'Whatever else she was lacking, she certainly knew how to spend my money. I think shopaholic is the best way to describe her.'

'Seems odd, going without her wedding ring,' observed Dave.

Bailey scoffed. 'In view of the fact that she'd left me, she probably thought she wouldn't be needing it any more, Sergeant,' he said, as though the reason for his absent wife's failure to collect her ring was blindingly obvious. 'But I don't see why any of this should interest you chaps.'

'Did her departure come as a surprise, Mr Bailey?' I asked, ignoring his veiled question.

'Not really, no. We'd been getting on each other's nerves for quite a long time before that.' Bailey relaxed slightly. 'I spend most of my waking hours working, but Eunice was, well, a party girl, I suppose is what you'd call her. She liked going out to dinner, visiting friends, nightclubbing, and all that sort of thing. But when I did get home, I was too damned tired to do anything but collapse in front of that.' He waved a hand at the television.

'What is your line of work, Mr Bailey?' asked Dave.

Bailey frowned, as though it was none of our business what he did, but then he relented. 'Property, mainly. Buying and selling.'

'So you're a property developer.' Dave liked to button up what he saw as loose ends.

'I suppose you could call it that, but that's not everything. I dabble in all sorts of things. I'm an entrepreneur, really. It's the way to make money in this world, young man.'

Looking round the elegant room in which we were sitting, it seemed that Bailey had been pretty successful at it.

I took back the questioning. 'You said just now that your wife went on expensive holidays, Mr Bailey, but you also said that you were too tired to do anything. Does that mean that she—'

'Exactly so,' Bailey interrupted. 'She went on her own. I'm not much of a one for holidays. The thought of just sitting in a deckchair watching the sea when I could be in London making money doesn't appeal. But Eunice's idea of fun consisted of disporting herself in her bikini on some hot beach.'

'When you say your wife went on her own, did you mean that? Or did she have a female friend she went with?' I'd said 'female', but that wasn't what I'd had in mind. And from his amused glance, Bailey knew I was fishing to see if there were other men in Eunice Bailey's life.

'I've really no idea, Chief Inspector, but if she was with a man, I'd've thought he'd've picked up the tab, wouldn't you? Unless he was some sort of fortune-hunter.' Bailey stood up and glanced at the Rolex watch on his wrist. 'Now, gentlemen, unless you have any more questions, I do have quite a lot of work to get through.'

'If you hear from your wife, perhaps you'd let us know, sir.' I smiled apologetically. 'My boss plays merry hell if I can't produce a result. Even for an enquiry that has an innocent explanation.' I handed him one of my cards.

Bailey laughed. 'Yes, I do understand,' he said. 'When I started out, some thirty years ago, I had a boss who always wanted results. I was working in a candle factory then.'

'And you've been burning it at both ends ever since,' observed Dave drily.

Bailey laughed loudly. 'You're not just a pretty face, are you, Sergeant?' he said.

'There is one other thing, sir,' I said. 'Do you have a photograph of your wife that might assist us in tracing her?'

'I think I've got one somewhere. Just a minute.' Bailey went into the next room and I heard him opening and closing drawers. He returned clutching a framed studio-portrait photograph of an attractive blonde in her mid-thirties. 'There you are, Chief Inspector, and you can keep it as far as I'm concerned.'

'D'you not want the frame, sir?' asked Dave.

'No,' said Bailey vehemently. 'You can throw the bloody thing away when you've finished with it, and the photograph.'

And that, as far as I was concerned, was that. I sent Dave home and told him that the next day would be early enough to work out what to do next. And I'd already decided that there was nothing else that could be done. Oh boy, how wrong can you be?

At nine o'clock the following morning, Dave appeared in my office with two cups of coffee. He sat down in my ancient armchair and threw me a Silk Cut.

'I'm trying to quit, Dave,' I said before lighting it. I've been attempting to give up smoking ever since a master at my school in Croydon caught me having a quick drag behind the bike sheds and told me a horror story about his brother who'd died of lung cancer. But I just don't have the willpower. And Dave's no help either. Even the Commissioner's diktat that smoking is forbidden in all police buildings didn't help me to curb the habit. Not that anyone takes any notice of that.

'So what do we do about Mrs Bailey's wedding ring, guv?' Dave asked.

'I don't see what else there is to do. She suddenly decides to leave her husband and go to America. Happens all the time, and I should think that being married to a workaholic like Martin Bailey is enough to drive any woman nuts. And these things happen suddenly: a blazing row and that's it. Bang! And off she goes. It's probably been brewing for a long time. In fact, Bailey said as much.'

'So NFA, d'you reckon, guv?'

'Unfortunately, Dave, "no further action" is something the commander will have to authorize. I don't know how or why we got lumbered with the bloody job in the first place. It's a missing-person enquiry, plain and simple. Well, in my view, it's not even that now. And it's certainly not something we should be dealing with anyway.'

Dave chuckled. 'I reckon the guv'nor at West End Central thought he'd offload it on us, guv, and saw an easy mark in the boss.'

That, of course, was a strong possibility. It was our misfortune that our illustrious commander was not really a detective at all. But someone in the quaintly styled Human Resources Directorate – we used to call it 'personnel' – obviously thought it was a great idea to foist him on us. And at the stroke of a pen, a commander who had spent his entire professional life in the Uniform Branch, curbing rebellious football hooligans and buggering up the traffic, became a CID officer. It had happened before, but many of those other 'sidewaysed' officers just sat behind their desks, enjoyed the ride, and let the lads get on with it. Regrettably, our boss thought he *was* a detective, and interfered.

Waiting until ten o'clock – the commander never appears before then, and never stays after six – I picked up my notes and made my way to his office.

'Mr Brock?' The commander took off his half-moon spectacles and gazed at me over a pile of files.

'The matter of Eunice Bailey's wedding ring, sir.'

'What about it?'

'It was a report from West End Central nick, sir, and—'

'Yes, yes, I know that. So what have you done?'

'We visited the jeweller's and obtained the phone number she'd given them. We also got a description from the technician who dealt with her. He reckoned she was in her mid-thirties, with a good figure, and long blonde hair. We traced the phone number, and last night we interviewed her husband at his house in Coburn Street, Holland Park—'

'Holland Park, eh?' This clearly impressed the commander. 'And she was there, I suppose. Did she say why she hadn't collected her ring?'

'She wasn't there, sir. According to her husband, she left him a month ago, and told him she intended going to America. It seems that their marriage is over.'

'Whereabouts in the States, Mr Brock?'

'Mr Bailey has no idea, sir. He merely said she'd gone to America and that, of course, could mean the USA or Canada, or even South America.'

'There's no need to split hairs, Mr Brock,' snapped the commander irritably. He was obviously riled that he'd jumped too quickly to a conclusion, and that I'd pointed it out. He hated being trumped.

'We obtained a photograph of her from her husband, sir.' I handed him one of the prints we'd had copied from the original. 'As you can see, sir, she's a very attractive woman.'

'In that case, Mr Brock, her details had better be circulated to Interpol. And perhaps we can seek the assistance of the press. Whet their appetite, perhaps. I can see from this photograph that, as you say, she is an attractive woman. Missing socialite, perhaps, that sort of thing?'

'But why pursue it, sir?'

'Because until we can satisfy ourselves that she is alive, she could be a murder victim.'

'But shouldn't we wait until we find a body?' I was appalled that the commander was making such a big thing of Mrs Bailey and her wedding ring. In my early days as a CID officer, wiser heads than mine said that a detective should try to make a molehill out of a mountain, not the other way round. But in those days, the bosses were real hard-nosed detectives, not the cardboard version that was sitting opposite me now.

'See to it, Mr Brock. Those are my directions.' The commander replaced his glasses on the end of his nose and pulled yet another file out of his pile.

'Very good, sir,' I said, but waited until I was outside his office before swearing volubly.

'All wrapped up, guv?' asked Dave, when I returned to my own office.

'No, it bloody well isn't,' I said, and repeated what the commander had said.

'Leave it to me, guv, I'll sort it.' Dave picked up the few bits of paper that comprised the great wedding-ring mystery and retreated to the incident room.

The upshot was that Dave passed what little information we had about Eunice Bailey to the United Kingdom's National Central Bureau of Interpol. They weren't too impressed, apparently, and, according to Dave, muttered a bit about the need to circulate the information at all. But eventually, and reluctantly, they agreed to send it to the NCB in the United States, via Interpol headquarters in Lyon. And that, of course, is in France. A result, I knew from previous experience, would take forever and a day. If one was forthcoming at all.

In the meantime, I spoke to the head of news in our own Press Department. It's probably got a much more fanciful name now, courtesy of the funny names and total confusion squad at the Yard. The head of news, however, was not much taken with the idea either, and suggested that he could only circulate information if we could give him any. To which he added that the media wouldn't be too interested in Mrs Bailey's wedding ring anyway.

I recounted this depressing response to Dave.

'There's an easy way round that, guv.'

'And that is?'

'Fat Danny.'

Fat Danny, a thoroughly odious creep, was the crime reporter of the worst tabloid in Fleet Street, a reputation for which there is much competition. Overweight, with a pudding face that was permanently greasy, Danny had a tendency to wave his podgy little hands about the whole time he was talking. He had acquired the distinction – envied by several other crime reporters – of being able not only to sniff out the most salacious of crimes, but also to track down the officers investigating it. He was the perfect man for our missing person.

'Give him a bell, Dave, and set up a meet at the Red Lion ASAP.'

'Mr Brock, how are you?' Fat Danny was already ensconced in the corner of the downstairs bar of the Red Lion in Derby Gate when Dave and I arrived.

'No better for seeing you, Danny,' I said. 'And as you're buying, I'll have a pint of best bitter. And so will Dave.'

'Mr Poole tells me you've got something for me,' said Danny, once he had bought each of us a drink. He extracted a notebook from the inner recesses of his creased jacket and looked hopeful.

'Only on the understanding that this is non-attributable,' I cautioned.

Danny spread his podgy little hands. 'You know me, Mr Brock.'

'That's what my guv'nor's worried about,' put in Dave.

I explained about Eunice Bailey and her wedding ring, and gave Danny a brief background sketch of Martin Bailey, his occupation, and the palatial house in which he lived.

'Personally, I don't think there's anything in it, Danny,' I continued, 'but my guv'nor's got this bee in his bonnet that some major crime's been committed.'

'I've got an editor like that,' said Danny mournfully. 'We all have our cross to bear. Anyway, if you give me this Bailey's address and phone number, I'll see what I can do.' He ran his tongue round his lips and glanced dreamily at the ceiling.

'Beautiful rich socialite missing.' He was already formulating the headline. 'Got to be something there.'

'Have you been talking to my boss?' I asked. Danny had used almost exactly the same phrase as the commander.

'Likes the bright lights, you said, Mr Brock? I've got a few snouts in the nightclub world. I'll see what I can do.'

'Thanks, Danny, but you didn't hear it from me.' I gave him a copy of Eunice's photograph. 'And you didn't get that from me either.'

'Mum's the word, Mr Brock. You can stand on me.'

'Stand on you? If it goes pear-shaped, Danny, I'll stamp all over you.' And breaking the habit of a lifetime, I bought Fat Danny a drink.

Whatever else I might think about Fat Danny, I can't deny that he's a fast worker. The following morning's edition of his rag had a story about Eunice Bailey on its front page. And far from using the photograph I'd given Danny, his paper carried a photograph of the woman that looked as though it had been taken at a nightclub. It was obvious from the report that Danny had visited the jeweller's shop and, doubtless, had greased a few palms with the newspaper's money. He had also managed to acquire more information about Martin Bailey's business activities than we had garnered from our conversation with him, and even published the address of his office, together with a photograph of his house. Something that, I imagine, had not pleased the security-conscious entrepreneur.

That Bailey had not been pleased was brought to my attention shortly after I'd finished reading Fat Danny's article.

'The commander would like to see you, sir,' said Colin Wilberforce.

I tapped lightly on the door and entered the presence. 'You wanted to see me, sir?'

'Have you seen this report, Mr Brock?' The commander held the offending organ of the gutter press between finger and thumb as though he might catch some awful disease from it. I was surprised he wasn't wearing latex gloves.

'Yes, I have, sir.'

'Well, I've just had Mr Bailey on the telephone complaining that the police have spoken to the press about the disappearance of his wife. He was extremely annoyed and is talking about writing to his Member of Parliament, the Commissioner, and the Independent Police Complaints Commission. He mentioned the Human Rights Act, too.'

'Did he really, sir? Oh dear!' This was going to be fun.

'Did you speak to the press, Mr Brock?' The commander's tone was definitely accusatory.

'It was you who suggested that the media be told the story of Mrs Bailey's wedding ring, sir.' I thought it unnecessary to mention my meeting with Fat Danny. 'If I remember correctly you said something about whetting their appetite. In fact the very words used in that article' – I waved at the newspaper – 'are almost identical with the words you yourself used yesterday morning when you directed me to inform the press.' My comment was tantamount to accusing the commander of having spoken to Fleet Street himself. 'Missing beautiful socialite, I think. Something along those lines.' I made a pretence of looking more closely at the paper.

'Well, I, er . . . ' The commander was floundering. 'What I really meant was that you should speak to someone in the Directorate of Public Affairs.'

So that's what it's called. 'But you didn't say that, sir. You told me to seek the assistance of the press. You also mentioned Interpol, and that's been done, but you didn't say anything about the DPA.' I realized that there was, after all, some advantage in having a commander who'd transferred from the Uniform Branch. If he'd been an old-fashioned career detective, he'd probably have denied ever giving me that order. You had to watch your step when you'd got a real detective for a boss.

The commander sighed and glanced at a photograph of a harridan that resided permanently on his desk. I think it must've been Mrs Commander. Either that or the boss was a photograph masochist.

'I think you'd better mark it up "no further action", Mr Brock, on my directions. In the meantime, I'd better go and see this Mr Bailey and apologize.'

I was horrified at this latest example of the commander's idiocy. 'Good God! Don't do that, sir. That would be as good as saying we were responsible for leaking the story to the

press. If you read that report, you'll see that the reporter –
Danny someone, I think is his name – actually spoke to people
at the jeweller's. No, sir, that information obviously came
from another source. It certainly wasn't from this office.'

'Perhaps you're right, Mr Brock,' the commander conceded
wearily, and waved a hand in dismissal.

Three

I had hoped that the enquiry about Mrs Bailey and her forgotten wedding ring was over and done with, but it was not to be. Much to my surprise, most of Friday morning's papers had picked up Fat Danny's story of the previous day and had run with it. Personally, I didn't think anyone would be interested, but there it was. And it was this later story that had brought an almost immediate response from a member of the public.

'A man called Tom Nelson telephoned the Yard earlier today, sir, and they passed the message on to us,' said Colin Wilberforce, the moment I arrived at Curtis Green.

'Have you contacted him, Colin?' I took a cup of coffee from Dave's tin tray as he passed by on his way to the sergeants' office, and lit a Marlboro.

'Yes, sir. I rang him, and he said that he saw the report in one of this morning's papers. He thinks he knows Eunice Bailey.'

'How did the Yard know we were interested?'

'I put Mrs Bailey's name on the PNC, sir, just in case anything cropped up,' Colin said.

I sighed. Although putting the details on the Police National Computer was the obvious thing to have done, efficiency can sometimes be too efficient. 'What's this guy's address, Colin?'

'Twenty-seven Costello Street, East Sheen.' Colin handed me a message form. 'Mr Nelson said he'd be at home all day. Incidentally, sir, he sounded American.'

'Car's ready to go, guv,' said Dave, having reappeared in time to overhear the conversation, and to read my mind.

Tom Nelson was indeed an American, and the house in which he lived would have vied in value with that of Martin Bailey.

'You guys sure don't waste any time,' said Nelson. 'I only

rang Scotland Yard this morning. Come on in.' He led us through the house to a conservatory that had a view of a beautifully tended garden, mainly of grass and a few trees, but with a large, colourful bed of roses in the centre of the lawn. Beyond the garden lay the rolling acres of Richmond Park.

'I gather from your phone call that you knew Mrs Eunice Bailey, Mr Nelson,' I said, once Dave and I were settled in comfortable wicker armchairs.

'*Mrs* Bailey, did you say?' Nelson seemed a little disconcerted at that, and frowned.

'Yes. She's married to a Martin Bailey, although I understand they're now separated.'

'I didn't know that.' Nelson reached across to select a meerschaum pipe from a stand of some twelve. Slowly he began to tease tobacco into the bowl while he mulled over the implications of what I'd just said. Well, I imagine that's what he was doing.

'I'm wondering if we're talking about the same woman,' I said.

'Hell, I don't know. I'm sure the photo in the paper was her. Which woman are *you* talking about?' Nelson struck a match and applied it to his pipe. 'There can't be too many Eunice Baileys about.'

The photograph that Nelson had seen was the one that had appeared in newspapers, and wasn't that good a likeness, so I showed him the studio portrait of Eunice Bailey that I'd obtained from her husband.

'I guess that's her,' said Nelson. 'No doubt about it.'

I explained about the wedding ring that Eunice Bailey had failed to collect, and the fact that she had left her husband a month ago.

'Perhaps you'd better tell me what you know,' I said.

Nelson turned in his chair and shouted for someone called Trudy.

A young woman entered the conservatory. She was a good-looking, suntanned girl in her twenties with short brown hair, and was wearing a red floor-length crinkle-cotton skirt, and a white vest-top.

'This is Trudy, my secretary,' explained Nelson, not that I believed him. 'Would you like some tea, Detectives?'

'Thank you.'

Nelson nodded to the girl and she left us.

'Now then, about Eunice. It was a month ago, or there-abouts, that I met her. I was at a charity function at the Dorchester and she was there. I'm tied up with a lot of charities, mainly medical stuff, cancer and the like. I got talking with her—'

'Can you tell me the exact date, Mr Nelson?' I asked.

Nelson pulled out a diary and thumbed through it. 'It was Saturday, May eighteenth.'

'Was she wearing a wedding ring?' asked Dave, even though he would have known that the eighteenth was the day after she had taken the ring to be enlarged. But Dave was a great cross-checker.

'No, *sir*,' Nelson answered instantly and vehemently. 'As a matter of fact, she wasn't wearing any jewellery apart from earrings. Neat little gold jobs, as I recall.'

'So you got chatting to her, did you?' I asked.

'Sure did. She was a real friendly girl. Attractive, too, and great perfume. Coco Chanel, I think she said it was.'

'How did that come about? Did she come up to you, or the other way round?'

'It was a wine and canapés affair, and I found her standing next to me at one stage during the evening. We got into conversation, as one does at these events. Fairly early on, she mentioned that she wasn't married and was very keen on travelling, and told me about all the places she'd been to. We were getting on real swell, so after this junket was over, I invited her to have dinner with me, in the grillroom at the Dorchester.'

'Did she spend the night with you, Mr Nelson?' asked Dave, a believer in getting to the nub of things.

Nelson grinned and shook his head. 'Not that night, no. She went home.'

'Did she say where home was?' I asked.

'She told me she lived locally. A flat in Marble Arch, I think she said. I offered to escort her there – I was staying over at the Dorchester that night – but she said not to bother, and that she'd take a cab.'

'And did you take her to the cab, Mr Nelson?'

'Sure I did.' Nelson looked a little offended by the question, as if I were impugning his gentlemanly courtesy.

'Did you by any chance hear what she said to the cab driver?'

'No. I guess she must've told him where to go once she was inside.'

'And did you see her again?' I asked.

'You bet. I asked her if she was free for dinner the following evening. That would've been the Sunday. She said she was and gave me her cellphone number.'

'D'you remember that number?' asked Dave, pocketbook at the ready.

'Yep.' Nelson reeled off the number from memory, and Dave wrote it down.

'Did she mention going to America?' I was beginning to wonder if there was a connection between this amiable American and Eunice Bailey's statement to her estranged husband that that was where she was going when she left him.

'Not as a given, no. She just mentioned that she'd been to Florida once for a holiday, and that she'd like to go again. I don't know that part of the States. Never been there, in fact. I'm from Pittsburgh, Pennsylvania, myself.'

'Do you live here in England now, Mr Nelson?' There seemed to be too many personal possessions about the house for it to be a temporary abode.

'Yes, I do. I love this country. It's because it's so . . . civilized, I guess. Yes, that's the word. And I love London. You can walk about here quite safely, and that means a lot.'

Tom Nelson obviously hadn't seen London through a policeman's eyes.

'And was that the last time you saw Eunice Bailey?' I asked.

'Hell no. We dated regularly until we went to Bermuda for a vacation. That would've been on May twenty-third, I guess,' he said, having consulted his diary again.

'Bermuda? That's expensive, isn't it?'

'I can afford it,' said Nelson with a boyish grin.

'As a matter of interest, Mr Nelson, what is your occupation?' asked Dave.

'I don't have one, Detective. I suppose I'm what you'd call an international playboy.' Nelson smiled apologetically, almost as if having a lot of money embarrassed him. 'You see, I don't only have this place.' He waved a hand around the room to emphasize his ownership. 'I've also got a villa in the South of France. That's where I keep my yacht. Oh, and I keep a little place in Ambridge.'

'Where?' snapped Dave. He was quick to react when he thought someone was making fun of him.

Nelson laughed. 'Hell, Detective, I'm not talking about that radio soap called *The Archers*,' he said. 'My Ambridge really exists. It's about twenty to thirty miles north of Pittsburgh. But I don't use it much these days.'

'Very nice,' commented Dave drily. He was always suspicious of people who seemed to have no visible means of support. His work ethic demanded that everyone had to do something – and be paid for it – and if they didn't, they must be villains.

'You see, my grandfather made lots of money out of oil. And I do mean buckets of the stuff. When he died and my father inherited, he made even more, and when he died, it all came to me. So I just enjoy myself.'

'So you took Mrs Bailey to Bermuda. For how long?'

'Two weeks. It's a great place. You ought to go there some time.'

'Yes, I'm saving up,' said Dave drily. 'And did you see Mrs Bailey after you got back here?'

'She didn't come back with me. I had to return because there was a big charity affair that I'd promised to host, but she said she wanted to stay on for a few days. So I fixed her up with a credit card and told her to spend whatever she wanted.'

'Am I to understand that you have not seen her since then, Mr Nelson?' I asked.

'No, sir, I haven't. I tried ringing her cellphone, but there was no answer. Mind you, if she'd gone on to the States, it probably wouldn't have worked there. Not unless it was one of the triband type. I guess she just moved on to someone else. Pity, she was a great girl.' Nelson shook his head, presumably at pleasures never to be repeated.

'As a matter of interest, did you ever visit this flat where she claimed to live?' I had doubts that she did in fact have a flat in Marble Arch.

'No, I never did.'

'And you never learned the address?'

'No, sir.'

I was rapidly coming to the conclusion that Martin Bailey had been misinformed by his wife when she'd told him she was going to America. My suspicious mind led me to wonder if Tom Nelson had had something to do with Eunice Bailey's disappearance, and whether she was now holed up in Ambridge, north of Pittsburgh. 'This credit card you gave Mrs Bailey; I presume the account was sent to you for settlement.'

'Yes. D'you want to see it?'

'Please.'

Trudy appeared with the tea at that moment, and Nelson asked her to get his June accounts file.

He poured the tea and handed round the cups. 'I love this English habit of taking tea at any time of the day,' he said.

I was beginning to think that this guy was too good to be true. Or perhaps he was just naive.

The girl returned with a box file, and Nelson dug around in it until he produced the account he was looking for.

'There you are, Detective,' he said, handing it to me.

I examined the account, which was in the name of Eunice Bailey at Nelson's East Sheen address, but without any reference to her marital status. It showed that she had stayed at Driscoll's Hotel in Paget Parish, Bermuda, for a further three days, had spent only moderate amounts at restaurants – moderate for Bermuda, anyway – and had made a purchase at Swimsuit Extravaganza. And you didn't have to be a detective to work out what she'd bought there. But that was it. The account ceased to have any charges against it after the tenth of June. Not even an airfare to the United Kingdom.

'I wonder how Mrs Bailey got back here,' I mused. 'If she did.'

'I left her an open return ticket. First class to Gatwick on British Airways. I suppose she used that.'

I noticed that Dave was scribbling in his pocketbook again. Doubtless a note to himself to check whether she did actually return.

'May I have a copy of this account, Mr Nelson?' I asked, certain that he must have a photocopier, and that his 'secretary' knew how to use it.

'Sure. You can take it. It's paid. It would have got chucked out anyway.'

'If Mrs Bailey gets in touch with you again, Mr Nelson, or you manage to contact her, perhaps you'd let me know.' I gave him one of my cards.

'Sure thing, Detective.' Nelson examined the card and looked up. 'Homicide and Serious Crime? I reckon this must be pretty serious.'

'I doubt it,' I said, but I was becoming slowly convinced that we were dealing with something more complex than a straightforward missing-person enquiry. 'We always look into reports of women who seem to have disappeared.'

On the way back to Curtis Green, Dave had stopped at the London Map Centre in Caxton Street to buy a map and a guidebook of Bermuda. He reckoned we might need them, and I was forced to agree.

Once in the office, Dave got busy. First of all, he rang the number of Eunice Bailey's mobile that Tom Nelson had given us. Predictably, there was no answer.

Next off, he put through a call to Bob Winston, a mate of his at Heathrow Airport, and asked him to make enquiries about Eunice Bailey's ticket from Bermuda International Airport to Gatwick. Bob Winston was a detective constable who'd been attached to the Port Watch unit at the airport for years. What he didn't know about the workings of Heathrow and its airlines wasn't worth bothering about.

'It'll be easier than trying to contact British Airways direct, guv,' explained Dave. 'Bob will pop over to their offices. He knows everybody there.'

While he was waiting for an answer, he spread out the map of Bermuda. 'If she did go from Driscoll's Hotel to the airport, guv,' he said, 'she didn't charge the taxi to her credit card, and it's too far to walk.'

'Perhaps she paid cash for the cab,' I said. 'Most people do, even in this age of plastic.'

But that puzzle was resolved when Bob Winston rang back from Heathrow.

Replacing the receiver, Dave shrugged. 'The return ticket wasn't used, guv. Bob spoke to some computer wizard at British Airways, and she said that it had been cashed in. That's how it showed up in their records. And to make sure, she telephoned the BA office at Bermuda Airport, and they confirmed it. So what do we do now? Go there?'

'We should be so lucky,' I said. But it was now apparent that we couldn't leave this damned enquiry hanging in midair.

If only the commander hadn't decided that Homicide and Serious Crime Command should take an interest, we'd've been happily dealing with some uncomplicated murder.

'I'm afraid the commander is going to have to decide where we go from here, Dave. But I bet it won't be Bermuda.'

I made my way to the boss's office with some feeling of unease. On the one hand, as a detective, I was not happy to leave the Eunice Bailey question unanswered. But on the other hand, I was sure that if the commander decided that further action should be taken, it would be Dave and I taking it. And that could turn out to be a long and difficult business.

'Ah, Mr Brock.'

'Eunice Bailey and her wedding ring, sir.'

The commander looked surprised. 'I thought I'd directed that it be marked "no further action", Mr Brock.'

'So you did, sir, but something's come up.'

'Oh?' The commander removed his spectacles and sat back in his commander-type chair, a disturbed expression on his face. Martin Bailey's threat to make a fuss about Fat Danny's newspaper article obviously still worried him.

I explained, as briefly as possible, about the information we had gleaned from Tom Nelson, and that, according to our recent enquiries, Eunice Bailey appeared neither to have returned to this country nor to be still in Bermuda. At least, if the dormant credit card was anything to go by.

'Anything from Interpol, Mr Brock?' asked the commander, apparently playing for time.

I shook my head and smiled. 'Early days yet, sir,' I said, which afforded him no comfort at all. He was not only a firm believer in 'the proper channels', but thought they worked.

The commander played a little tattoo on his desktop while he considered what to do next. 'I think I shall have to speak to the DAC,' he said eventually.

That came as no surprise. We have a saying in the Metropolitan Police: when in trouble or in doubt, wave your arms and run about. But in the commander's case, it was to consult the Deputy Assistant Commissioner.

In a rare moment of compassion, I made a suggestion. 'I could telephone the Bermuda Police, sir, and ask them to make some enquiries locally, and particularly at this Driscoll's Hotel.'

The boss nodded sagely, as if it were he who had just thought of the idea. 'Yes, do that, Mr Brock. I think we'll await a result from there before we take any action that might prove to have been precipitate.'

'Very good, sir,' I said, hiding a smile. The commander was never one to take precipitate action. 'I thought I might also go and see Martin Bailey again, just in case—'

'Most inadvisable, Mr Brock,' the commander said hurriedly.

'I'll smooth him over, sir, don't worry. I'll explain to him that the newspaper reports were as much of a surprise to us as to him. In fact, I shall emphasize that, if anything, they've hindered our enquiries rather than helped. Furthermore, I shall tell him how annoyed we are about the whole business.'

'D'you think you can manage that, Mr Brock?' asked the commander, a question that displayed his lack of detective expertise.

'No problem, sir,' I said, 'but we'll see what Bermuda has to say first.'

I got the impression that the commander was beginning to look at me in a more favourable light. He might even be regarding me as a suitable candidate for promotion. *Oh, you fool, Brock! What are you thinking of?*

I returned to the incident room. 'What's the time difference between here and Bermuda, Colin?' I asked.

The one thing about Colin Wilberforce is that he never appears to be fazed by anything that's thrown at him.

'One moment, sir.' Colin seized a copy of *Whitaker's Almanack* from his personal library and thumbed through it. 'Given that we're now on British Summer Time, sir, and they're on Eastern Standard Time, they'll be four hours behind us.' He glanced at the clock over the door. 'It'll be nine o'clock in the morning there, sir.'

'Thank you, Colin,' I said, as though this immediate response was in no way out of the ordinary, which, of course, it wasn't. 'Would you find out the telephone number of the Police Headquarters at . . . .' I paused.

'Hamilton, sir,' said Colin, without batting an eyelid. 'But if it's to be a long message, it might be quicker to send them an email.'

'Good thinking. I'll draft something out. Would you be able to send that for me.'

'Of course, sir.' Colin frowned.

With the help of Dave, I composed a message telling the Bermuda Police what we knew of Eunice Bailey, right from when she deposited her wedding ring, through to our interview with Tom Nelson.

Colin Wilberforce sent it, and informed me that the Bermuda Police had immediately confirmed its receipt. Oh, the wonders of modern science.

'And now, Dave,' I said, 'despite what the commander said, I think we'll pay another visit to Martin Bailey. You never know, he might have heard from Eunice since we spoke last.'

'That means a late night, I suppose,' said Dave mournfully.

'Yes,' I said, 'I suppose it does.'

Four

As nine o'clock in the evening seemed to be the earliest time at which we'd find Martin Bailey at home, that was when we arrived at Coburn Street.

Once again we went through the rigmarole of showing his CCTV camera our warrant cards, and eventually Bailey opened the door.

He was not at all pleased to see us. In fact, he was almost vibrating with anger when he admitted us to his house, presumably at our temerity in returning to see him after the newspaper exposé of his wife's disappearance. From his attitude, he obviously blamed us for the report, because this time there was no offer of a drink. But that didn't stop him pouring a large Scotch for himself. However, his manners did not entirely desert him, and he invited us to take a seat.

'I have to say, Chief Inspector, that I'm extremely bloody angry at having found the story of my wife's desertion spread all over some gutter-press newspaper two days after you'd called here. For God's sake, man, my wife's left me, walked out. It happens to hundreds of people. I spoke to some fool at Scotland Yard and told him exactly what I thought of the whole business. I also told him that I intended to take legal action, and furthermore I shall make a formal protest to the police complaints people, whatever that organization's called. It's a bloody disgrace that my private life has been plastered all over some damned rag. And all because you fellows decided to leak it.'

I waited patiently until Bailey had finished his tirade knowing that, like a Catherine wheel, he would eventually fizzle out.

'I was extremely annoyed about it, too, Mr Bailey,' I said mildly.

That caught him wrong-footed. He put down his glass and

stared at me. 'Are you saying that you weren't responsible for leaking it to the press?' he asked incredulously.

'Most certainly we weren't,' I said, conjuring up a bit of contrived anger of my own. 'I've been a detective for a long time, Mr Bailey, and in my experience such revelations tend to hinder our investigations rather than help them. The last thing we would do is talk to the press.' I'm pretty good at lying when it's expedient.

Bailey seemed somewhat mollified by that. 'Then how the hell did they get hold of the story? Not that there is a story. My wife left me a month ago. *End* of story. It happens all the time, but you don't see reports in the paper every time someone's wife runs away, not unless it's a film star, or a footballer, or some lowlife of that sort. But the fact that my wife has left me doesn't warrant that sort of coverage. And it was even repeated the following day. Now then, you say you've been a detective for a long time, so tell me how in hell's name the press got hold of it.'

'I've no idea, Mr Bailey, but I think it's called chequebook journalism. And I suspect it came about because the jeweller informed the police that your wife had failed to collect her wedding ring. And, as a result, two Scotland Yard officers turned up to make enquiries.'

'How does that affect the issue?'

'The most likely scenario would be that an employee of the jeweller's rang up a newspaper and told them just that. And I dare say his palm was crossed with silver. Some people have very low moral thresholds, you know.'

'I'll sue the damned newspaper, then.' Bailey was exactly the sort of man who had to blame someone, and would not be satisfied until he'd had his pound of flesh. He was the sort of hard-nosed businessman who always got his own way, and became very angry when he was thwarted.

'If you don't mind me giving you a word of advice, Mr Bailey,' said Dave, 'you won't get very far. Newspapers are very defensive of their informants. In fact, there've been cases where the editor would rather go to prison for contempt of court than reveal his source. Apart from anything else, it wasn't libellous as far as I could see.'

'It was an invasion of my damned privacy,' snapped Bailey, but appeared at last to accept that the tabloid revelations that had so offended him were not of our doing. 'D'you chaps want a drink?' he asked, as he stood up to replenish his own glass.

Ah, so we'd been forgiven. 'No, thank you, sir,' I said, replying for both of us.

'Anyway, why are you back here? Eunice has buggered off and left me, and that's that.'

'We have received information that leads us to believe that some harm may have befallen your wife, Mr Bailey.'

'Oh?' Bailey took a sudden interest. 'What sort of information?' It seemed to be typical of the man that he was only interested in the information, not the suggested harm.

'As a result of the report that appeared in several of this morning's newspapers, we were contacted by a man who'd met your wife. On or about the date that you told us she left you.'

'That comes as no surprise. I suspected she might've been seeing someone else.'

'We interviewed this man earlier today, and he told us that he and Mrs Bailey spent a fortnight's holiday in Bermuda between the twenty-third of May and the sixth of June.'

'Bermuda! Ye Gods! And I suppose he slept with her.' Bailey seemed to be unreasonably angered by this piece of news, despite having told us that his wife had left because she felt neglected by him. And presumably that neglect was sexual as well as social. 'What's his name? I'll cite the bastard in the divorce courts.' He punched his right fist into the palm of his left hand. 'Oh yes, I'll make him pay. And her.'

'I'm sorry, Mr Bailey, I'm not at liberty to divulge that information. It's privileged.'

'Privileged be damned. I'll subpoena you when I start divorce proceedings. The pair of you. Then you'd have to reveal his name.'

'That, of course, is your right, sir,' said Dave smoothly, 'but I doubt you'll be very successful in your action.'

'Oh? Why's that?'

'Because it seems that your wife was not wearing a wedding ring at the time. You may recall that it's still at the jeweller's where she left it for work to be done on it. And according to our informant, Mrs Bailey told him she was unmarried, and he claims that he had no reason to disbelieve her.'

'Did he indeed? So where the hell is my wife now? Can you answer me that, or is that privileged too?' Bailey demanded sarcastically.

'I'm afraid we wouldn't be allowed to tell you her whereabouts unless she gave us permission to do so, sir,' said Dave, who appeared to be enjoying himself. 'But the fact of the matter is that we have no idea where she is. That's why we're here.'

'But you said she'd been to Bermuda for a fortnight, so she must've come back, in which case you should've been able to check with the airline—'

'She appears not to have returned, Mr Bailey,' I said. 'We have been told by the man who was with her that when he came back to this country on the sixth of June, Mrs Bailey remained in Bermuda. At least until the tenth of June. Our informant told us that he gave her a first-class ticket for Bermuda to Gatwick, and a credit card, but there were no charges on it after that date. We've checked with British Airways, and the ticket wasn't used; in fact, it was cashed in at the airline's Bermuda office.'

'So why the hell aren't you looking for her?'

I ignored that question. 'Have you had any contact with her since she walked out on the eighteenth of May?'

'No, none at all, and frankly I don't want to hear from her, or see her again.'

'If she does contact you, perhaps you'd let us know,' I said.

'Have you ever been to Bermuda, sir?' asked Dave casually, as we stood up to leave.

'No, I haven't,' said Bailey. 'Too damned expensive for my liking.'

And that, from a man who must've been a millionaire several times over, seemed a strange comment. But not unusual. As I said before, a lot of rich men I've met were very mean with their money.

When we got back to Curtis Green – at eleven o'clock – we checked with Gavin Creasey, the night-duty incident-room manager, that no reply had yet been received from Bermuda. As there was little we could do about the missing Mrs Bailey until we heard from them, we went home.

'I'll see you on Monday, Dave. Give my regards to Madeleine.'

When I arrived home at my flat in Surbiton on the Friday evening, there was another acerbic note from Gladys Gurney, my lady who 'does':

> Dear Mr Brock
> Owing to your flat being in such a mess, I didn't have no time to put your washing on, or do none of your ironing. It would help if you was to put things in a bit of order before you go to work, then I could do some of the other things.
> Yours faithfully
> Gladys Gurney (Mrs)

As a consequence, I spent most of Saturday gathering up my dirty clothing and putting it in the washing machine. Then I occupied an hour or so ironing enough shirts to see me through the ensuing week. But it was no good me complaining. Gladys Gurney is an absolute treasure, and I don't know why she puts up with me. She would be extremely difficult to replace.

The same probably goes for my girlfriend, Gail Sutton, a gorgeous, mid-thirties, tall blonde with a figure to die for. I'd met her a while back when I was investigating the murder of a chorus girl at the theatre where she was appearing.

Gail is an actress and trained dancer, although she hasn't done much work lately. But that's of her own choosing. Some years ago, she'd been appearing in Noel Coward's *Private Lives* at the Richmond Theatre. Feeling unwell after the matinée one afternoon, she'd handed over to her understudy for the evening performance, and returned home earlier than expected. To her intense fury, she found her then husband – Gerald Andrews, a theatre director – in bed with a nude dancer. At least, she was nude when Gail found them. They both were. The unremarkable result was a divorce, and Gail reverted to using her maiden name. But she was convinced that Andrews, out of spite, had sabotaged her acting career, and she's been unable to get a decent part since. That's why she was 'hoofing' in the chorus line of *Scatterbrain* at the Granville Theatre when I met her.

Having dealt with all the domestic chores that Mrs Gurney had not had time to complete, I rang Gail and suggested dinner out that evening.

I collected her from her town house in Kingston and we walked along the river to the town centre.

'I thought we'd try this new bistro that's just opened, darling,' I suggested.

'Fine by me,' Gail replied. She was, as usual, dressed in the height of fashion. Her bronze-coloured dress, with large flaps over the shoulders and pockets, was, she assured me, the latest from Burberry. And I thought they only made raincoats and distinctive scarves. But Gail has often told me that I lack any knowledge of haute couture. What interested me about the dress was that it had buttons all down the front.

'Do those buttons undo, or are they just for show?' I asked, touching one of them.

She slapped my hand away. 'You may find out later,' she said. 'Then again you may not. Depends how good the dinner is.' But I discovered later that I was not to investigate the buttons.

It was during the meal that there came one of the interruptions to which I'd become accustomed.

'I'm sorry to intrude . . . ' A man, who had been sitting at an adjacent table, sidled up to us still clutching his napkin. He was a balding, stooped fellow of about sixty, and wore a blazer with a device on the pocket that featured a tennis racquet. 'It is Miss Sutton, isn't it? Miss Gail Sutton?'

'Yes.' Gail looked up wearily.

'I saw you in *Private Lives* years ago,' continued the man. 'I'm a great admirer of the late Noël Coward. And, er, you, of course, Miss Sutton.' He gave an embarrassed little laugh.

'Thank you,' said Gail. 'That's very kind.'

'I wonder if I could bother you for your autograph?' The man produced a piece of paper.

'Certainly.' Gail turned to me with a mischievous expression. 'May I borrow your pen, my lord,' she said.

I produced a ballpoint, and handed it over.

Gail scribbled her name on the paper, and with a fetching smile, returned it to her admirer.

'Thank you so much, Miss Sutton.' The man turned to me. 'I do apologize for the interruption, my lord,' he said, half bowing, and crossed to his own table where he engaged in a whispered conversation with a woman who could only have been his wife. She glanced at me, rather than Gail, and then resumed the conversation, more earnestly than before.

'Watch the gossip columns,' said Gail, and speared a French bean.

'I'm going up to Nottingham tomorrow, darling, to see my parents,' Gail said, as we strolled home arm in arm. 'I want to make an early start, and I need to have an uninterrupted night's sleep.'

Oh well!

'Your father's a property developer, isn't he, Gail?'

'You know darn' well he is, darling. Why? Looking to buy up some property and develop it?' Gail smiled impishly at me.

Of course I knew how George Sutton had made his money. I'd met him and his wife Sally, herself a former dancer, at Gail's home. George talked endlessly about Formula One motor racing and the land-speed record, but had made sufficient money to pay Gail a handsome allowance while she was 'resting'.

'Would you mention a name to him, in confidence, of course.'

'What's that all about?'

I knew I could trust Gail, and I told her as much as she needed to know about my enquiry into the missing Eunice Bailey. 'I wondered if your father had ever heard of a guy called Martin Bailey, that's all.'

'Is he a suspect of some sort?' asked Gail.

'In my book, everyone is until they're not,' I said.

Gail stopped and turned to face me. 'D'you know what you are, Harry, darling?'

'Surprise me.'

'You're a cynical old copper, and I don't know why I love you.'

'It's my irresistible charm,' I said.

'Really? I must've missed that.'

* * *

Monday morning brought a reply from the Bermuda Police. They'd not only got their skates on, they had been thorough.

> To Metpol London FAO DCI Brock Scotland Yard
> Eunice Bailey and Tom Nelson shared room at Driscoll's Hotel 23 May to 6 June. Nelson left Bermuda International Airport that day on flight BA 2232 to London Gatwick 2210 hrs local. Eunice Bailey stayed on. On Sat 8 June man named Nigel Skinner arrived at hotel and struck up close friendship with Mrs Bailey that neither of them disguised. Were seen swimming together at private hotel beach. Booked out together Monday 10 June. No trace of air departure but not believed to have remained in Bermuda. Possible they took a flight under assumed names.
> Regards
> Donald Mercer Det Supt.

'So now we've got another player in the puzzle, Dave,' I said, handing him the message. 'I wonder who the hell this Nigel Skinner is.'

'I reckon Martin Bailey was right when he said his missus was a party girl, guv. Looks as though she goes after anything in trousers. Or better still, anything out of trousers.' Dave took an orange from his briefcase, and began to peel it. I think he only does it to antagonize me; I hate the smell of oranges. 'What's more, I reckon it was her who made the running when she picked up Tom Nelson at the Dorchester.'

'I suppose we'd better keep the boss in the loop,' I said gloomily and, taking Dave with me, made for the commander's office.

'Did you see Mr Bailey on Friday, Mr Brock?'

'Yes, sir. Smoothed him over, no trouble at all. Mind you, he's threatening to subpoena DS Poole and me.'

'Subpoena? Great Scott! Whatever for?'

I told the commander about our interview with Tom Nelson on Friday morning. 'We were obliged to question Bailey about Nelson, not that we mentioned him by name. However, when we asked him if he knew that Mrs Bailey had gone to Bermuda with this man, Martin Bailey started talking about divorce

proceedings, and said that he would subpoena us to attend
court to identify Nelson.'

'Great Scott!' the commander said again. 'We can't have
officers giving evidence in divorce cases. Apart from anything
else, it's only hearsay, from what you tell me.'

'I'm afraid a High Court judge may take a different view,
sir,' said Dave. 'And hearsay evidence is often allowed in
contested divorce cases. If Bailey keeps his promise, we'll be
trotting up the Strand and hopping into the witness box.'

I didn't know whether Dave was right or wrong about any
of that, but I was fairly sure that the commander didn't know
either. Policemen are largely ignorant of the civil law.

'You may care to see the report we received from the
Bermuda Police, sir,' I said, proffering the email printout.

The commander almost snatched it out of my hand. He
loves anything on paper.

'Who is this Nigel Skinner, Mr Brock?'

'At the moment, we've no idea, sir. He could be another
casual acquaintance that Mrs Bailey picked up. In the same
way that she appears to have picked up Nelson. I'm beginning to think that she was quite keen on casual sex.'

The commander shook his head, and made one of his inane
comments. 'I really don't know what the DAC will say.'

But I did. He'd laugh and say, 'So what?'

'What d'you propose to do next, Mr Brock.'

'I was hoping you'd give me directions, sir,' I said smugly.
After all, the boss had started this wild-goose chase, and it
was only fair that he should decide what to do next.

For a few moments, the commander sought inspiration
from the uninspiring view afforded by his office window. 'I
think you'll have to pursue it to the bitter end now, Mr Brock.
If this poor woman has been murdered, we'd finish up looking
frightfully unprofessional if we didn't resolve it.'

I don't know how the hell our noble chief arrived at the
point where he'd assumed that Eunice Bailey had been
murdered, but it looked as though we'd not finished yet.

'Are you suggesting that DS Poole and I go to Bermuda,
sir?'

'Good heavens, no, Mr Brock.' The commander was seized
with horror at the very idea. 'That'd be much too expensive,

and we do have to watch the budget, you know.' And once again he lapsed into silent thought. But then he surrendered. 'You're an experienced detective, Mr Brock. I'll leave it to you to decide your course of action.'

'Very good, sir.' In other words, if it all goes pear-shaped, it'll be down to me. But I'd already decided what to do next.

Five

I decided that another visit to Tom Nelson was called for. From what I'd gathered from reading travel books about Bermuda – and I'd done a crash course in them over the past few days – it's a close-knit community that likes to gossip. It was possible, therefore, that Nelson might have come across Nigel Skinner or perhaps had heard the name.

The door was answered by Trudy, the young glamour-puss whom Nelson had described as his secretary, although I was in little doubt about her precise status. Good luck to him. I wish I could find a secretary with a derrière like hers. She smiled sweetly and showed us into the conservatory.

Nelson cast aside his copy of the *Financial Times*, stood up, and shook hands.

'Had you been to Bermuda before the occasion when you took Mrs Bailey, Mr Nelson?' I asked for openers.

'Several times. Why d'you ask?'

'We have been in contact with the Bermuda Police regarding her disappearance, and they informed us that she made the acquaintance of a man named Nigel Skinner. This was after you'd left Bermuda.'

Nelson laughed. 'I'm not surprised,' he said.

'Really? What makes you say that?'

'She enjoyed sex. In fact, I doubt she could do without it for long. She'd had several affairs, you know.'

'She told you that?'

'Oh sure. She didn't make a secret of it. Said she'd had a lot of affairs, but I didn't give a damn. Well, why should I? I've had a few in my time, and a fair number of one-night stands.'

'And she told you this when you first met?'

'Yes, sure she did, but to be honest, it wasn't so much a meeting as a case of her coming on to me. Although I say it myself, it was pretty obvious that she fancied me.' Nelson paused, and then laughed. 'Or to be realistic, fancied my money.' He paused again. 'To be honest, it did cross my mind that she might be a high-class hooker.'

'Did she mention who any of her affairs were with?'

'Only one. She said that she'd been to some business dinner with her husband. A rare outing with him, apparently, and—'

'When we saw you last, Mr Nelson,' said Dave, 'you implied that you didn't know that Mrs Bailey was married. As a matter of fact, you said she'd told you she wasn't.'

Nelson gave a rueful smile. 'Yeah, well, it's not the done thing to admit to having a fling with a married woman, is it? Can lead to complications. Like divorce courts.'

This was not the time to tell him of Martin Bailey's intentions regarding divorce.

'I hope you're not obstructing us in what could be a murder enquiry, Mr Nelson,' I said sternly. I was by no means certain that that's what we were looking into, but I was starting to get some worrying thoughts about the way this so-called missing-person investigation was going.

'Hell! D'you really think someone's murdered her?' Nelson gave the impression of being deeply shocked, but I've met some good actor-murderers in the past.

I shrugged. 'I don't know, but it's beginning to look increasingly serious. However, you were telling us about this affair that she had.'

'Yeah. She met this guy at a business dinner and the upshot was that she had a fling with him.'

'Did she say when and where?'

'Nope, she just said that she'd arranged to meet up with him a few days later, and that it lasted about two weeks. Then they went their separate ways.'

'Did she tell you this man's name? Was it Skinner, by any chance?'

'No, sir. She never named names. I reckon she was a pretty discreet sort of girl, thank the Lord.'

I knew that I'd've been damned lucky to learn the man's identity, and even more so to learn that it was Skinner, but it was worth a try.

'Have you ever heard of this man Nigel Skinner?' I asked. 'Particularly in Bermuda.'

'Doesn't mean a thing to me, Detective.' Nelson furrowed his brow. 'No, not a thing. You say he picked up with Eunice after I left?'

'That's our information.'

'Sorry, I can't help you.' Nelson looked genuinely disappointed that he was unable to assist.

'And you're quite sure that you didn't meet Eunice Bailey after you returned to London on the sixth of June.'

'Absolutely. Like I said, I tried ringing her cellphone, but there was never any reply. And she never told me her address. Other than to say it was in Marble Arch someplace.'

'You said previously that you'd had to return to London to attend a charity function. Where was that?'

'Palmer's Hotel in Park Lane, and it was on the seventh of June. Here . . . ' Nelson opened the drawer in a side table and took out a handful of pasteboard invitations. He riffled through them and handed me one. 'That's the one.'

But I was still unconvinced by Nelson's story. Given that Mrs Bailey had apparently not left Bermuda didn't necessarily mean that she was still there. As the Bermuda Police had suggested, she might have travelled out under an assumed name, and met Nelson in London. And if she was dead, he might be the murderer. On the other hand, and in view of what Nelson had said about the woman's discretion, she could well have been conducting yet another clandestine affair, this time with the mysterious Nigel Skinner. And that, I supposed, would be a good enough reason for travelling incognito if she'd happened to be with him. We knew that the ticket Nelson had given her had been cashed in, but she could have used the money to buy another. I was beginning to build up a picture of a devious woman.

'I would like you to make a written statement about all of this, Mr Nelson,' I said.

Nelson raised his eyebrows. 'Should I have an attorney present?' he asked, a worried expression settling on his face.

Now it was my turn to assume raised eyebrows. 'Whatever for?'

'Well, this is beginning to sound like it's getting a bit heavy, Detective.'

'Mr Nelson, this is merely the way in which the British police gather evidence. We can't remember everything that's said to us. We have to have it written down. I imagine it's much the same in the United States.'

'Yeah, I guess so.'

But Nelson's reluctance made me feel a little suspicious, but maybe he hadn't previously been involved in a police investigation. On either side of the big pond that separates Britain from the United States.

For the next hour, Nelson dictated a detailed account of his first meeting with Eunice Bailey, and continued until the point when he'd left Bermuda at the end of the two-week holiday he'd enjoyed with her. Then, at my suggestion, he added a rider claiming that he had not seen her since returning to this country. After reading it several times, he eventually signed it.

'As I mentioned last time, Mr Nelson,' I said, as Dave and I stood up to leave, 'if Mrs Bailey does get in touch, I'd be obliged if you'd let me know as a matter of urgency.'

'Sure thing, Detective.'

I got the impression that Tom Nelson was pleased to see the back of us. But something told me that it would not be the last time we'd talk.

We returned to Curtis Green and handed Nelson's lengthy statement to Colin Wilberforce. Within minutes, he'd photocopied it, logged it on the computer, indexed it, and filed it. As I've said many times, I'm convinced that if Colin ever got himself promoted, and thus posted elsewhere, the incident room would descend into chaos.

'What's next, guv?' asked Dave.

'I reckon it's time to have another chat with Martin Bailey,' I said.

Dave groaned. 'Another late night, then.'

'That's what the coppering game's all about, Dave, but try ringing him. You never know, it might be one of the days when he's working at home.'

And he was.

'He's there, guv, and the arrogant bastard will be pleased to grant us an audience at three o'clock.'

'How very civil of him.'

I suppose that seeing us on his CCTV was sufficient for Bailey this time, because he did not demand that we showed our warrant cards. We were making progress, but not with our enquiry.

'Have you come to tell me that you've found my wife, Chief Inspector?' Bailey waved us to seats in his opulent living room. 'Not that it's of any interest to me.'

'No, Mr Bailey, but if you are able to answer some questions, it might help us to do so.'

'Go ahead.' Bailey sat in an armchair facing us, crossed his legs and folded his hands in his lap.

'Nigel Skinner.' I threw in the name in the hope that it would awaken a memory. But not this time.

'Who the hell's Nigel Skinner?'

'I was hoping you'd be able to tell me,' I said.

'When we were here last, Mr Bailey,' said Dave, 'we told you that we'd interviewed a man who was with your wife in Bermuda for two weeks until the sixth of June, but that he then left. However, we've since learned that following this man's departure, Mrs Bailey made the acquaintance of a man named Nigel Skinner, and spent some time with him over the next four days. They then booked out of the hotel together on the tenth of June, but there the trail ends.'

'And I suppose she spent most of the time in bed with him,' commented Bailey acidly. But this time he made no mention of divorce.

'I'm afraid we don't have that information,' said Dave blandly, trotting out one of his standard phrases.

'How did you find all that out?' demanded Bailey.

'We've been in touch with the Bermuda Police,' I said. 'They've been very helpful.'

'So who the hell is this man Skinner? Did they tell you that?'

'No, they were unable to trace him. There's only so much the police can do, you know.'

'Yes, I suppose so,' conceded Bailey grudgingly. 'So what happens next?'

'We keep looking,' I said. 'I suppose you've not heard from your wife since our last visit.'

'Not a bloody word, Chief Inspector, but then I didn't expect to. And I don't really want to.'

'There is another lead we'd like to follow up, Mr Bailey.'

'What's that?'

I related the story told us by Tom Nelson about Eunice Bailey meeting one of Martin Bailey's business associates at a dinner. And her claim that they had a brief affair.

To my surprise, Bailey laughed. 'I knew about that,' he said. 'So what?'

'You didn't object?' I asked.

'What's the bloody point? If you've got a wife who goes over the side, you either put up with it or divorce the bitch. And to tell you the truth,' Bailey continued with, for him, rare candour, 'I was seeing someone else at the same time.'

'Can you tell us the name of this man your wife was seeing, sir?' asked Dave.

'Dickie Richards. Actually his name's Peter Richards, but everyone calls him Dickie.'

'Do you have an address for him?' Dave asked, pocketbook already open on his knee.

Bailey gave us the details without hesitation. 'That'll shake him,' he said. 'I'll bet he thinks I didn't know about it. You can mention my name if you like,' he added with an evil grin. 'Just to let him know he can't pull the wool over Martin Bailey's eyes.'

'Doesn't that constitute grounds for divorce?' queried Dave, puzzled that Bailey had been very keen on the idea when we'd originally mentioned Nelson.

'Apparently not,' said Bailey. 'My useless lawyer told me that as I took her back into the marital home, I'd condoned her adultery. We all make mistakes,' he added with a sigh.

We'd left it until seven o'clock to call on Peter Richards on the assumption that he would have been at work. And we were right. We met him on the doorstep of his house in Notting Hill just as he was putting his key in the lock.

'Mr Richards?'

'Yes.' Richards withdrew the key, and turned to face us, glancing at Dave somewhat apprehensively. Perhaps he thought we were a multiracial mugging team.

'We're police officers, Mr Richards,' I said, and produced my warrant card.

'What d'you want?' The nervous expression was still there, and his right hand twitched at his top-pocket handkerchief.

'We'd like to talk to you about Mrs Eunice Bailey.'

'Really?'

I don't know what was going through Richards's mind but, despite his offhand response, he seemed extremely shaken by that announcement. Putting his key back in the lock, he opened the door.

A good-looking Titian-haired woman in a pink satin robe appeared in the hall as we entered. She glanced at Dave and me with a lift of her chin, and then looked at her husband, a quizzical expression on her face.

'These gentlemen are from the police, darling,' said Richards, and improvising rapidly, added, 'They want to talk to me about some fraud that's happening.'

'Are you involved, Dickie? You haven't been up to something criminal, I hope.' A frown descended on the woman's face that could have implied 'something criminal *again*'.

'No, no, nothing like that,' said Richards hurriedly. It seemed that he had only succeeded in exchanging one tricky situation for another. 'I'll talk to them in the study.' Somewhat belatedly, he introduced her. 'Incidentally, this is my wife, Fiona.'

Fiona Richards afforded us a cursory nod, and I got the impression that it was not the first time that Richards had been involved with the police. I didn't have to say anything; I knew that Dave would be making a mental note to search the Yard's records when we got back to Curtis Green.

'I'm going to take a shower, Dickie, but I hope you won't be too long,' said Fiona frostily. 'Don't forget we're going out tonight,' she called over her shoulder as she turned away.

Richards's study was thickly carpeted and furnished with a large leather-topped desk, the obligatory computer, and a few books on a shelf. They were not particularly interesting: a dictionary, a world atlas, a few popular paperbacks, and an encyclopaedia that, judging by its size, couldn't have contained much information. But I wouldn't have minded betting that one of the locked drawers in his desk contained a few explicit girlie magazines. I don't know why; I just had that feeling. But that was of no interest to us right now. There's a Porn Squad that deals with that sort of rubbish. Not that they have much success these days.

Richards seated himself in a captain's chair behind the desk, and invited us to sit in the two other leather armchairs that the room contained. He seemed to have recovered his composure now that he'd got over the shock of two coppers arriving to talk to him about Eunice Bailey. And that he'd managed to fend off his domineering wife.

'May I offer you gentlemen a drink?' he asked, oozing urbane charm.

'No, thank you. I understand that you had an affair with Eunice Bailey some time ago, Mr Richards.'

The composure vanished; we'd got him. 'That's absolute rubbish. I'm faithful to my wife, and always have been. I demand to know where you got such a preposterous story from.' But the colour had drained from Richards's face and he'd begun perspiring. To be fair, however – unusual for me – it was a warm day in late June and the study was insufferably hot.

'As a matter of fact, Eunice Bailey's husband told us.'

'*What?*' Unsurprisingly, that seemed to have made matters worse. 'How in hell's name did he find out?' Richards's arms slipped from the arms of his chair, and hung loosely at its sides. Outside a police car raced down the road, its siren penetrating the Richardses' double-glazing.

'I've no idea, Mr Richards. Perhaps his wife told him. But I gather from what you've just said that you did have an affair with her.'

'I suppose Martin Bailey was being vindictive, telling you people about it, but I can't think why he should have done.' Richards glanced at the door, presumably to make sure it was firmly closed. 'Yes, it's true,' he admitted quietly, a note of resignation in his voice. 'Eunice and I did have an affair.' But then he rallied, and out came the indignant self-righteous citizen. 'But what has that got to do with the police? Surely to God you've enough crime to deal with without poking your noses into law-abiding people's private lives. We've been burgled twice in a year.'

'If only it were that easy,' sighed Dave. 'But Mrs Bailey has disappeared and the police are concerned that she might have come to some harm.'

'Oh God! What d'you think might have happened to her?' Richards ran a finger around the inside of his sweat-stained collar, and little beads of perspiration crept out from beneath an ill-fitting toupee.

'The worst-case scenario is that she's been murdered.' I sat back and waited.

'Murdered? She can't possibly have been.' Richards shook his head in disbelief, and perspired even more. I wasn't sure that he could cope with these revelations, coming, as they had, one on top of another.

'Why not?' I asked. 'People do get murdered. All too often these days.'

'When did you last see Mrs Bailey, Mr Richards?' asked Dave. By now his pocketbook was open, and he was waggling his pen in the sort of menacing way that only he could achieve.

'Now look, you can't think I had anything to—'

'Just answer the question, please, Mr Richards.' Dave waggled his pen again.

'It was last year. Yes, just about a year ago.'

'And how did you meet her?' Dave started writing.

Richards gave an account of his meeting with Eunice Bailey that accorded, almost word for word, with the story that Tom Nelson said she'd told him. In short, two weeks of sweaty unbridled lust, played out in the afternoons in a hotel in Kensington.

'How well d'you know Nigel Skinner?' I posed the question quietly.

'Who?'

'Nigel Skinner,' I repeated.

'I don't know anyone of that name. Why? What's he got to do with it?'

'Just a name that came up in the course of our enquiries. Have you heard from Mrs Bailey since you last saw her?'

'No, I haven't, and I don't want to either.'

'And why's that? Did you have an argument?'

But Richards seemed to sense that I was leading him into saying that he and Eunice had argued, and that the argument had ended in violence.

'No, nothing like that. She told me that she intended seeking a divorce from her husband. Well, the last thing I wanted was to be cited in some tacky divorce case, so we split. I had a nasty feeling that I was being set up. She was a very persuasive woman, and I suspected that she could be quite deceitful when the mood took her.'

And if Martin Bailey had threatened to expose Richards in

court as Eunice's lover, Richards may have been tempted to murder Eunice rather than risk his marriage to Fiona. Particularly if she was the one with the money.

The door opened and Fiona Richards stood on the threshold, silently pointing at her wristwatch.

'Yes, all right,' snapped Richards. 'I won't be long.'

'Don't forget you've still got to change into your dinner jacket.' Fiona tossed her head and left, slamming the door behind her.

'Have you ever been to Bermuda, Mr Richards?' asked Dave.

'Bermuda? No, why?'

'Or the States?'

'I've been to New York twice, and several times to Las Vegas. On business.'

'And what is your business?' I asked.

'I'm a director of a company that owns a number of overseas casinos. Both in the States and Europe.'

'So how come you met Martin Bailey, a property developer, at a business dinner?'

'Because, Chief Inspector, casinos have to be accommodated in property,' Richards said, rather tartly I thought, 'and we prefer to build our own. Either that or convert suitable premises. And Bailey has interests abroad.'

'So you've bought overseas property from Mr Bailey,' commented Dave, 'as well as making a cuckold of him.' My sergeant can be very cutting at times.

'It's not something I'm proud of,' said Richards, 'and if Fiona ever finds out, that'll be the end of our marriage. And given the recent amounts of alimony that the High Court has awarded, that could cost me a small fortune.'

That, of course, could be a motive for murder. But murdering Martin Bailey rather than Bailey's wife.

'If you should hear from Mrs Bailey again, Mr Richards,' I said, as Dave and I prepared to leave, 'perhaps you'd let me know.' And I handed him one of my cards. I seemed to be distributing quite a few of them lately.

Richards examined it. That the card indicated that we were attached to the Homicide and Serious Crime Command didn't seem to do anything to cheer him up. Added to which, I suspected he was about to be subjected to an in-depth interrogation by his wife that would make ours seem quite friendly by comparison.

The following morning Dave sent DC John Appleby to Palmer's Hotel in Park Lane to verify Nelson's claim that he had attended a charity function there on the seventh of June.

Then Dave did a search of records.

'Richards has got previous, guv.'

'What for?'

'Tax evasion about six years ago.' Dave looked up from his file and grinned. 'He was running an import and export agency at the time. Got weighed off with a fine of ten thousand pounds, and went bankrupt when the Inland Revenue pursued him as a primary creditor.'

'Well, there's a surprise,' I said. 'He seems to have recovered, though.'

'Ah, Mr Brock.' And there was the commander. I hadn't realized it was ten o'clock already. 'Any developments in the Bailey case?' he asked airily.

I gave him a very quick rundown on what we had achieved so far. Which wasn't much.

'D'you think this Peter Richards is a likely suspect?' The commander had clearly been influenced by the fact that Richards had a previous conviction for tax evasion. But a real detective would have known that, generally speaking, a tax evader does not usually progress to murder. Unless it was a tax collector he murdered.

'Could be, sir,' said Dave. 'But then I never trust a man with a dodgy Irish.'

'An Irish?' The commander turned to me with a puzzled expression. 'What on earth is Sergeant Poole talking about, Mr Brock?'

'It's rhyming slang, sir. Irish jig: wig.'

'I don't approve of slang of any sort,' said the commander huffily, and disappeared to his own office. I think he thought that because we wear smart suits – apart from Dave, that is – we should behave like gentlemen. Well, gentlemen don't catch villains. But it was typical that his remark was directed at me rather than Dave. It was noticeable that he had been wary of Dave ever since he had been put politely in his place after posing a question about Dave's racial origins.

It had been a hilarious encounter. The commander had asked Dave where he came from. Dave had said London. That, and one or two other exchanges, had made Dave choose to infer that the commander was being racist.

The truth of the matter was that Dave's grandfather, a doctor, had come from the Caribbean in the fifties, and settled in Bethnal Green. Dave's father was an accountant, but, following university, Dave himself joined the police. 'And that, sir,' he had said to the commander, 'makes me the black sheep of the family.'

The commander hadn't been able to cope with a black officer being racist about himself, and he'd retired hurt.

'Dave, when DI Ebdon gets in would you ask her to arrange for covert photographs to be taken of Martin Bailey, Tom Nelson and Peter Richards. I've a feeling that we'll need to show them around.'

'Yes, sir.' Dave obviously didn't think much of the idea. He always called me 'sir' when I made a fatuous suggestion.

Six

Young John Appleby returned from Palmer's Hotel at about two o'clock the following afternoon. 'I spoke to the banqueting head waiter, who was on duty on the evening of the seventh of June, sir, and he remembers Mr Nelson quite clearly. He confirms that he was definitely there.'

'How can he be so sure, John?' Given the number of people who attend functions at big hotels, I was surprised that the head waiter was able so confidently to recall someone who had been there nearly three weeks previously.

'Mr Nelson was the organizer of the charity event that took place that evening, sir, and he gave the head waiter a sizeable tip. Two hundred pounds, apparently.'

'Yes,' I said, 'that would tend to stick in his mind, I suppose.'

'Isn't it bloody marvellous?' commented Dave. 'Someone gives a couple of hundred quid to his favourite charity, and it finishes up in a head waiter's back pocket.'

Disregarding Dave's acerbic comment, valid though it was, I concluded that there would still have been time for Nelson to return to Bermuda the next day. And it wasn't until the tenth of June – three days later – that Mrs Bailey's credit card had ceased to be used. The snag in that reasoning was that the staff at Driscoll's Hotel would surely have recognized Nelson if he'd returned a day or two later masquerading as Nigel Skinner. Unless he'd bought someone's silence by handing out a tip as substantial as the one he'd given the head waiter in London.

There again, if Nelson had returned to Bermuda, he might have met Eunice when she wasn't in the company of Skinner. Perhaps Eunice Bailey's body was mouldering in some shallow grave there, or even at the bottom of the Atlantic. If Nelson could afford to have a yacht on the French Riviera, he might also have one in Bermuda. If not, he could certainly have afforded to charter one. I imagine that a weighted body dropped somewhere in the six hundred miles between Bermuda and the North Carolina coastline would take a long time to find. And if it were discovered, it would be down to the Bermuda Police or the FBI, not me. I should be so lucky. But the real question was why he should have murdered her.

'There's another thing that doesn't make sense, Dave,' I said.

'There are a lot of things that don't make sense, guv.' Dave tossed me a cigarette, and sank into my only armchair. 'What in particular?'

'Where was Eunice Bailey for the five days between going absent from the marital home, and pushing off to Bermuda with Nelson on the twenty-third?'

'Does it matter . . . sir?' Dave was calling me 'sir' again. I suppose he thought it was a stupid question. 'If she has been topped, it won't have been between those two dates because we know she was alive in Bermuda later on.'

'Good point, Dave,' I admitted. Dave can always be relied upon to stop me from going off at a tangent.

'And Nelson said he met her every night on those days.'

'Yes, but we've only got his word for it.' I thought I'd got my own back. Wrong!

'But she was still alive later on, according to the Bermuda Police.'

I gave up on that. Dave was absolutely right, of course. As usual.

I did, however, think it might be profitable if we were to look into Martin Bailey's background a little more thoroughly.

I wandered out to the incident room and spoke to Colin Wilberforce. 'Colin, can you get a General Register Office search organized?'

'Yes, sir. Who d'you want to know about?'

'Find out when Martin Bailey was married, and anything else about him that might be useful.'

And, that apart, there seemed to be little else we could do for the time being. But no sooner had I returned to my office than the phone rang.

'Miss Sutton's on the line, sir,' said Colin. 'Shall I put her through?'

'Yes, please, Colin.'

It was most unusual for Gail to telephone me at work, and I hoped that nothing was wrong.

'Sorry to bother you at work, darling, but my parents are coming down for the weekend.'

I failed to see the urgency in Gail telling me about this, but I guessed what was coming next.

'How nice for you,' I said.

'Would you join us for dinner on Saturday evening at my place?'

'That would be wonderful, darling.' I couldn't think of a reason to refuse, save the possibility that I might be called out, and said so.

'My father has something important to tell you that he didn't want to discuss on the phone.'

'Any idea what it's about?'

Gail sighed, loudly. 'Of course not. I just told you he wouldn't discuss it on the phone.' I think she sometimes wonders how I catch criminals.

The only new information of any importance in connection with the Eunice Bailey case came through the next day, Thursday.

Colin came into my office clutching a computer printout from the police-liaison officer at the General Register Office in Southport.

'Martin Bailey, sir.'

'What've we got, Colin?'

'He was married to Eunice Webb, as she then was, five years ago. Incidentally, his present address was the one shown on the marriage certificate. But he was previously married to a Gina Nash, whom he divorced a year before his marriage to Eunice. That previous marriage lasted five years.'

'Interesting. Any indication where the first Mrs Bailey is living?'

'I've got the address where she was living at the time of the divorce, six years ago, sir,' said Colin, 'but whether she's still there is anyone's guess.'

'Ask DI Ebdon to make a few discreet enquiries, Colin, but not to interview the woman. If she finds her.'

Kate Ebdon, a flame-haired Australian who usually dressed in jeans and a man's white shirt, was in charge of the legwork team that did all the background enquiries. She was a damned good detective, and terrified most villains . . . and the commander. He strongly disapproved of the way she dressed, but hadn't the guts to take her to task about it. She has an engaging technique of getting the maximum information out of witnesses, as well as having literally charmed the pants off one or two of the Flying Squad officers with whom she'd previously served.

Colin made a note or two on the clipboard he always carried, and departed.

I arrived at Gail's Kingston town house at seven o'clock on the Saturday evening, clutching a bottle of champagne that I'd bought on the way. I'd walked from my flat in Surbiton because I knew I'd be having a drink or two, and I intended to take a taxi back. There's nothing the Black Rats – as we of the plain-clothed cognoscenti call the traffic boys – like better than to breathalyse a CID officer. But why, you may wonder, was I not staying the night? Simple. Gail tries to pretend to her parents that she and I do not frequently share a bed. But I wouldn't mind betting that her parents did so before they were married. Strange that, how parents suddenly develop a puritanical streak once their relationship is solemnized.

George Sutton shook hands, and his vivacious wife Sally gave me a hug and a kiss.

Once I'd got a Scotch in my hand, George steered me down the stairs and out to the garden.

'Gail tells me that you're interested in a man called Martin Bailey, Harry.'

'Yes, that's right.' I'd forgotten having asked Gail to find out if her father knew anything about Bailey.

'I've run across him from time to time. He's a dodgy character.' Sutton paused to watch an aircraft on its final flight path into Heathrow Airport.

'I'd more or less formed that opinion myself, George.'

'Talk to anyone in the property game, and they'll tell you not to do business with Bailey if you can possibly do business with anyone else. And don't even shake hands with him if you can avoid it.' Sutton took out his pipe and began to fill it. 'There are rumours that he's got a substantial amount of cash invested in a tax haven. The Cayman Islands, I think.

And he has a place in Bermuda. Might even have business interests there, but I can't be sure. I only got the information second-hand from an acquaintance of mine.'

Marvellous! Just as the enquiry was beginning to stall, Gail's father had thrown a bloody great boulder into my tranquil lake.

'What sort of place in Bermuda?'

Sutton shrugged. 'I don't know, Harry, old boy, but I was told that he's got a holiday home there somewhere.'

I pulled out my mobile and rang Gavin Creasey at the Curtis Green incident room. While I was waiting for him to reply, it occurred to me that Gavin always seemed to be on night duty. I made a mental note to enquire into it. As a senior officer, I'm supposed to worry about the welfare of my subordinates.

'Gavin, get a message off to the Bermuda Police ASAP. Address it to Detective Superintendent Donald Mercer, and ask him if he would be so good as to have discreet enquiries made regarding Martin Bailey. I've received information that he has a place there, and may also have business interests. Just to spice it up a bit, add that we're working on the possibility that Eunice Bailey, the subject of our previous messages, might have been murdered somewhere on the Bermudas.'

I cancelled the call and drained my Scotch.

'Bloody hell, you blokes don't hang about, do you?' said Sutton, obviously impressed by this example of the speed and efficiency of the Metropolitan Police. But then he does live in Nottingham.

We went in for dinner. As usual George Sutton began talking about Formula One motor racing, but once that was exhausted, he threw in a few thumbnail sketches of previous land-speed record attempts. His monologue was peppered with names like Malcolm Campbell, Frank Lockhart, Lee Bible, Henry Segrave and Parry Thomas. But eventually, Sally Sutton told him he was being a bore and should shut up. It was just as well: I hadn't heard of any of them.

I had dutifully returned home on the Saturday evening, but Gail rang me at two o'clock on the Sunday afternoon.

'The coast's clear, darling,' she said. 'Why don't you come round?'

This was an exciting invitation, and I presumed that she

intended to compensate me for not having been allowed to stay the previous night. I was wrong.

'You've not met Charlie and Bill, have you?' said Gail, the moment I arrived. 'They live at Esher.'

'No. Are they . . . ?' I waggled my hand.

Gail laughed. 'Charlie's a woman. Her name's actually Charlotte, but everyone calls her Charlie. And Bill Hunter is the guy she's married to. She's an actress, but Charlie Hunter's not her stage name. As a matter of fact, I can't remember what she does call herself. And Bill is something in the City, awfully rich.'

'So what about them?'

'We're going to see them. They've got this big house at Esher, and they've invited us over for a swim.'

'I don't have any swimming things with me,' I protested.

Gail shot me an arch smile. 'I don't think that matters too much,' she said.

Oh, so it's to be one of those parties.

Bill and Charlie Hunter were a delightful couple – probably in their late thirties – and made us immediately welcome. They were already attired for swimming, and I needn't have worried about Gail's earlier teasing comment, which was a shame really because Charlie was a very shapely brunette.

'So you're the famous Harry Brock,' said Charlie, shaking hands. 'I've heard a lot about you.'

'Nothing bad, I hope.' I don't know why people always say that, but I responded to her trite comment with one of my own.

'Come on through,' said Bill, and led the way through their sumptuous house to a secluded open-air swimming pool in the large garden.

Bill Hunter lent me a pair of trunks and Gail and I got changed in separate purpose-built wooden cabins complete with showers. Oh yes, he was rich all right.

'Aren't you coming in?' asked Gail, by now wearing a risqué bikini.

'You swim, I'll watch,' I said, nursing the first of several whisky sours as I reclined under a large parasol. It was as well that Gail had volunteered to drive.

It seemed that Bill Hunter was as uninterested in swimming

as I was. While the girls frolicked in the pool, he dispensed another whisky sour and sat beside me.

'Gail says you catch murderers.'

'Only when I'm lucky,' I said. I don't know why people always have to quiz me about my job on a day off. I'll bet they wouldn't if I was an accountant.

'Sounds jolly interesting,' persisted Hunter.

'Most of it's not,' I said. 'Much of it's routine.'

'I've never understood that. What d'you chaps actually mean when you say, "It's just routine"?'

'They only say that on television,' I said. 'We don't say it in case someone asks what you've just asked.'

'Eh?' Hunter sat up and turned to face me.

'We don't say it, because I've no idea what it means,' I said.

Despite all that, it was an enjoyable and relaxing afternoon. And when eventually Gail and I got back to her house, she *did* compensate me for the previous evening.

The moment I arrived at the office on Monday morning, Colin Wilberforce handed me a message.

'Reply from Bermuda, sir,' he said.

'They didn't waste any time,' I said. 'Where's Dave?'

'Getting the coffee, sir.'

I turned, but then paused. 'Colin, why does Gavin Creasey always seem to do night duty?'

'He likes it, sir. He's not married. In fact, he once told me that he hasn't got any family at all. He reckons that doing nights leaves him all afternoon to do whatever he wants to do.'

Oh well! It takes all sorts, I suppose. Personally, I was delighted when I stopped doing night duty on a regular basis. Mind you, there are occasions when I do day duty *and* night duty all rolled into one. But that's what being a CID officer is all about.

Dave appeared in my office bearing coffee. I related what George Sutton had told me on Saturday, and then scanned the message from Bermuda.

'This is interesting, Dave,' I said, handing him the printout. 'It seems that Martin Bailey – who, you remember, denied ever having been to Bermuda – has a holiday cottage at a place called Flatt's Village, wherever that is.'

'Soon tell you, guv.' Dave went to the sergeants' office and returned moments later with a map that he spread on my desk. 'There it is,' he said, planting a forefinger on a point just south of Harrington Sound. 'That's Flatt's Village.'

'Superintendent Mercer also says that enquiries are continuing regarding any business interests that Bailey may have there, and he'll let us know if anything turns up.' I threw Dave a Marlboro. This week I'd decided to give up giving up smoking. Apart from anything else, I continue to derive some childish pleasure from smoking where I shouldn't. Bit like smoking behind the bike sheds at school. 'But I don't see how Bailey having a place in Bermuda alters anything very much.'

'But he said he'd never been there, guv. That puts him in the frame, surely.'

'Not necessarily. He might have some dodgy business dealings going down over there, something that might interest Her Majesty's Revenue and Customs. Or even the Fraud Squad. And that would be a very good reason for staying shtum. There is another thing, too. If Bailey had anything to do with his wife's disappearance – like he'd murdered her – why didn't he do a runner once we started asking questions?'

'Because he's an arrogant bastard who thinks that he can outwit the bumbling Old Bill, guv. So what are we going to do about it?'

'Front him with it. See what he has to say. If he then does a runner, I think we might be on to something.'

'Very good . . . *sir*.' Dave glanced at his watch. 'Now?'

'Better give him a ring. I don't want to waste time going out to Holland Park if he's not going to be there.'

But that course of action was delayed by the arrival of DI Ebdon.

'G'day, guv,' she said, waving a piece of paper. 'I've dug up some information about this Gina Nash sheila.' As usual, she was hamming up her Australian accent.

'Bailey's first wife?'

'That's her. I did a bit of poking about, and eventually tracked her down to an address on Richmond Hill in Surrey.'

'Good work, Kate. Is she married again?'

'Doesn't look like it. Uses her maiden name. Seems as though she's what you might call a woman of independent means.'

'What, no occupation?'

'Not that I could discover, but I didn't get too close.'

'Well,' I said, glancing at Dave, 'I reckon we'll have a chat with the Lass of Richmond Hill before we talk to Martin Bailey again.'

It wasn't quite on Richmond Hill. Gina Nash's big old house was in Talavera Road, and had a marvellous view of the River Thames.

'If she lives there on her own, she must rattle around in it,' commented Dave as we drew up outside. 'And by the look of the place, she's got some loot.'

The woman who answered the door had her long brown hair clipped back into a ponytail. She was wearing a paint-bespattered smock and held a paintbrush in one hand, and greeted us with a quizzical smile. I reckoned she was in her late thirties.

'Ms Nash?' I enquired.

'Yes.'

'We're police officers, Ms Nash,' I said, and introduced Dave and me.

'That's a shame. I was hoping you'd come to buy a painting.'

'Oh, you're a painter, are you?' Dave glanced pointedly at the woman's smock and paintbrush, and gave her a devilish smile.

'How very clever of you,' responded Gina Nash, and smiled too. 'Well, whatever it is, you'd better come in. I'm in the middle of something.'

She led us through the house and down a back staircase to a conservatory not unlike Tom Nelson's, except that this one had been converted into a studio. On an easel there was a painting depicting a view of the river that we'd seen from the front door. Canvases lined one wall, some of which were partly completed paintings. A table covered with the paraphernalia of Gina's craft stood in the centre of the room.

'You don't mind if I just put the finishing touches to this bit of sky while I still have it in mind, do you?'

'Not at all.'

Indicating a settee on the far side of the table, Gina invited us to sit down. 'Mind your clothes,' she cautioned. 'I don't want you to get paint all over them.' She added a few brush-strokes of white to the blue of her painting's sky, laid down her brush and palette, and perched on a stool. 'Well, now, gentlemen, this is all very intriguing. What can I do for you? Are you from the Arts and Antiques Squad? I don't do forgeries.' She flashed another smile.

'No, Ms Nash, we're from the Homicide and Serious Crime Command at Scotland Yard.'

'My word. Has someone been murdered?'

I didn't want to get into that too early on. 'I understand that you were once married to Martin Bailey,' I said.

Gina Nash gave a girlish giggle. 'Don't tell me that someone has finally murdered Martin,' she said. 'Yes, we were married for five years, but it ended in divorce about six years ago. He had an affair with some tart he picked up and, as that wasn't the first, I left him. But it hurt.'

'D'you mean he was violent?' asked Dave.

'No, nothing like that. What I meant was that the divorce hurt him. I took him for two million pounds.'

'Who was this woman you named, Ms Nash?' I asked.

'Oh, for goodness' sake call me Gina. Everyone does. He eventually married her, I believe. Her name was . . . ' She paused in thought, searching for the name. 'Yes, it was Eunice Webb. Thought a lot of herself, did that one. Is it her who's been murdered?'

'I don't know. But we are looking into her disappearance.'

'How can I help, then?'

'Did Mr Bailey have a place in Bermuda when you were married to him, Gina?'

'Yes, he did. We went there a few times. It was a lovely little cottage at a place called Flatt's Village. Not that I saw much of him when we were there. He had some business to attend to, so he said. Personally, I think he spent as much time chatting up the local talent as he did on business. I actually spotted him in a bar one evening, talking to some suntanned American bimbo with legs up to her arse. But I let him get on with it. I just lounged about on the beach every day. It's a wonderful place for swimming.'

'Have you any idea what his business was?'

'Apart from an overweening urge to make pots of money, any which way he could, d'you mean? No, Martin never volunteered information. I wouldn't be at all surprised if you told me he was up to something illegal.' Gina thought about that for moment or two. 'Was he?'

'Not as far as we know, but that's not what we're interested in.' Not that that would stop me from passing any interesting titbits to the Fraud Squad, of course. 'As I said just now, Eunice Bailey, as she now is, has disappeared, and we're concerned to discover her present whereabouts.'

'If she's got any sense, she'll have left the bastard,' commented Gina, with a trace of bitterness. 'He's got to have been one of the most selfish, self-centred men I've ever met. And arrogant too. It was bad enough being married to him, but I should think it's even worse doing business with him.'

'He told us that he was in the property-development business,' said Dave.

'Probably,' said Gina. 'But as I was saying earlier, his main business was making money, no matter how he did it, or who he put down in the process. He was quite ruthless.' She took a packet of cigarettes from the pocket of her smock. 'D'you guys smoke?' she asked.

'Have one of mine,' said Dave, leaping from his chair and proffering his packet of Silk Cut.

'Thanks.' Gina shot Dave a warm smile, and waited until he'd lit her cigarette before continuing. 'We never went out anywhere together, you know,' she said, expelling a plume of smoke towards the glass roof of the studio. 'He'd be working from morning to night. I lost count of the number of times I went out on my own. That wouldn't have been so bad, but I found out that it wasn't all work. There were other women, but then I just told you that.' She took a pull on her cigarette, and switched her gaze to Dave. That she was studying him through an artist's eye became obvious from her next question. 'Have you ever posed for a life study, Sergeant Poole?' she asked.

'No,' said Dave.

'I'd like to paint you. Would you be prepared to pose for me? Nude, of course.'

'Not a chance,' said Dave. 'I can't remember the last time my guv'nor allowed me to sit still for an hour doing nothing.'

'Pity,' commented Gina, and reverted to the reason we were there. 'I don't see that I can help you very much about Martin's present wife, unless you have some more questions.'

'Only one or two. When did you last see Martin Bailey?'

Gina laughed. 'Coming out of the Law Courts in the Strand,

six years ago,' she said. 'He didn't look at all well, but then I'd just taken two million pounds off him. Serve the sod right. I'd originally been willing to settle for quite a bit less than that, but when he decided to fight the divorce, I thought, well, fuck you, mister, and I took it to the wire.'

'Did you ever meet the current Mrs Bailey?' asked Dave.

'Only in court that same time. My solicitor subpoenaed her, and named her as the woman in the case. That's what cost Martin so much, I think. But I'm surprised to hear that she's still with him. She must have a hell of a lot of stamina. Ah, but you just said she'd disappeared. Good for her.'

'Did you ever hear mention of a man called Nigel Skinner, particularly when you were in Bermuda, Gina?'

'No,' Gina replied immediately. 'I've never heard the name.'

'Well, thank you for your time. I hope we didn't interrupt your painting too much.'

'That's OK. If I think of anything else, I'll give you a ring. How do I reach you?'

I gave her one of my cards and she escorted us to the front door.

Gina Nash shook hands with each of us, her hand lingering longer in Dave's hand than in mine. 'If you ever change your mind about posing for me, Sergeant Poole, telephone me,' she said.

Seven

'Are we going to pay Bailey another visit, then, guv?' asked Dave, as he put the gearlever into drive.

'Yes. Make for Holland Park.'

'What, now?' Dave sounded horrified. 'Shouldn't we ring first? Might be a wasted journey.'

'I'll risk it,' I said. 'I'd rather like to catch him unawares. If we give him notice we're coming, it'll give him time to prepare, and for all we know, he might've picked up that we've discovered his Bermuda connection. If he's not there, so be it.'

Dave sniffed. He was obviously unimpressed by this suggestion.

Crossing Kew Bridge, and cutting through Chiswick, we reached Holland Park in record time. Judging by Dave's driving – positive driving, he called it – I got the impression that he was hoping for an early night. But he shouldn't have joined if he couldn't take a joke.

From the Shepherd's Bush roundabout – which Dave navigated like it was a straight piece of motorway – we turned into Coburn Street, and approached Martin Bailey's house. Just in time to see a figure descending the steps, and walk away from us.

'I know that bloke,' said Dave, slowing down.

'So do I. He's an ex-detective sergeant called John something.'

'He got eighteen months for helping himself to some tomfoolery at the scene of a burglary that he was supposed to be investigating. If I remember correctly, it was a necklace that was only worth about fifty quid. Just goes to show what a prat he is.'

'Yes, I know. Pull up, Dave,' I said, as we drew level with the disgraced detective. I wound down the window. 'Hello, John. Fancy seeing you in Holland Park.'

The former policeman glanced briefly over his shoulder and started to run.

'Guilty knowledge,' said Dave, but he always said that.

'Well, don't sit there, Dave. Go get him.'

Dave leaped from the car, and with an estimable turn of speed set off in pursuit of the bent detective.

I slid across into the driving seat, and slowly followed the speeding figure of my sergeant. I'm too old to pursue villains on foot. Rank hath its privileges.

John turned into Gospel Street, but was obviously running out of steam. Dave, who was rapidly closing the gap, was almost within reaching distance of John's collar when he disappeared around the corner. And there's nothing Dave likes better than feeling a collar.

By the time I'd rounded the corner, Dave had John in a crippling wristlock.

I turned off the engine and got out of the car.

'Oh, I didn't know it was you, Mr Brock.' The bent ex-copper spoke nervously. 'I thought it was someone I owed money to.'

'Well, it wouldn't have been me, would it, John?'

John laughed nervously. 'No, I s'pose not.' He didn't seem at all pleased to see us, but as he'd just come out of Bailey's house, he must've guessed why we were in Coburn Street. Although I'm not too sure he's that bright.

I jerked a thumb in Dave's direction. 'You seem to have met DS Poole.'

'We have actually met before,' said Dave pleasantly, and gave the wristlock a little twist.

John yelped. 'All right, all right, I'm not going anywhere.'

'Very true,' said Dave

'Get in the car, John,' I said. 'I want a word with you.'

'I'm in a bit of a hurry, Mr Brock.' John lamely attempted to avoid the unavoidable.

'So are we,' I responded.

John slid into the back seat of our car and looked unhappy.

'What were you doing in Martin Bailey's house, John?' I asked.

'He wasn't there, but I couldn't tell you anyway, Mr Brock. It's confidential. I'm a private investigator now, and I've been retained by Mr Bailey. It's privileged information.'

'It would be if you were a priest, a doctor, or a lawyer,' commented Dave. 'But your rubbishy little job doesn't have that sort of privilege. You're just a bent ex-copper trying to make a crust. And probably failing.'

'Drive to the nearest nick, Dave,' I said. 'And don't try and get out, John, because there are prisoner-locks on the rear doors.'

'Here, are you nicking me?' John's voice rose an octave in alarm.

'If that's what it takes,' I said. 'Obstructing the police in the execution of their duty is a serious offence. As you probably remember.'

'All right, all right. But not here. Can't we go to a pub for a chat?'

I made a pretence of mulling over that suggestion. 'Yes, OK. But you can buy the drinks and charge them to expenses when you send Martin Bailey his account. If I remember correctly, you were quite good at fiddling expenses.'

Dave is very skilled at locating public houses, and he found one within five minutes.

John bought a round of drinks, and we settled at a table well away from the handful of other clients.

'So,' I began, 'what've you got to tell me?'

'You're asking me things I can't answer, Mr Brock,' wailed John.

'The guv'nor hasn't asked you anything yet.' Dave took a mouthful of tomato juice and grimaced.

'But if Mr Bailey finds out I've been talking to you, that'll be the end of my contract. Between you and me, Mr Brock, Martin Bailey's a nasty bastard.'

'I shouldn't worry too much about that,' said Dave. 'If we happen to mention your form to Bailey, you'll be out on your ear anyway. That's if you're lucky enough to stay out of the nick again.'

'Let me put it to you in simple terms, John,' I said. 'I'm investigating the disappearance of Eunice Bailey, who may well have been murdered.' I was by no means sure of that, but this excuse for a PI needed a little encouragement.

'*Murdered?* You're joking.' A few beads of perspiration broke out on John's brow as he suddenly realized that he was in the middle of something rather heavy.

'I'm sure you remember my methods, John,' I said, taking a sip of beer. 'But just to remind you, anyone – and I do mean *anyone* – who obstructs me in a murder investigation is likely to finish up gripping the dock rail in Number One Court at the Old Bailey.' I drained my glass and pushed it across the table. 'I'll have another pint while you're thinking about that.'

John made his way unsteadily to the bar, but it wasn't the alcohol that was causing him to weave an uncertain course.

'Now then, what exactly has Bailey hired you to do for him?' I asked, once John had returned.

'I'm gathering evidence for a divorce.' John spoke softly, licked his lips and glanced over his shoulder, as though expecting to find Martin Bailey standing behind him.

'What, Bailey's divorce?' I found that hard to believe. 'I hope you're not spinning me a fanny, John,' I said, leaning closer to him.

'Who else?' John moved back an inch or two. 'He's married to this woman called Eunice, like you said, and Mr Bailey reckons she's over the side.'

I laughed. 'Really? And when did he engage your invaluable services?'

John took out a pocket diary and flicked through the pages. 'The eighteenth of May.'

I glanced at Dave, but didn't need to say anything. It had obviously registered with him that that was the date upon which Eunice Bailey had quit the marital home.

'And what have you found out so far?' I asked.

'Nothing, really.'

'I can see you're as good at this job as you were as a copper,' commented Dave. 'So what have you done in pursuit of this difficult divorce enquiry?'

'I've been to Bermuda. That cost Mr Bailey a few quid, I can tell you.' John grinned crookedly.

'Bermuda? What on earth were you doing there, John?' I asked, feigning innocence.

'Mr Bailey seemed to think that's where his wife had gone. Reckoned she was shacked up with some bloke over there.'

'Did he tell you the name of this bloke?

'No, he never said.'

'And was she shacked up over there?'

'I don't know.' John glanced about furtively. 'I couldn't find out anything.'

'Sounds right,' commented Dave.

'When was this?' I asked. 'That you went to Bermuda, I mean.'

John consulted his diary again. 'The eleventh of June.'

And that was the day after the last charge on the credit card that Tom Nelson had given Eunice Bailey.

'But you found out nothing?'

'Not a thing, Mr Brock.'

'Whereabouts in Bermuda did you make your enquiries?'

'A few hotels around Hamilton. That's the capital. Didn't seem much point trying anywhere else. But no one had heard of her anyway.'

'Just Hamilton?' Dave was having as much difficulty as me in believing this tale.

'Well, I reckoned that's where she'd be if she was anywhere.'

'At which hotels did you make these enquiries?' Now it was Dave's turn to lean closer to John.

John licked his lips again. 'I can't remember now, but as I drew a blank, there didn't seem much point in making a note of 'em.'

'I can see your detective abilities haven't improved since you got slung out of the Job, John,' said Dave, finishing his tomato juice. 'When did you return from Bermuda?'

'The thirteenth. Two days later.'

Neither of us had mentioned Driscoll's Hotel. If we had done so, I was pretty certain that the information would be relayed to Bailey by this odious ex-detective. I was quite happy for Bailey to know about that particular hotel – when it suited me – but I wanted to be the one to tell him. Just to see his reaction.

'How often d'you report back to Bailey, John?' I asked.

John gave that a bit of thought before replying. 'Er, once a week, on a Friday,' he said hesitantly.

'And do you always report to him in person?'

'Most times, yeah. Sometimes Mr Bailey will ring me and ask if I've got anything for him.'

'Can you remember when those occasions were?'

'No, I never made a note of when I saw him in person, and when he rang me.'

'And you said that you didn't make a note of the hotels where you made enquiries,' said Dave. 'Are you telling me that Bailey pays you without asking where you'd made those enquiries? Doesn't he want to see receipts or anything of that sort?'

'He trusts me,' said John unconvincingly.

'More fool him,' commented Dave.

'One more thing before we cut you loose, John,' I said. 'If one word of this conversation gets back to Bailey, I'll start thinking conspiracy, and I'll come looking for you.'

'You needn't worry about that, Mr Brock,' said John, now thoroughly shaken by his enforced interview with us. 'This job's a nice little earner, and I don't want to lose it.'

But I knew it wouldn't last. Whatever else there was to be said about Martin Bailey, he was a sharp cookie. If he could afford to give Gina Nash two million pounds – even though it had hurt his pride if not his pocket – he knew how to make money. And for that he needed to be quick-witted. The moment we started questioning him, he was almost bound to put two and two together, and John's days as Bailey's personal PI would be over. Of course, there might come a time when it would be in my interest to tell Bailey that I'd questioned his private detective.

'Goodbye, John,' I said.

'You couldn't give me a lift to the station, I suppose?' John asked hopefully.

'The only station we'd give you a lift to is the police station, John,' said Dave, who never disguised his loathing for bent coppers. 'With the intention of charging you with something. Now piss off.'

And with that, John departed with commendable speed.

I presumed that when we'd spotted the bent ex-copper leaving Martin Bailey's house, he'd been hoping to visit his client with the intention of making yet another report. I didn't believe his story that Bailey wasn't at home and decided to check. We drove the short distance from the pub back to Coburn Street.

There was a brief pause while the CCTV camera was remotely swivelled to examine us, but a much longer delay before Bailey opened the door. So either John had lied, or Bailey had decided not to admit him.

'My God, the police again.' Bailey expressed surprise, but his sophisticated security equipment would have told him who was on the doorstep. 'What is it this time? Found her, have you?'

'No, Mr Bailey, but we are establishing some useful leads.'

'You'd better come in, then,' Bailey said grudgingly.

I waited until we were seated, once again, in the sitting room.

'I understand that you have a holiday home at a place called Flatt's Village in Bermuda, Mr Bailey,' I said, hitting him with what I thought was a piece of surprise information.

'Have you been talking to my ex-wife?' Bailey betrayed no sign of shock at our discovery of his hidey-hole.

'Your ex-wife? If you mean Eunice, I've just said that we haven't traced her.'

'No, of course not. Eunice isn't my ex-wife yet, not officially, anyway. No, I'm talking about that bitch Gina.'

'I'm sorry, I didn't know you'd been married previously,' I lied.

'Well, I was, and the bleedin' cow took me for two million quid when we split.'

For the first time, I noticed that Bailey possessed a cockney accent that only became noticeable when he was excited or annoyed. Then I remembered that the printout from the General Register Office showed that he'd been born in Bow. No doubt he would occasionally boast that he was an East End boy made good. And had taken elocution lessons.

'So you do have a place in Bermuda,' I persisted.

'Yes. So what?'

'When we spoke to you previously, you denied ever having been to Bermuda.'

'So what? It's got bugger-all to do with you lot. What I do in my private life is private.'

'Mr Bailey, we are attempting to find your wife,' I said patiently, 'and to deny you'd been to Bermuda when we'd told you that some of our enquiries were centred there is not helpful.'

'OK, so I'm sorry.' Bailey spread his hands apologetically. 'But have you found her yet?'

'No. I told you that when we arrived.'

'Then what the hell are you doing here? Rather than

cluttering up my sitting room, stopping me from working, you should be out there looking for her.'

'Why are you so concerned?' I asked. 'I got the impression that you were glad to see the back of your wife. In fact, I seem to recall that you said you didn't want to see her again.' I decided to throw the ex-con private-detective John to the wolves. 'I understand that you've been seeking evidence to support a divorce.'

'Who the bloody hell told you that?' Bailey's face suffused with rage. 'Was it that bloody ex-copper I've hired?'

'Ex-copper, Mr Bailey?' Dave conjured up his most innocent expression. 'What ex-copper's this?'

Bailey's rage subsided. 'He was some broken-down hack I picked out of Yellow Pages. He reckoned he was good at matrimonial enquiries, and boasted about being ex-Scotland Yard, but I suppose they all say that. I sent the idiot to Bermuda to see if he could find anything out, but he came back with zilch. Cost me a bloody fortune, too, the useless tool. D'you mean you haven't spoken to him.'

'No, but it might be helpful if we did,' said Dave. 'What's his name?'

Bailey left the room to return moments later clutching a cheap business card. 'There you are,' he said. 'But if he's able to tell you anything, let me know, because he's told me sod all.'

'What, and have you threaten us with a subpoena again? Not likely.' Dave took the card and, for show, copied the details into his pocketbook.

'Did your current wife ever go to Bermuda with you, Mr Bailey?' I asked.

'A few times, yes. She liked parading herself in her bikini on the beach.'

'Yes, I seem to remember you telling us that. And you also said that you weren't keen on beaches.'

'Too bloody right. No, I had a bit of business to deal with. That's why I went, but I took Eunice with me to give her a break.'

'What's the point of having a holiday cottage in Flatt's Village if you don't like holidays?'

'Useful base for my business,' said Bailey curtly. 'Anyway, what's any of this got to do with finding Eunice?'

'I was wondering why you wanted to find her, Mr Bailey.'

'Because I want to divorce the bloody woman, Chief Inspector, and I can't do that until I find out where she is. I don't know how much you know about divorce, but I need to have papers served on her.'

Oh boy! What didn't I know about divorce?

'I suppose so,' I said. 'Well, in that case, we'll leave you, Mr Bailey. But with the usual request. If you should hear from your wife—'

'Yeah, yeah! Don't worry about that, Chief Inspector, you'll be the first to know.'

'Well, we didn't learn much there,' I said, as Dave and I drove back to Curtis Green.

'Except that Martin Bailey's a lying git,' Dave said. 'Incidentally, guv, did you hear what I heard?'

'You mean the door slamming?'

'Yes, upstairs.'

I'd noticed it while we were talking to Bailey. Somewhere a door had slammed, and it sounded as though it had come from the floor above. Bailey had heard it too, and his face had briefly registered annoyance, but he'd made no comment. And I didn't ask. It seemed very much as though Bailey was sharing his house with someone else. It was too late in the day for it to have been his cleaning woman – not if she was anything like my Mrs Gurney – and I doubted that it was Eunice. But there again, I'd formed the opinion that Bailey was a devious bastard. Both by encounter and from what Gail's father had told me.

It was, however, worth further investigation, and when we got back to the office, I sent for Kate Ebdon and told her about the slamming door.

'Get a couple of people to keep an eye on the place, Kate. I should think that two days would be enough. You can put a nondescript obo van in the street without any fear of it being rumbled. If, as I think, he's got a woman living with him, I want to know as much about her as possible. But discreetly, mind.'

'No probs, guv,' said Kate. 'D'you think it might be Eunice?'

'If it is her, Kate, it means that Bailey's playing some sort of game that's beyond me. No, I very much doubt it's her,' I said. 'Probably some girl he's picked up with.'

'Perhaps he's a white-slave trafficker,' said Dave.

'I doubt it. From what I read in the papers, prostitutes are being brought into the country these days, not exported.'

It didn't take Kate Ebdon very long. On the Tuesday afternoon, she breezed into the incident room when I was reading the statements. Again! Not that they told me anything about the missing Eunice Bailey.

'Found her, guv.'

'Found who?'

'The sheila who's shacked up with Martin Bailey.'

'Tell me more.'

'I put DCs John Appleby and Nicola Chance in the obo van first thing this morning. About nine o'clock, this bird comes waltzing out of the house and grabs a cab. The obo van followed and they finished up in the King's Road, Chelsea. It seems that the subject works in some poncey boutique there, selling overpriced perfume and silly bits of expensive jewellery. Nicola followed her in, pretended to look around, and clocked her name badge.'

'So who is she?'

'She's called Jane Grant.' Kate flicked open her pocket-book. 'She's aged about twenty-five, five-ten, blonde hair worn shoulder-length.' She looked up. 'Don't they all?' Kate was not impressed by the slavish devotion to prevailing fashion adopted by most young girls, however unsuited it was to their particular shape and size. 'According to the way the other girls deferred to Grant, Nicola reckons that she's probably the manager, but there was nothing to indicate who owns it. I suppose it might be Jane Grant herself, but it could be Martin Bailey. As you say, he's got a lot of fingers in a lot of pies.'

'Thanks, Kate. That was a good bit of work.'

'Wasn't down to me, guv. It was Nicola. I gave her a pat on the back.'

'We shall interview Jane Grant, Dave,' I said. 'Forthwith.'

'Where, guv? At Bailey's house?'

'Not with him breathing down our necks. And down hers. No, we'll interview her at work.'

'But she'll tell Martin Bailey.'

'I hope so,' I said. 'I'm sure he's up to something, although

I don't know what exactly. So we'll lean on the bastard, and push him into a corner. In short, I want him to feel threatened. Bailey's been jigging us about for too long, and he's due a little bit of pressure.'

'About bloody time,' said Dave, and began to peel an orange.

Eight

We left it until half-past ten the following morning to visit the boutique in the King's Road where Jane Grant worked. There was a space on a double-yellow line right outside the shop. Dave parked the car, left the police logbook on the dash, and vowed vengeance on any traffic warden who issued us with a ticket.

Skilfully avoiding a yob on a bicycle who was riding on the pavement – where else? – we entered the shop.

There were two girls behind the counter. Each was in her mid-twenties, and either of them could have been Jane Grant, which just goes to prove that what Kate Ebdon had said about young women's adherence to prevailing fashion was true. But in the event, neither of them was the woman we wanted to talk to.

'Is Jane Grant here?' I asked the one who came sashaying up to serve me.

'No, she's in the stockroom, but I'm sure I'll be able to help you, sir.'

'It's Miss Grant I need to talk to,' I said.

The girl seemed a trifle put out by that, nevertheless she smiled sweetly. 'I'll fetch her. Who shall I say it is?'

'My name's Harry Brock.'

'Are you a rep?' The question was accompanied by a slight frown.

'Certainly not.' But I wasn't going to tell her what I really did for a living.

'I won't keep you a moment, Mr Brock.'

The girl who emerged from the stockroom was dressed in a similar outfit to the other two, and with her shoulder-length blonde hair they could've been triplets.

'I'm Jane Grant, the manager. I understand you want to talk to me.'

'Yes,' I said, motioning her to the other end of the counter. Fortunately two customers entered the boutique at that moment, and so Jane's colleagues were fully occupied. 'We're police officers, Miss Grant,' I said quietly. 'It is *Miss* Grant, is it?'

'Yes, it is, but what on earth d'you want to see me about?'

'Is there somewhere we can talk?' I asked.

'There's a coffee shop next door but one. I'm due for my break, anyway.'

Jane Grant escorted us out of the shop and along the street to a sparsely populated and rather twee coffee shop that showed all the signs of terminal bankruptcy. Dave bought three cups of coffee, and for days afterwards was to be heard complaining about the price.

'I can assure you that all our goods are legitimate.' Once we were sitting down, Jane immediately made an assumption as to why we wanted to talk to her. The wrong assumption. 'I know there are a lot of counterfeit perfumes on the market, but we're very careful and always buy from established stockists.'

'We're not here to talk about your stock, Miss Grant.'

'What, then?'

'I understand that you live with Martin Bailey.'

The girl's eyes opened wide in surprise, and she flushed. 'Yes, I do, but what's that got to do with the police?'

I wondered briefly how it was that an attractive girl like Jane Grant was happy to be living with a man at least twenty years her senior. But I knew the answer to that: it was his money. Unless, of course, she was just a lodger. Not that I could see Bailey needing to take in lodgers. On the other hand, given Bailey's track record, it would have been a drastic change of lifestyle if he had suddenly starting spending money on his womenfolk. At least, according to Gina Nash; and indeed Bailey himself, who'd said that Eunice had left him because she was fed up with never being taken out.

'I'm a detective chief inspector with the Homicide and Serious Crime Command, and Sergeant Poole and I are investigating the disappearance of Mr Bailey's wife.'

'His *wife*? You must mean his ex-wife, surely.'

Oh dear! 'No, his present wife, Miss Grant.'

'But he's divorced. He told me so. He was married to a

dreadful woman called Gina, but the marriage ended about
six years ago.'

'And five years ago, he married Eunice Webb, now Mrs
Bailey. It's her disappearance that we're investigating.'

'My God!' Jane Grant was clearly shaken by this revela-
tion and, presumably, by the consequent realization that Martin
Bailey had been lying to her.

'What exactly is your status in the Bailey household, Miss
Grant?' asked Dave, scooping some froth from what passed
for coffee.

'What d'you mean by that?' asked the girl, bristling
noticeably.

'Well, are you a lodger, or a secretary, or a companion? Or
are you related to Mr Bailey, perhaps?'

'I don't see that it's any of your damned business,' said
Jane heatedly, 'but if you must know, I'm his girlfriend. And
yes, before you ask, I sleep with him. There, satisfied?'

Good. We were getting to her.

'Not quite,' said Dave. 'How did you meet?'

'At a nightclub.'

'In England?'

'Of course in England. In the West End.'

'How long ago?'

'It was the nineteenth of May,' Jane Grant answered un-
hesitatingly.

'Why d'you remember that date so clearly?' asked Dave.

'It was my birthday,' Jane replied smugly. 'I was out cele-
brating with a couple of girlfriends, and Martin came up and
asked me for a dance. Then he bought us all champagne, and
paid for our supper. At the end of the evening, he took us all
home in his Rolls-Royce. He asked if he could see me again,
and it sort of developed from there. I was living in an awful
bedsit in Fulham and a week later he invited me to move in
with him.'

*So, the day after his wife walked out, Martin Bailey hit the
fleshpots of London's West End, and found a replacement.
And was willing to spend money in order to do so.*

It was no wonder that this rather immature young lady had
fallen for all the wealth that was being flashed around.

'Have you ever been to Bermuda with Mr Bailey?' I
asked.

'What a funny question. No, I've not been to Bermuda at all. Why?'

'Because that's where Mrs Bailey – Mrs Eunice Bailey – was last seen.'

'I don't believe any of this,' said Jane, but she was clearly disturbed by our probing, and apparently irrelevant, questions. 'Are you suggesting that Martin might have had something to do with his wife's disappearance?'

'What d'you think?'

'I think it's a ridiculous idea. And I'm not sure I believe you, anyway, when you say he's married.'

'Miss Grant, my chief inspector and I have visited Mr Bailey three times at his home,' said Dave, embarking on a different subject. 'On none of those occasions were you in evidence. What happened? Did Mr Bailey banish you to your room like a naughty schoolgirl?'

Jane shot Dave a murderous glance. I think she'd taken umbrage at the implication that she could be ordered about. 'He said he had business clients calling and that I'd only be bored. He suggested I went upstairs and watched television, or had a shower, or something.' She shook her head, obviously puzzling over why Bailey did not want her to know that the police were calling on him. 'It's ridiculous. Martin's a very nice man, and very generous too.' She paused for a moment. 'Did you say you were from the homicide squad?'

'Yes,' I said. 'The Homicide and Serious Crime Command.'

'Oh God! Does that mean you think this woman's been murdered?' It wasn't difficult to guess what was passing through Jane Grant's mind at that moment. Perhaps she spent too long in her room watching television.

'I don't know, Miss Grant. That's why we're investigating Mrs Bailey's disappearance. But I gather from what you were saying that Mr Bailey has never mentioned his current wife to you.'

'No, only his ex-wife, Gina. This is all too silly for words.' Jane attempted to be dismissive, but it was clear that the inference she'd drawn had worried her.

'That remains to be seen,' I said, 'but we may have to talk to you again. Either here or at Coburn Street.' Dave and I stood up, leaving behind us a very concerned young woman.

As we walked back to our car, a scruffy individual approached us. 'Spare a quid for a cup of coffee, guv'nor.'

'You'll need more than a quid,' said Dave, the cost of the coffee he'd just paid for still vexing him.

'Our Miss Grant didn't seem very happy,' I said.

'It'll certainly give Bailey something to think about when she gets home and tells him all about her confrontation with the wicked police, guv,' said Dave.

We didn't have long to wait. That same day, at about six o'clock, Martin Bailey was on the phone. And he was mad.

'What the bloody hell d'you people think you're playing at?' he demanded. 'My girlfriend was almost in tears when she got home. She says that you turned up at her workplace, badgered her about her private life, and asked her about her relationship with me.' The words came tumbling out, and it was apparent that Bailey was boiling over with rage. 'She said that you more or less suggested that Eunice had been murdered. You're in trouble over this, mister. Big trouble. I want to see you, and I want to see you this evening.'

I put the telephone receiver close to my desk diary, and riffled the pages loudly enough for Bailey to hear.

'I'm afraid that won't be possible, Mr Bailey,' I said mildly. 'I have appointments this evening, and tomorrow I'm giving evidence at the Old Bailey. I'm afraid I shan't be available to see you until, er, shall we say, eight o'clock tomorrow evening.'

'I'm going out tomorrow,' barked Bailey down the phone.

'It's up to you, sir,' I said. 'If not tomorrow, it could be several days before I can see you.'

'I suppose I could put them off, but it's damned inconvenient. All right, tomorrow at eight.' And with that Bailey slammed down the receiver of his phone.

'I think he's upset, Dave,' I said, once I'd recounted the details of the call.

'Oh good!' said Dave.

But Martin Bailey had another trick up his sleeve. The following morning, I received a telephone call from a man who claimed to be his solicitor. It was an entertaining exchange, at least from my point of view.

'I have to inform you, Mr Brock, that earlier today I lodged an official complaint against you with the authorities at Scotland Yard.'

'Really? What for?'

'Harassment. I have been told by my client that you have not only been unreasonably harassing him, but that you have also been pestering his ward, a Miss Jane Grant.'

'I see,' I said, having stifled a laugh at the solicitor's description of Martin Bailey's bedmate as his 'ward'.

'What d'you have to say about that?'

'Nothing.'

'What d'you mean, nothing?'

'Exactly that. As you have now made an official complaint against me, I am not permitted to discuss the matter. It is, in a sense, sub judice.'

'But that's ridiculous.'

'I couldn't agree more,' I responded.

Without another word, the solicitor terminated the conversation. But a quarter of an hour later he was back again.

'I'm ringing to inform you that I have now withdrawn my complaint, Mr Brock.'

'I see,' I said.

'Now will you discuss this matter with me?'

'No,' I said.

Bailey must have been watching out of the window for our arrival, because no sooner had I rung the bell than the door was wrenched open.

'Ah, about time,' snapped Bailey. 'Come in.' And he marched away, leaving Dave to shut the door.

By the time we caught up with him, he was standing four-square in front of the empty fireplace in the sitting room. The hi-fi was playing a Humphrey Littleton recording, but he made no attempt to turn it off.

'What the hell's this all about?' demanded Bailey crossly. 'I've no bloody idea where Eunice has gone, and Jane has even less knowledge of her whereabouts. So why the blazes did you go to her workplace and harass her?'

'We did not harass her, Mr Bailey,' said Dave. 'We actually had a friendly chat over a cup of coffee. For which I paid.' The cost of the coffee was still rankling, mainly because there was no way in which he could charge it to expenses. Not legitimately, anyway.

'But to answer your question, Mr Bailey,' I said, 'I shall interview anyone I think may be able to assist me in my enquiries into the suspicious disappearance of your wife.'

'Suspicious? What's bloody suspicious about it?'

'As I have explained before, Mr Bailey, your wife has not been seen since the tenth of June, neither has there been a charge on her credit card since that date.'

Rather than discussing that irrefutable fact, Bailey played what he thought was his trump card. 'I think you should know that I have instructed my solicitor to lodge an official complaint of harassment against you,' he said.

'He's withdrawn it,' I said, playing my own trump.

'*What?* How did you manage that? Another bloody whitewash, I suppose.' The fact that his solicitor had seemingly acted without further instructions merely served to fuel Bailey's anger.

'I've no idea,' I said. 'But I had a brief conversation with your solicitor on the telephone this morning, and I can only assume that he thought that to proceed with a complaint would be counterproductive to my enquiries.'

'I'll bloody well read his fortune for him,' muttered Bailey. It must have appeared to him that he was being thwarted at every turn.

'Now, sir, having got that out of the way, what was it you wanted to see me about?' It was a pointless question. I knew what he wanted to see me about: it was to have a bitch about me questioning his girlfriend.

'Just to give you a bloody warning, Mr Chief Inspector.' Bailey attempted the sort of ruthlessness that must have terrified any of his employees who crossed him, but it was lost on me. 'This poking about in my private life has got to stop, and if it doesn't I shall complain personally to the Commissioner. I have no idea where my wife is, but questioning Jane about it will get you nowhere.'

'I think that's probably right, Mr Bailey. When I spoke to her, she told me that she didn't even know that you were married to Eunice. But she does now.'

'You had no bloody right to tell—'

'Goodbye, Mr Bailey.'

*   *   *

'D'you reckon there's anything in this job, guv?' asked Dave, the next morning. 'We don't seem to be getting anywhere.'

He and I were sitting in my office, having a cup of coffee.

'I'm beginning to wonder, Dave. There's no doubt that Bailey's an obnoxious bastard, and it's no wonder that Eunice buggered off. I think if I'd been in her position, I'd've done the same. And I certainly wouldn't have told him where I'd gone.'

'But she did,' Dave reminded me. 'Bailey said she'd told him she was going to America.'

'I think she was just spinning him a yarn, Dave,' I said. 'She didn't want him to know where she was going. Indeed, she might not even have decided.' Frankly, I didn't know what to think. For over two weeks now, we'd been messing about trying to track down the elusive Eunice Bailey, but we'd come up with nothing of any import. One thing a detective learns from his earliest days in the CID is that anyone who really doesn't want to be found won't be found. We'd discovered quite a bit about Martin Bailey, but that was of no use at all. The whole thing could have an innocent explanation, and thanks to our beloved commander, we had somehow got embroiled in what the police call 'a matrimonial'.

Then, suddenly, it all changed.

Colin Wilberforce came into the office. 'The acting commander would like to see you and Dave, sir,' he said. 'When you've got a moment, he said.'

'The *acting* commander? Where's the boss?'

'I understand he's taken a few days' leave, sir.'

This was very good news indeed. Detective Chief Superintendent Alan Cleaver was the commander's deputy, and stood in for him whenever he was away. Furthermore, Cleaver was a career detective, and spoke detectives' language.

'You wanted to see us, guv?' I said, as we entered the commander's office.

'Yes, Harry. Park your arse. You too, Dave. How's this Eunice Bailey job going? Anything in it, or is it time to knock it on the head?'

I gave Cleaver a quick summary of how the commander had lumbered us with the enquiry in the first place – at which he sighed – and then gave him a rundown on what we'd learned so far.

Cleaver swung round in his chair, and for a few moments stared out of the window.

'There's only one way to sort this bloody thing out, Harry,' he said, turning to face us again.

'I'd be grateful for any advice, guv,' I said. I knew that anything Cleaver had to offer, based on his wide experience, would be worth heeding.

'Go to Bermuda.'

'We'd never get authority for that,' I said, much as the prospect of a few days in the sun appealed to me.

'It makes sense, Harry. The woman disappeared in Bermuda, and has not been seen in England since. From what you've told me, the Bermuda Police have confined themselves to making enquiries on your behalf. Which is fair enough; they think it's a London job, but it could well be their job. I think you need to get over there and have a chat with this Superintendent Mercer, and get it sorted. If Eunice Bailey's been murdered in Bermuda, Mercer'll need all the help he can get. And you've done a lot of the spadework for him already.'

'D'you want a report, guv?' I asked.

'A report? What about?' asked Cleaver, an amused expression on his face.

'Applying for permission to go to Bermuda.'

The acting commander did not reply. Instead, he tapped out a number on his telephone.

'It's Alan Cleaver here, guv, Acting Commander H and SCC. I want to send Harry Brock and his bag carrier to Bermuda to sort out a suspected murder. The woman's called Eunice Bailey, and she was last seen in Bermuda on the tenth of June. Since then, nothing. Harry's been doing some work on it, and her husband is a dodgy character, but until Harry can get over there he's unlikely to get a result.' There was a pause, and then, 'Thanks, guv.'

Cleaver replaced the receiver. 'The DAC says you can go, Harry. See whoever arranges these things and get your flight sorted out. And you're entitled to tropical suits, so get that fixed up too. I'll see you when you get back. And don't get too pissed on the rum swizzles.'

Back in the office, Dave got busy on the telephone, arranging the tickets to Bermuda International. Colin Wilberforce sent an email to Detective Superintendent Mercer, telling him our ETA, and asking him to book us into a hotel. In the afternoon we journeyed to Charing Cross Road and were fixed up with lightweight suits by the Metropolitan Police accredited supplier of tropical gear.

Oh boy! If only things moved that quickly when the commander was here.

Nine

Dave and I arrived at Gatwick just before one o'clock and checked in for the Bermuda flight that was due to leave at five past three.

'Looks like we've wandered in to some sort of select club, guv,' commented Dave, gazing around at the throng of well-dressed people chatting to each other in the departure lounge. Most of them seemed to be Bermudians, and if the abundance of bags marked Harrods, Harvey Nichols, and Hamleys was anything to go by, they had spent most of their time – and their money – shopping in London.

The six-and-a-quarter-hour flight was uneventful apart from a nasty patch of turbulence somewhere in mid-Atlantic. The seatbelt sign came on, and the stewardess came down the aisle to check that we were belted up. She seemed mildly amused that I was gripping my armrests until the knuckles showed white.

But after that little bit of excitement we watched a film for a while, and then slept for the rest of the way. Which was just as well, because we guessed we'd have a long evening in front of us. Although we arrived in Bermuda at about half-past nine our time, it was only five-thirty in the afternoon there. We'd both done duty abroad before, and we knew that host detectives usually made a beeline for the nearest bar.

We descended the aircraft steps into the Bermuda sun, and felt as though we had walked into an oven.

There was a police car near the plane, and next to it a guy in Bermuda shorts, a collar and tie, and a smart jacket.

There is something about detectives that other detectives recognize instantly. I don't know how or why, but it happens. And it happened now. The man strode across to Dave and me, and shook hands.

'Chief Inspector Brock, I presume. I'm Don Mercer. Welcome to Bermuda.'

'The name's Harry,' I said, 'and this is Dave Poole, my DS.'

'I've fixed you up at a hotel in Hamilton itself, Harry,' said Mercer. 'Not that it matters much where it is; there isn't anywhere on Bermuda that's very far from anywhere else. First thing is to dump your things there, and then we'll have a bite to eat, if that suits you. I don't suppose you want to start work until tomorrow. I'll get the driver to put your bags in the car. Have you got stuff in the hold?'

'No, what we're carrying is all we've got.' I was beginning to like Mercer already, which is an advantage when you have to work together at short notice. If you don't hit it off straight away, the work doesn't get done. 'Don't we have to go through immigration and customs first, Don?' I asked.

Mercer grinned. 'I'm an immigration officer and a customs officer, as well as being a copper,' he said. 'Consider yourself landed.'

It was about cight miles from the airport to the hotel in Pitts Bay Road, Hamilton, but it didn't take Mercer's driver very long. Although the speed limit is twenty miles an hour – and in parts of the islands, even less – he chose to ignore it.

Don Mercer was about my age, and during the journey he told us that he originated from Guildford in Surrey. 'Twenty years ago, I looked at the way England was shaping up, Harry,' he said, 'and decided to get the hell out of it. And I'm bloody glad I did.'

'I wish I had too,' I said. 'I looked at the adverts in the *Police Review* for constables in Bermuda, and was sorely tempted. But I finished up joining the Met.'

'Bad mistake, Harry,' said Mercer with a laugh, as he dropped us at our hotel. 'Eight o'clock suit you for dinner, and you, Dave? Give you time to settle in, have a shower, and change.'

The hotel was luxurious, and I tried not to think what our expenses claim would look like when we got back to London. I just hoped it would be worth it.

Dave and I went down to the reception area at just before eight. By now, given that our body clocks told us it was nearly two in the morning, we were both feeling pretty worn out. But we are CID officers, and long hours come naturally, although not always from choice.

Don Mercer was sitting in an armchair, reading a copy of that day's *Royal Gazette*.

'We'll go to Jasper's, Harry,' he said, setting aside the newspaper, and standing up. 'It's a good restaurant, and it's only a few yards along Pitts Bay Road from here.'

The maître d'hôtel at Jasper's greeted Don Mercer like the old friend he obviously was. 'Good evening, Superintendent. Good to see you again, sir.' He glanced at Dave and me. 'Good evening to you, gentlemen. A drink at the bar?' His arm was already extended in that direction as if to brook no opposition. 'And then a table for three?'

'Thank you, George,' said Mercer.

The barman had that mixture of confidence and deference and professional skill that doubtless meant that he was on a good wage, and that that wage was reflected in the bar prices. Not that I cared. I had a feeling that Mercer wasn't going to pay for the drinks anyway.

'Mr Mercer, how are you, sir?' The barman smiled broadly at the superintendent, nodded towards Dave and me, and asked what we would like to drink.

'My usual shipwreck, please, Alec,' said Mercer.

'What in hell's name's a shipwreck?' I asked.

'It's made from loquats and served on ice with a twist of lemon, sir,' said the barman automatically. He had obviously been obliged to explain this very Bermudian drink to tourists many times before. 'And for you, sir?'

'I'll have a pint of bitter if you have any, please,' I said.

'So will I,' said Dave.

'Bermuda Triangle Full Moon is the nearest thing to your English bitter, gentlemen. Two pints coming up.' The barman turned away and busied himself preparing the drinks.

'Why's it called a Bermuda Triangle, Don?' I asked.

Mercer laughed. 'Because, like the Bermuda Triangle itself, if you have too many of them, you'll disappear without trace,' he said, as the barman placed the drinks in front of us.

The head waiter appeared at precisely the moment we finished our drinks, escorted us to our table, and presented each of us with a menu.

'I hope you're going to try the fish chowder while you're here,' said Mercer. 'It's a local speciality.'

'I'm not too keen on chowder,' I said. 'I'll settle for a fillet steak, if it's all the same to you.'

'Me too,' said Dave, never backward when a free meal was on offer.

The waiters possessed an air of quiet efficiency that tells you immediately that the bill is going to be astronomical, and that they expected a tip of at least fifteen per cent. Thank God the Bermuda Police was paying. Well, I hoped it was. If only for the sake of the commander's blood pressure.

Over dinner, Don Mercer told us a little of Bermuda and the problems faced by the local police.

'I don't suppose it's too bad compared with what you have to deal with in London, Harry. For a start, we don't have any terrorism any more, but we have our fair share of muggings and drugs, although the judiciary cracks down hard on possession. Believe it or not, the epidemic crime here is moped theft. We have about two hundred of the damned things nicked every month. The trouble is that visitors are only allowed to hire mopeds, not cars, and they think this a crime-free paradise. They leave them lying about all over the place, and, believe me, the local villains take rotten advantage.' He paused while the waiter poured more wine. 'Most of them finish up being cannibalized.' Mercer laughed. 'The mopeds, that is, not the villains. Unfortunately. I hate to admit it, but we've more or less given up on it. Quick entry in the crime book, and then write it off.'

Following dinner, we consumed more Bermuda Triangle Full Moons than were good for us, and spent a couple of hours talking about the Job, as coppers do the world over. Consequently, after what seemed like only an hour in bed, I awoke to the ringing of the telephone.

It was Don Mercer. 'Good morning, Harry. How's your head?'

'I've had better wake-up calls,' I mumbled. My head felt as though little men with hammers were trying to escape from inside my skull.

'Well, it's nine o'clock, pal. Time to get moving.'

I glanced at the clock to confirm what Mercer had said, and sprang out of bed. A mistake! My hangover was even worse than I thought.

'Give me ten minutes, Don, and we'll be with you.' I rang Dave and gave him the glad news.

We showered, and skipped breakfast. But missing out on food was no hardship. We didn't fancy anything.

Our first stop was at Police Heights in Devonshire Parish, where we paid a courtesy call on the Commissioner of Police.

Jimmy Willis was a jovial black man dressed in shorts and a colourful Hawaiian shirt. He shook hands with each of us, and promptly offered Dave a job, presumably because he, too, was black. 'We could use young men like you in the Bermuda force, Sergeant,' he said. And although it was only ten o'clock in the morning, he invited us to join him in a rum swizzle. We declined, and settled for the welcome alternative of black coffee.

'Don is a good policeman, Mr Brock,' Willis said, 'and I'm sure that he'll be able to provide anything you need.' And then – although I shouldn't have been surprised – he demonstrated that he knew exactly why we were here. 'I hope this young woman, Eunice Bailey, has not been murdered on Bermuda.'

'I hope so, too, sir,' I said, 'but at the moment Scotland Yard is treating it as a missing-person enquiry.'

Willis nodded thoughtfully. 'Yes, but missing persons often turn out to be dead persons, Mr Brock. Although murder here is not unusual, it is rare. You probably know that the Governor was assassinated back in nineteen seventy-three, as was one of my predecessors, but we pride ourselves on having been pretty law-abiding since then.' He took a sip of his rum swizzle. 'We've had our moments, of course. During the Second World War, we had a team of code-breakers working in the basement of the Princess Hotel. And you probably know that Ian Fleming invented James Bond here. But enough of the history lesson.' He waved a hand, and stood up. 'And now, if you'll excuse me, gentlemen,' he said, 'I have an audience with the Governor at eleven.' He laughed infectiously. 'I have to put on my fancy dress for that, you see.'

We shook hands again, and took our leave.

'I'm assuming you'd like to have a look at Bailey's place in Flatt's Village, Harry,' said Mercer as we walked back to the car. 'I took the precaution of obtaining a search warrant, and I've arranged for the CSI boys to meet us there in case you want to lift any prints.'

'Great,' I said. This was service indeed.

Martin Bailey's picturesque cottage was washed pink with a stepped limestone roof, and shutters that were painted a pale blue. It was an idyllic setting.

There was a van outside the house, and a couple of black Bermudian technicians emerged from it as we arrived. Both were in their twenties.

'These are the scientific guys, Harry,' said Mercer, and introduced them to us. 'Brownie is the chief, and Jacko is his number two.'

The two men laughed uproariously – although it wasn't clear what had amused them – and shook hands.

Brownie spent a few moments skilfully deploying a picklock before throwing open the cottage's front door. He turned to Mercer with a wide grin on his face. 'OK, boss?'

The furniture in the cottage was basic, wooden, and comfortable, and there were rugs on the stone floors. But the search was disappointing in terms of advancing our enquiries into the missing Eunice Bailey. It took an hour, the CSIs examining every square inch of the cottage, but there was little to interest us. A few paperback books sat alongside some out-of-date magazines on a shelf in the sitting room, and that was about all. There wasn't even a computer. Crockery had been washed up and put away, the beds had been stripped, and the cottage thoroughly cleaned. There were no personal possessions or correspondence of any description to indicate that Martin Bailey, or his wife, had ever been there. In fact, there was nothing to indicate that *anyone* had been there.

I suppose I shouldn't have been surprised. Either Bailey was an extremely cautious man who never left anything suspicious lying about, or he'd never had anything incriminating there to start with. Dave expressed doubts about that, but then he's the sceptical type.

'It all looks very neat and tidy, Don,' I said. 'Not a thing out of place.'

'He's probably got a woman who comes in to clean every so often,' said Mercer.

'I think it might be a good idea to lift a few prints, Don,

if this cleaning woman hasn't wiped them all,' I said. 'You never know, we might find a match in our collection at the Yard.'

The CSIs set to work, and found about fifteen useful sets of fingerprints that they transferred to glass with transparent adhesive tape. Dave took charge of them, and did the necessary paperwork to preserve continuity of evidence. They'd probably turn out to be useless, but if you did have to take them to court the last thing you wanted was some smart-arse barrister proving that the chain of evidence had been broken.

'There's bound to be some fibres and that, boss,' said Brownie. 'Want us to have a go with the e-vac?' He was obviously very keen on his job.

'No, thanks, Brownie,' I said. 'I don't think it would help us much.' The e-vac, a sort of miniature Hoover for collecting the minutest pieces of evidence, was a handy piece of equipment, but I could see little value in collecting anything from here. At best it would prove that the Baileys had been in the cottage, and that was not in dispute. And if any alien fibres or hairs were discovered, we had nothing with which to compare them.

'Where d'you want to go next, Harry?' asked Don.

'I thought it might be a good idea to have a word with the people at Driscoll's Hotel.'

'Sure, but I doubt if they've got anything to add to what they told me.'

'Yes, but we've got these now, guv'nor,' said Dave to Mercer, producing the photographs of Martin Bailey, Tom Nelson, and Dickie Richards that had been taken covertly by Kate Ebdon's team. And one of Jane Grant that had been taken after our brief chat with her. We'd also brought copies of the portrait photograph of Eunice that Martin Bailey had given us.

But that exercise proved disappointing. Both the manager and the receptionist at Driscoll's studied the photographs carefully. Each denied ever having seen either Bailey or Grant, but as they were surveillance photographs taken at a distance, that was not altogether surprising. They did, however, confirm what we knew already: Tom Nelson was the man who'd stayed with Eunice Bailey from the twenty-third of May to the sixth of June, and that Eunice had stayed on for another four days. But they were unable to help us in identifying the mysterious

Nigel Skinner who had befriended Eunice after Nelson had left.

Don Mercer demanded to see the register.

'The register is actually a computer these days, Mr Mercer,' said the manager with a smile, and found the relevant entry.

'I'm sorry, Harry,' said Mercer. 'I should have spotted this before.' Nigel Skinner had furnished a United Kingdom address in Notting Hill, West London. Dave jotted down the details, but he, like me, was not optimistic that we would find Skinner there.

'I don't see what else we can do, Don,' I said. We'd adjourned to a pleasant open-air restaurant on Elbow Beach for lunch, and were chewing over what we'd found out. Or rather, what we hadn't found out.

The view was breathtaking. Yellow and white parasols were dotted about the golden beaches; muscular men, and girls in micro-bikinis, were dashing in and out of the surf. A man of sixty with leathery suntanned skin trudged ahead of an equally tanned woman, and complained in a strong Bronx accent that he didn't know where he'd left his towel.

'When I got your latest message, Harry,' said Mercer, 'I put the word out among my informants to see if they'd come across Mrs Bailey or this Nigel Skinner. Before I picked you up this morning, I got a call from a guy called Darrell Nightingale. He's a well-known jobbing boat carpenter with a place out at Shrewsbury, and he reckons he's got something.' He glanced at his watch. 'We'll have a run out there this afternoon, if that's OK.'

'Did he say what it was about?'

Mercer smiled. 'Not on the phone. He's afraid that unless he meets me in person, he might not get a ten-dollar bill slipped into his grubby hand. Mind you, I shouldn't hold out too much hope. He's not come up with much in the past.' He shrugged. 'You never know though, Harry, it might be your lucky day.'

Darrell Nightingale, a huge black man with a bushy white beard, emerged from his ramshackle workshop as we drew up.

'Hello, Mr Mercer. How you doing?' Nightingale grinned broadly and extended a large callused hand.

'These two gentlemen are from Scotland Yard, Darrell.'

Nightingale opened his eyes wide in a parody of surprise. 'Not *the* Scotland Yard?' he asked.

'There isn't another one, Darrell,' said Mercer drily. He was obviously accustomed to Nightingale's theatrics. 'So what've you got to tell me?'

The old carpenter licked his lips. 'Why don't we go to the pub up on Middle Road, boss? Much more comfortable up there.'

Mercer laughed. 'It had better be worth it, you crafty old rogue.'

It was a short walk to Darrell Nightingale's favourite watering hole, where he was hailed by practically the entire clientele as he walked in. But he was not the only one who was known there. Although Don Mercer was greeted with similar cordiality, the customers displayed a measure of reservation about the arrival of a senior policeman in their midst. Funny how CID officers have that effect on people in pubs.

'I suppose you'll be wanting a dark-'n'-stormy, Darrell,' said Mercer, but the drink – rum and ginger beer – was already on the bar. This time, Dave and I settled for rum swizzles. Well, you've got to try the local beverages when you're abroad, haven't you?

The four of us carried our drinks to the far end of the long bar, Nightingale greeting acquaintances as he went.

'I hope you've got something good for me, Darrell,' said Mercer.

'This woman you were talking about, boss. I saw her in here with a man.'

'How d'you know it was her?'

'She was called Eunice, the same name as my missus. That's what the man was calling her, and they weren't exactly speaking softly.'

Dave deliberately produced the photograph of Jane Grant, rather than that of Eunice, and showed it to the carpenter. 'That her?'

Nightingale examined it closely and then shook his head. 'No, boss, that ain't her. She was older than that.'

Dave substituted the photograph of Eunice Bailey. 'How about her, Darrell?'

This time there was no hesitation. 'That's the woman, boss. She was in here with some guy, like I said.'

'When did you see these two people in here, Darrell?' I asked.

Nightingale pulled thoughtfully at his beard. 'I remember it was a Saturday.' He leaned over the counter and shouted for the barman. 'Hey, Bernie, when did I settle my slate?'

The barman roared with laughter and opened a book that he took from behind the till. 'That was some event, Darrell. Ask anyone in here and they'll tell you it was the fifteenth of June. I've got it written down here, and I put a red ring round it. What you call a red-letter day.'

'Are you sure about that, Bernie?' asked Mercer.

'Sure as I'm standing here, Mr Mercer. Here, look for yourself.' And he displayed the book.

'Well,' said Dave, 'that's a bloody turn up. Five days after she was last seen at Driscoll's Hotel, she was still here. So where was she staying in the meantime?'

'This man she was with, Darrell, what did he look like?' I asked.

Nightingale gave a sketchy description that could've been anyone.

'Show him the other photograph, Dave,' I said, not wishing to name Martin Bailey.

Nightingale took some time looking at the shot of Eunice's husband. 'I don't know, boss. It could've been, but I'm not sure. A lot of white folk look the same to me.' He returned the photograph to Dave. 'Don't you have that problem, sir?' he asked.

'Not a lot,' said Dave, and laughed. He could hardly object to a veiled racist comment from another black man.

I was not surprised at Nightingale's inability to make a positive identification, any more than I'd been disheartened at the doubts expressed by the staff at Driscoll's. The legwork team who'd taken Martin Bailey's photograph had done its best, but, like the carpenter's description, it could have been almost anyone.

'You said that they weren't talking quietly, Darrell,' I said. 'Did you hear what they *were* talking about?'

'This and that,' said Nightingale. 'Mostly about where they were going the following day.'

That sounded interesting. 'And where were they going?'

'Swimming, boss. At Elbow Beach.'

'I wonder . . . ' began Mercer.

'You wonder what?' I asked.

'There are some cottages along there. What we call colony cottages. They're usually owned by hotels, but they're actually self-contained bungalows. I'm wondering if Eunice Bailey and this guy Nigel Skinner took one of them for a few days.'

'Would it be difficult to find out?'

'I don't know until I try, Harry,' said Mercer, and turned back to Nightingale. 'Did these two people leave before you did, Darrell?'

'Sure did, boss. Bernie called a cab for them. Hey, Bernie,' said Darrell. 'What cab company did you call for them two people the night I settled my slate?'

'Same one as always, Darrell. Want the number?'

'No,' said Mercer, 'he's walking, but I want it.'

Bernie scribbled the telephone number on a bar mat and handed it over.

Finally, Dave showed the photographs to the barman and to the clientele of the pub. Most were able to identify Eunice Bailey, but the photographs of the two men were met with shaking heads.

'Trouble is,' said Dave, 'they were probably so busy looking at the gorgeous Eunice that they didn't even notice there was a man with her.'

Ten

After we'd left Darrell Nightingale carousing with his mates in the pub on Middle Road, we returned to police head-quarters. Don Mercer had borrowed our collection of photo-graphs, and instructed one of his detective sergeants to make enquiries at the cab company that Bernie had called.

Dave and I went back to our hotel for a shower and an hour or two's sleep. At eight o'clock, we joined Don Mercer down-stairs, and the three of us returned to Jasper's for dinner. We were foolish enough to follow dinner with more Bermuda Triangle Full Moons. Will I never learn?

Even though the following day was a Sunday, Mercer roused me at about nine o'clock. I had another hangover, but Don appeared impervious to the local brew.

'I think we may have something, Harry,' he said, when we met him in the foyer of our hotel. 'My sergeant found the cab driver who took Eunice Bailey and her partner to a bungalow on Elbow Beach on Saturday the fifteenth of June. Ready to take a trip out there?'

We called first at the hotel that owned the bungalows.

'Yes, Mr Mercer,' said the manager, 'we did rent a bungalow to a Mr Skinner and his wife.' He consulted a register. 'From the tenth of June to the sixteenth.'

'And is this the wife?' asked Dave, producing the photo-graph of Eunice Bailey.

'Yes, indeed, that's her,' said the manager. 'A very attrac-tive lady,' he added, somewhat diffidently.

'Did you see either of these men?' Dave showed the manager the photographs of Martin Bailey and Tom Nelson.

The manager took some time studying the photographs before eventually shaking his head. 'No, sir. I'm fairly sure that neither of those gentlemen was with Mrs Skinner. Although . . . ' He looked again at Nelson's photograph. 'It's just possible that's the gentleman, sir, but I'm not really certain.'

'Have you any idea where the Skinners went from here?' I asked, dismissing the manager's doubtful identification of Tom Nelson. I was fairly sure in my own mind that it couldn't have been him.

'I'm afraid not, sir. It's not a question we usually ask.'

'How did Mr Skinner settle the bill?'

The manager tapped a few details into a computer. 'In cash, sir. Quite unusual these days.'

'Did the Skinners leave a forwarding address, in case any mail arrived for them?'

The manager referred once again to the computer. 'No, sir. There'd be a note of it here if they had. We do, however, have a London address for them.' He repeated the Notting Hill address we'd discovered at Driscoll's Hotel. 'Was it something important, Superintendent?' he asked, turning to Mercer.

'Just a couple we're trying to trace.' Mercer spoke casually, considering it unwise to mention that we thought the woman might have been murdered. 'I presume that the bungalow's now occupied by someone else.'

'No, it's not. As a matter of fact, it's been empty since Mr and Mrs Skinner departed. But, of course, it's been thoroughly cleaned.'

'Did they leave any property behind?' I asked, knowing that many hotels have a property store full of abandoned items, some of them quite bizarre.

'No, sir, nothing. Did you want to have a look at the bungalow?'

'What d'you think, Harry?' asked Mercer.

'I don't think there'd be much point, Don,' I said. 'There are probably fingerprints all over the place, but it'd be like looking for a needle in a haystack. Those we lifted at Flatt's Village are probably our best bet.' I turned to the manager. 'Thank you for your assistance.'

'My pleasure, sir,' said the manager.

And that, I was sorry to say, seemed to be all we could do in Bermuda.

That evening Dave and I caught the ten-past ten flight from Bermuda International, and landed at Gatwick at the unearthly hour of six forty-five on Monday morning.

'Go home and recuperate, Dave,' I said. 'I'll see you tomorrow morning.'

Fortunately the commander was still on leave, otherwise he might have gone ape when he learned that we'd spent a few expensive days in Bermuda. Particularly when all we'd come back with was an address for Nigel Skinner that would probably turn out to be duff anyway.

It reminded me of a story told me by a detective constable, years ago. He'd spent ten days travelling the length and breadth of the United States on a fraud enquiry at a cost to the Commissioner of nearly ten thousand pounds. But had come back with nothing evidential.

A few days later he'd had the misfortune to meet the Commissioner in the lift at Scotland Yard. Unfortunately the Commissioner was fully cognizant of the amount that the DC had cost the police fund. The Commissioner's only comment was that he and the DC had each reached the zenith of his profession. Ouch! I made a mental note to avoid the Commissioner at all costs.

'What's on the cards for this morning, guv?' Dave breezed into my office with a quite sickening display of energy.

'I suppose we'd better do something about this Nigel Skinner,' I said.

'He appears to exist,' said Dave, putting a cup of coffee on my desk. 'I had a word with the Notting Hill police this morning, and there is a Nigel Skinner on the electoral roll for the address we got from the manager of Driscoll's Hotel.'

'Well done, Dave.'

'There is also a Sally Skinner shown for the same address.'

'Ah! Wife?'

'The voters' list doesn't show marital status, sir.' Dave spoke as though I should have been aware of this elementary fact. 'It could be his mother, sister, or daughter. Or even grandmother, I suppose,' he added with a sniff.

'What about the fingerprints we lifted at Bailey's cottage, Dave?'

'I popped into the office yesterday, guv,' Dave said, almost guiltily.

'But I told you to take the day off.' I'd got my welfare hat on again.

'Yeah, I know, but I thought it'd be a good idea to get the fingerprint check under way.'

'So, did you get a result?'

'Yeah, but not the right one, guv. No trace of any of them in records. By the time the boys and girls in Fingerprint Bureau had checked them, the fifteen sets that were lifted came down to just three people. But if two of them are Martin and Eunice Bailey's, we know they haven't got any previous convictions. There was a third set, but there was no trace of those either. If they are Nigel Skinner's, he hasn't got any previous either. I ran a name check on the PNC, but we don't have his date of birth, and there are too many Nigel Skinners to make a positive match.'

'Only one thing for it, Dave,' I said. 'We'll have to go and see him. See if you can find a phone number for him.'

'Done already,' said Dave. 'Want me to ring him?'

'Yes.' I glanced at my watch. 'See if we can see him today.'

'Probably out at work, but I'll give it a try.'

Dave returned a few minutes later. 'He's there and he's willing to see us, guv. But he couldn't understand why the police should want to interview him.'

'Perhaps we can put him out of his misery,' I said. 'But first of all, we'll have some lunch.'

'Thank God for that,' said Dave.

We went to our favourite Italian restaurant that, good though it was, wasn't a patch on Jasper's in Hamilton.

The terraced houses in Reeder Street, Notting Hill, were nothing out of the ordinary, but in today's spiralling property market were probably worth a small fortune. Dave pointed out that Reeder Street was not very far from where Dickie Richards lived, not that anything could be read into that.

The man who answered the door was in his early thirties, was casually dressed, and promptly introduced himself as Nigel Skinner.

'I've been puzzling over why the police should want to talk to me ever since I got your telephone call,' he said.

'It might be better if we spoke to you alone, Mr Skinner,' I said, 'rather than in the presence of your wife.' If a married man's wife is present, it is always difficult talking to him about an affair that he might have had, and sure as hell you won't get the truth. And, to be on the safe side, I presumed that Sally Skinner was his wife, rather than his mother. His age ruled out having a daughter called Sally who was old enough to vote.

'I've no secrets from Sally,' replied Skinner, a little tartly, I thought. But at least it confirmed that Sally *was* his wife. 'Anyway, she's gardening. Come into the sitting room, please.' Either this man was a consummate liar, or we'd got the wrong man. 'So, what's this all about?'

'When did you leave Bermuda, Mr Skinner?' I asked, deciding to go straight in.

'Bermuda?' Skinner laughed. 'I've never been to Bermuda in my life.'

'How long have you known Eunice Bailey?' I tried another tack.

'Two or three years, I suppose. Why?'

'Would you mind telling me how you met?'

'If you tell me why you want to know,' responded Skinner. He was beginning to get a little annoyed, and I wondered if he had something to hide. It turned out that he had, but I didn't find out what until later.

'We are investigating her disappearance, Mr Skinner,' said Dave. 'A disappearance in suspicious circumstances.'

We weren't sure that they were suspicious circumstances, but such a statement does tend to concentrate the minds of recalcitrant witnesses.

'Good God! I didn't know she'd disappeared. When did this happen?'

'You're quite sure you've never been to Bermuda?' I asked.

'Positive. But what's Bermuda got to do with it?'

There was no other way. 'In the course of our enquiries, Sergeant Poole and I travelled to Bermuda. We made enquiries at Driscoll's Hotel in Hamilton, and found your name on the computer that records guests.'

'Well, it must've been another Nigel Skinner. It's not exactly an uncommon name.'

'Your address was the address recorded in the hotel computer, Mr Skinner. That's why we're here. We also learned that the same Nigel Skinner rented a bungalow on Elbow Beach from the tenth to the sixteenth of June, together with Eunice Bailey, who was calling herself Eunice Skinner.'

'This is all quite bizarre,' protested Skinner. 'I first met Eunice, and her husband Martin, at a property owners' confederation dinner.'

'Two or three years ago, you said.'

'That's right. But what's all this about her disappearing? D'you think something's happened to her? Did she actually go to Bermuda? Is that why you're asking about it?' The questions tumbled out.

'We know for certain that she was there, Mr Skinner, and she's not been seen since the sixteenth of last month.'

'I'm sorry I can't help you, but any suggestion that I was ever in Bermuda is completely without foundation. I do know, however, that Martin Bailey has a place there.'

'Yes, we discovered that. When did you last see Eunice Bailey, Mr Skinner?'

'Nigel . . . ' The voice came from outside the room.

'Ah, here's my wife,' said Skinner, and glanced at the woman who'd appeared in the doorway.

'Oh! I'm sorry, I didn't know that anyone was here.' Sally Skinner was probably no more than twenty-six or so, and a real beauty. Her long black hair was loose, and she was wearing tight black leather trousers and a black shirt. She certainly didn't look as though she'd been gardening. Perhaps she'd been watering a window box.

'These gentlemen are from the police, Sally,' said Skinner.

'The police? Whatever's the matter?' Mrs Skinner looked enquiringly at Dave and me, an expression of concern settling on her face.

Skinner briefly recounted what we'd been talking about. It was met with gales of laughter, and apparent relief. 'Nigel in a love nest in Bermuda with Eunice?' queried Sally Skinner, addressing me. 'How superbly delicious. I'd love to go to Bermuda, or anywhere else for that matter, but Nigel's always working too hard. D'you know, the last holiday we had was in the south of France two years ago. Anyway, he was here for the whole of June, working.'

'I was just asking your husband when he last saw Eunice Bailey, Mrs Skinner.'

'Well, I can answer that.' Sally Skinner reached up with both hands and flicked her hair back over her shoulders. It was something that she did every few minutes. 'It must have been a year ago,' she continued. 'We'd met them at some association dinner, what, three years previously?' She glanced at her husband for confirmation, and he nodded. 'After that, we saw them fairly regularly, but then it cooled. I don't think it was anything to do with us personally, but I got the impression that there was a bit of a rift between Martin and Eunice, and we saw them only rarely after that. To be perfectly honest, I think another man was involved. Eunice is a very attractive woman, and I'm not speaking out of turn when I say that she wasn't above flirting, even with Nigel.' She smiled briefly at her husband. 'Martin always pretended not to notice, but I think he might have got a bit fed up with it after a while.'

'Your wife says that you were working here all June, Mr Skinner. What exactly is your profession?'

'I own a couple of office blocks in central London, and one in Bristol. It's a full-time job looking after them, but it's very lucrative.' Skinner smiled, almost ruefully, and made a little apologetic gesture with his hands.

'I'm sorry to have bothered you, Mr Skinner, and you too, ma'am,' I said, 'but I'm sure you understand that when we receive information, we have to follow it up. Particularly in serious cases.'

'Of course,' said Skinner. 'You don't think Eunice has been murdered, do you?'

'I really don't know,' I said, 'but nothing's been heard of her since the sixteenth of June. She'll probably turn up safe and sound.' But the more I looked into this mystery, the less confident I was that it would have a happy outcome.

There are times when the police have to accept that they are going no further with a particular enquiry. We never admit it, of course, but instead come up with some apt verbal palliative. Like 'enquiries are continuing', or 'police are following up a promising new lead'. The truth is that the investigation has been put on the back burner, and after a few weeks has been forgotten about. Unless a new lead *does* turn up.

But right now, we struggled on.

'D'you reckon that Skinner was telling the truth, guv?' asked Dave.

'Yes, I'm afraid I do, Dave. Sally Skinner's reaction was so spontaneous that I don't think she was lying about her husband having been there for the whole of June. Unless she's a good actress.'

Dave peeled a banana. 'Yeah, I know Skinner played the innocent, but if he *was* in Bermuda, he'd've known why we wanted to see him. And he and his wife had ample time to concoct a story between the time I rang him, and we arrived on his doorstep.'

'There's only one flaw in that, Dave. Why would his wife cover for him if he was having it off with Eunice Bailey in Bermuda?'

'Money,' said Dave, waving his banana skin before dropping it in the waste bin. I assumed that there was some symbolism in that little pantomime.

'Meaning?'

'Skinner seems to be very well off – by my standards, anyway – and it might be that Sally Skinner would rather let him play the field than divorce him. I think she'd prefer to put up with his philandering than give up the pleasant lifestyle she's enjoying at the moment.'

'You're a cynic, Dave.'

'Yes, guv. Perhaps I've been working with you for too long. On the other hand, she might be playing fast and loose as well. She's a very good-looking bird.'

'But if it wasn't Skinner in Bermuda, sharing a bed with Eunice Bailey, who the hell was it? And if it wasn't him, why should someone else use his name and address in the register at Driscoll's? And again when he and Eunice took that bungalow for a few days.'

'Haven't a clue,' said Dave, and threw me a cigarette.

I sent for Kate Ebdon.

'Kate, I want you to arrange for searches to be done at Companies House. Look into the businesses of Martin Bailey, Tom Nelson, Peter Richards, and Nigel Skinner. They're all connected in some way with Eunice Bailey. I don't know whether it'll prove anything, but it's something we've got to do.'

When Companies House was in London, a detective would jump on a bus, shoot up to Stoke Newington, and, with any luck, come back with the answers in a couple of hours. But the office was now in Cardiff, and that meant sending emails to the police-liaison officer there. That's progress for you, I suppose.

'Could take a bit of time, guv,' said Kate, confirming what I'd just been thinking, and made a few notes on her clipboard. 'There's one other thing that might be of interest.'

'What's that?' I always sat up and took careful note when Kate said something like that. She was a tenacious detective, and hated leaving loose ends. Even though they weren't her loose ends to tidy up.

'That bent ex-copper that was doing work for Martin Bailey. Dave said in his statement that Bailey told you he'd found him in Yellow Pages . . . '

'That's right, that's what Bailey said . . . *guv.*' Dave grinned at the DI.

'Don't take the piss, *Sarge,*' said Kate, and turned back to me. 'Well, he's not in Yellow Pages. I had a run through, and he's not listed.'

'Now, I wonder why Bailey should have said that. But there's one way of finding out. We'll ask him,' I suggested.

'Who, Bailey, guv?'

'No, Dave,' I said. 'John, the aforementioned bent ex-detective sergeant.'

'You don't think he was the guy in Bermuda with Eunice, do you?' asked Dave.

'If he was, we'd've found his fingerprints at Flatt's Village. And we know he's got form. He's not clever enough to have cleaned every square inch of that place. There'd've been no reason anyway.'

'But he has been to Bermuda, guv.' Dave was unwilling to leave it.

'Exactly, but he said he'd been no further than a few hotels in Hamilton. Frankly, I don't think he was ever there.'

'Martin Bailey said he sent him there.'

'Martin Bailey also denied having been to Bermuda, but we know that was a lie. Ergo, Bailey's a liar.'

According to the business card that Martin Bailey had shown us, our disgraced detective sergeant had an office on the Tottenham Court Road.

It proved to be a room on the second floor of an old building, and was reached by ascending a rickety, uncarpeted staircase.

There was a badly printed card pinned to the door. Apart from John's name it also falsely claimed that the occupant was 'Ex-Scotland Yard', and optimistically professed that he was skilled in matrimonial and fraud enquiries. I didn't doubt the latter; he was pretty good at fraud himself.

But the door was locked.

The dowdy office next door was occupied by an individual whose sign described him as an accountant. Given that Dave's father was an accountant, it was obvious that Dave deduced from the poor state of the furnishings and decor that this guy was not very good at his job.

The accountant was an emaciated individual in his fifties. He pointedly ignored our arrival, but after a moment or two, looked up, a hostile expression on his face. 'Whatever it is you're selling, I don't want any, or I've already got some,' he said.

'We're police officers,' I said to this rather anaemic number-cruncher, and was pleased to see that this information caused him a measure of apprehension. 'I'm looking for the private investigator who occupies the office next door.'

'He's gone. Left. Skedaddled. Why, is he doing some work for you? Seems to spend most of his time spying on husbands who are having it off with some bird. Or did.'

'Any idea where he went?'

'No. He disappeared about a week ago. Beginning of the month. No idea where he went.'

'Who's got the key to his office?' asked Dave.

'Try the caretaker. He's got an office on the ground floor.'

'Interesting,' said Dave, as we descended the staircase. 'If John did a runner at the beginning of the month, it would have been straight after we'd had a chat with him when we caught him coming out of Bailey's drum.'

The caretaker had a pile of sandwiches and a thermos flask in front of him. He looked to be the sort who hadn't got a television licence, was fiddling the social security, reneging on the Child Support Agency, and getting tax credits for tax he didn't pay.

'Dunno where he's gone, guv'nor,' said this classic example of pitiful human detritus. 'Nothing to do with me.'

'Who collects the rent, then?' asked Dave.

'No idea, guv'nor. I only look after the place an' that.'

'Thanks very much,' said Dave sarcastically.

Having established that John hadn't left a forwarding

address, we obtained the key to his poky little office, but there was little to see. It looked to me as though he'd been expecting a visit because there wasn't a scrap of paperwork anywhere, except for a few circulars on the floor behind the door. Apart from the basic furniture, there was only a kettle and a couple of unwashed mugs. The filing cabinet was empty save for a parking ticket issued in early June for an infraction of the regulations that obtained in Southwark Bridge Road.

I handed it to Dave. 'See what you can do with that.'

'It might not even be his, guv,' Dave said, 'but I'll run a check on the index number. He might have notified the DVLA of a change of address, I suppose.' But his cynical laugh betrayed exactly what he thought were the chances of that.

Eleven

I was agreeably surprised when Kate came into my office the following morning with the result – quicker than I'd expected – of the Companies House search. Although it confirmed some of what we had already learned, it also posed a further question.

Martin Bailey was indeed the managing director of a private limited company ostensibly specializing in property development, the activities of which appeared to be above board. It was to be expected that Peter Richards' assertion that he was a director of a group of overseas casinos was not recorded, presumably because the company was registered somewhere abroad. Had I still been on the Fraud Squad this might have interested me slightly, but I had other things to think about. It came as no surprise that Tom Nelson wasn't shown anywhere, but he'd told us that he didn't do anything apart from supporting a number of charities. All well and good so far.

The enigma was Nigel Skinner. Skinner had claimed to own two office blocks in London and one in Bristol, but he was not shown as a director of any registered company.

'If Skinner owns a number of office buildings, Dave, I should think it's financial suicide not to form himself into a limited company.' My years investigating fraud had taught me that the creation of a limited-liability company was a safety measure ensuring that, if it went belly up, the directors could walk away with very little personal financial harm.

'Perhaps he wasn't telling us the truth, guv.' Dave always worked on the theory that everyone told lies until the contrary was proved. 'It's an easy thing to say, but a difficult one to prove.'

'In which case, Dave, he might not have been telling the truth when he said he'd never been to Bermuda.'

'I seem to recall having hinted at that . . . *sir*,' said Dave.

'Put him on the PNC, Dave.' Entering Skinner's name on the Police National Computer was like putting a message in a bottle and chucking it in the sea. But if he came to the notice of police in any way, I would be informed.

'I've done it, guv. And John what's-his-name's on there already, of course.'

And that jogged my memory. 'Kate, Dave's got a parking ticket that we found at our bent PI's office yesterday. Get someone to check the index mark and see who owns it, and where he lives. But knowing our luck, it's probably nothing to do with John. Secondly, see if the Avon and Somerset Police know anything about a Nigel Skinner who's supposed to own an office block in Bristol.'

It took Kate an hour.

'The index number you found on the parking ticket at John's office goes out to his vehicle, but the Tottenham Court Road address is the one recorded at the DVLA,' said Kate. 'And the Avon and Somerset Police have never heard of Nigel Skinner. They also said that it's impossible to find out whether or not he owns an office block in Bristol without some more information. Like where it is.'

'Well, so much for that,' I said. Not that I'd held out any hope of the Bristol law being able to discover anything useful about Skinner. If I'd been asked if someone owned an office block somewhere in London, I wouldn't've known where to start.

'At least we can do John for failing to notify the DVLA of a change of address,' commented Dave drily, reluctant to let anyone get away with anything.

'However, guv,' said Kate, 'I rang the number on the business card that John gave Bailey. The one that went out to the Tottenham Court Road address.'

'And?'

'And there was a recorded message transferring all calls to a number in Putney. I did a subscriber check, and then the electoral roll. He's listed at this address.' Kate jotted the information down on my pad.

Dave laughed. 'No wonder he got nicked,' he said. 'John's not as clever as he thinks he is.'

'Maybe, Dave, but I think we can let him sweat for a while. I'm more interested in Skinner.'

'Aren't we going off at a tangent here, guv?' asked Dave. 'Unless we can prove that Skinner was in Bermuda, we don't have much of a case.'

'What's your manpower strength like, Kate?' I ignored Dave's observation, even though it was a good one.

'Depends what you want to do, guv.'

'Can you stretch your team to a couple of days' obo on Skinner? Say two shifts: seven to three, and three to eleven.'

'I reckon so,' said Kate. 'What are you looking for?'

'As there was no trace of him at Companies House, I've got doubts about the story he told us of owning office blocks. I'd like to find out what he really does, and where he goes. Perhaps he goes to Bermuda.'

'Right, I'll give it a go.'

It was not until two o'clock the following afternoon that Kate's early-turn observation team radioed in with a message.

'Skinner and his wife left their Notting Hill address at thirteen oh five, guv,' said Kate, 'and drove to a warehouse in Hounslow. They're still there.'

'Any indication as to what this warehouse is, or what it contains?'

'Not as yet, but we're making enquiries.'

'Good. Keep me posted.'

A further message at five thirty reported that the Skinners had left Hounslow and returned to Notting Hill.

'I wonder what that's all about, Dave?'

'Could be drugs, guv, given that Hounslow's next door to Heathrow Airport,' said Dave. 'Drugs are very popular these days,' he added cynically. 'But there's one sure way of finding out: give him a pull.'

'Not until we've found out a bit more about this warehouse. Doesn't exactly come into the category of a central London office block, does it?'

'And sure as hell Hounslow's not in Bristol,' remarked Dave.

'Do we keep the obo on, guv?' asked Kate.

'No, take it off. But I intend to get a warrant to search this warehouse. I'll want the obo back on when we go in, just to make sure that the Skinners don't surprise us in the act. And on second thoughts, don't bother about making further enquiries.'

It was not until Monday morning that I was able to see a district judge in his chambers at the City of Westminster magistrates' court, and persuade him that we had a case for a search warrant. The judge thought the information was a bit thin, but when I mentioned the possibility of finding the body of a murder victim in the Hounslow warehouse, he capitulated. We got our warrant.

I briefed Kate to resume the observation on the Skinners' place at Notting Hill, and got Dave to make a duff telephone call to them, just to confirm that they were at home. They were.

I rang a mate of mine on the Drugs Squad and suggested he might like to send one of his officers to meet us in Hounslow. He was a bit dubious, and said that if illegal substances were likely to be found there a full team should go. I responded by saying that if we did find drugs, he was welcome to call up the cavalry immediately and do what he liked. Eventually he agreed that one of his officers – a detective sergeant called Joe Patel – would meet us at the warehouse.

We drove to Hounslow, along with a lock expert hand-picked by Linda Mitchell, my favourite senior forensic practitioner. I decided against taking a full search team, because we weren't looking for evidence of a crime, even though we might find such evidence. It was, as the district judge had acidly suggested, more of a fishing expedition.

A man of Indian appearance, wearing jeans and a flowery shirt, got out of a car that had seen better days. He was bearded, had long hair, and was adorned with an excessive amount of bling.

'Mr Brock?'

'Yes.'

'DS Patel, Drugs Squad, guv.'

I checked again with Kate Ebdon that the Skinners were still at home, the lock expert did the business, and in we went.

The warehouse was small, not much bigger than a double garage, but there was steel racking covering most of the two sidewalls and the end wall.

The racks were full of DVDs and, in the centre, a number

of machines for duplicating them. There was also a DVD player.

Dave selected a DVD at random and glanced at the photograph on the cover. 'Well, well,' he said, holding it up for us to see. It depicted a busty naked bimbo emerging from a swimming pool. 'Anyone speak Dutch?' he asked.

'I did an attachment to the Drugs Squad in Amsterdam for a year,' said Joe Patel. 'Picked up a bit of the lingo. Let's have a look.' He took the DVD and laughed. 'Roughly translated it means: Fun and Games at the Lido.'

Dave crossed to the opposite side of the warehouse, and selected another DVD. 'These have all got English titles, guv. I reckon our Mr Skinner imports those' – he gestured at the other rack – 'copies 'em, and knocks 'em out in Soho somewhere. Or, for that matter, anywhere else he can find a market.'

'Like Bristol,' I said.

'I reckon that lets me out, guv,' said Patel. He shook hands and departed.

There was no immediate action that I could take, not that I wanted to take any anyway. I had quite enough on my plate, and this was clearly a matter for the Porn Squad. Possibly even Her Majesty's Revenue and Customs. It did, however, cause me to wonder if Skinner was up to any other sort of nastiness. Nastiness that might in some way be connected to the disappearance of Eunice Bailey.

'I suppose we'd better make sure it is porn,' said Dave, his lascivious streak coming to the fore. He took a DVD and put it in the player. There was no doubt at all that the subject matter was not only porn, but hard-core porn.

'Bloody hell!' said Dave. 'Just look who's here, guv.'

I peered closer at the image of a naked couple performing vigorous sex. The woman was undoubtedly the demure Sally Skinner. And she seemed to be thoroughly enjoying herself, but with a man who was not her husband.

'Not so much Sally Skinner as Sally Skin,' commented Dave. 'Oh well, it takes all sorts, I suppose.'

We were careful to leave everything as we'd found it. I didn't want the Skinners to know we'd searched their warehouse until I'd decided what needed to be done next.

'As the Skinners weren't here, guv, we're supposed to leave

a copy of the warrant in a prominent place,' observed Dave, ever mindful of the law.

'Yes,' I said, putting the warrant in my pocket. 'I remember hearing that somewhere.'

I did a bit of decision-making on the way back to Curtis Green, and once there telephoned the headquarters of what I believed to be the National Investigation Service of Customs and Excise at Lower Thames Street in the City of London. I asked to speak to the surveyor, my old friend John Fielding.

But it turned out that that organization seems also to have its own funny names and total confusion squad. Fielding explained that, although he used to be called a surveyor in the National Investigation Service, he was now called a senior investigating officer in something called Detection of Her Majesty's Revenue and Customs. 'Detection', he further informed me, was a 'business strand' of HMRC. Whatever the hell that meant.

'Well, now we've got that out of the way, John, I've come across something that might interest you.' And I went on to explain what we'd discovered in the Hounslow warehouse.

'I wonder how he's bringing that stuff in,' said Fielding, half to himself. 'Anyway, Harry, I think this is likely to be of more interest to SOCA rather than us.' It was unfortunate that he pronounced SOCA 'soccer'.

'What the hell's football got to do with it, John?' I asked.

Fielding laughed. 'You're winding me up, Harry. SOCA is the Serious and Organized Crime Agency . . . as you well know. But I think they're the people to talk to.'

Of course I was winding him up. I knew perfectly well that SOCA, another monolith created by a panic-stricken government, had gobbled up the National Crime Squad, the National Criminal Intelligence Service, and half Revenue and Customs. And God knows what else.

The problem with such amorphous organizations is that one can never find the right person to talk to. My experience told me that I would get shunted from one officer to another, each claiming that it wasn't his – or her – area of expertise. I set Dave the task. And he, of course, knew how to short-circuit the system.

The first officer that Dave spoke to at SOCA got the benefit of his ploy. 'We've come across a massive porn-DVD-smuggling operation near Heathrow. Get someone to ring my guv'nor, will you?' With that he provided my name and phone number and replaced the receiver. 'That should wind 'em up a bit, guv,' he said.

The upshot of Dave's phone call was that I received an answer within ten minutes.

The caller, who introduced himself as 'Agent Madison', eventually, and under intense questioning, admitted to being Detective Sergeant Patrick Madison.

'Can you tell me a bit more about this job of yours, sir?' Madison enquired.

I gave him a rundown on what we'd found, and how we'd come to discover it.

'Interesting,' was Madison's comment.

'It is, isn't it? But what are you going to do about it?' I asked.

There was a longish pause, and then, 'I think we'll have to mount an observation. But what's your interest in this, sir?'

I explained briefly about the missing Eunice Bailey, and the reason we'd interviewed Nigel Skinner.

'So you've really no further interest in the porn side of it.'

'None at all, but I am interested in whether or not he murdered Mrs Bailey. Possibly in Bermuda.'

'Yes, I suppose so.'

'There's no suppose about it, Sergeant,' I said. 'And if and when you nick the Skinners, I want to be there.'

'Yes, of course, sir.'

It took SOCA a week to come up with a result.

'I'm Agent Madison, sir,' said the man who entered my office.

'Sit down, *Sergeant*,' I said pointedly. I couldn't be doing with all this 'agent' stuff. I rang through to the sergeants' office and asked Dave to join us.

Madison sat down and took a bulky file from his briefcase. 'We mounted an observation,' he began.

'Congratulations,' said Dave. He didn't have a great deal of time for what he called fancy organizations.

'And on Friday last, the nineteenth of July, sir,' said Madison, glancing up, 'we followed both the targets—'

'I presume you mean Nigel and Sally Skinner,' I said.

'Yes, sir.'

'And what time was this?'

Madison consulted his file. 'Twenty-three thirty, by which time it was dark.'

'Would be,' commented Dave drily. 'It's the rotation of the earth on its axis that does it.'

It was obvious that Madison didn't know what to make of Dave, but he struggled on. 'We followed Skinner and his wife from twenty-five Reeder Street, Notting Hill, to Park Road, Staines, which is immediately on the north side of the Staines reservoir. A few minutes later, a light aircraft landed on the reservoir.'

'*On* the reservoir, did you say?'

'Yes, sir. It was a Cessna one-seven-two floatplane. But it has wheels too. The aircraft then taxied across to Park Road, and the pilot delivered a plastic crate – measuring about two feet by eighteen inches, and a foot deep – to one of the targets. That is to say Nigel Skinner, sir. The aircraft took off straight-away, and Skinner put the crate into a Range Rover and drove to the warehouse at Hounslow. He and his wife spent twenty minutes inside and then they returned to their home address.'

'Any idea where this aircraft came from?'

'Not at this stage, sir. We spoke to air-traffic control at Heathrow, but they had no record of a Cessna floatplane arriving at that time. They suggested that it probably flew low enough to stay beneath the radar screen.'

'Didn't anyone get the registration number of this aircraft?' I asked.

'Unfortunately no, sir. It was too dark, and we didn't want to show out. However, now we know what the form is, it's almost certain that there'll be another run. Then we'll be able to speak to our foreign liaison.'

'Like the Netherlands,' said Dave.

Madison looked surprised. 'Why d'you say that?'

'Because when we looked at the DVDs in the Hounslow warehouse,' said Dave, 'half of them had titles written in Dutch, and the Netherlands has a thriving porn industry.'

'Ah, yes, quite so.'

I just hoped that Madison wouldn't suggest that Dave should join SOCA. He was likely to get a pretty dusty answer. Dave had a thing about being a sharp-end copper.

'So what do you propose to do next, Sergeant Madison?'
I asked.

'Maintain observation on the Skinners, sir, and the next time they go to Hounslow, which will probably be this coming Friday, arrest them and the pilot of this Cessna.'

'And how d'you intend to do that, given that he'll probably take off the moment he sights the Old Bill?' asked Dave.

'We have plans in place,' said Madison, which is what policeman always say when they haven't a clue what to do next.

Twelve

'What the hell d'you want this time?' Martin Bailey's hostile demeanour made it blatantly obvious that he was not best pleased to see us. 'Look, I've told you that I have no idea where my bloody wife has gone, and I don't damned well care. This harassment has gone too far,' he protested. 'I've told you I intend to make a formal complaint about it, but you just won't take no for an answer.'

'D'you wish to carry on this conversation on the doorstep, Mr Bailey, or shall we go inside?' Although I spoke mildly, I was getting irritated by Bailey's boorish attitude.

Bailey turned abruptly from the door, leaving us to follow him into the sitting room. 'Well, what now?' he demanded, once we had settled.

'On a previous occasion, I mentioned a man named Nigel Skinner,' I began, 'who we believe may have stayed with your wife at a hotel in Bermuda.' I'd decided to interview Bailey again, just to see what he'd say about Skinner's assertion that he knew Bailey and his wife.

'Yes, I remember. What about him?'

'We have now located Skinner and interviewed him.'

'Have you indeed? And did he tell you what he's done with my wife? Not that I care. He's welcome to her.'

'I don't think he's done anything with her. In fact, I'm reasonably satisfied that he's never been to Bermuda in his life.' This was not the time to tell Bailey that Skinner and his wife were being investigated for importing hard-core pornographic DVDs. Or that Sally Skinner was a porn actress.

'Why are you telling me all this, Chief Inspector?'

'Because when I mentioned Nigel Skinner previously, you told me that you'd never heard of him.'

'That's perfectly correct. I don't know him. The name means nothing to me.'

'When we spoke to Mr and Mrs Skinner a fortnight ago, each of them separately claimed to have met you and your wife some three years ago at a . . . ' I turned to Dave. 'What exactly did Mr Skinner say, Sergeant?'

Dave opened his pocketbook. 'To quote his exact words, sir: "I first met Eunice, and her husband Martin, at a property owners' confederation dinner." He then went on to say that this was about two or three years ago.'

'Absolute nonsense. I've never heard of the man, nor his wife.'

'We then asked Mr Skinner when he'd last seen Mrs Bailey,' Dave continued, 'and at that point Mrs Skinner entered the room, having overheard the conversation.' He referred to his pocketbook again. 'And she said: "We'd met them at some association dinner, what, three years previously? After that, we saw them fairly regularly, but then it cooled." '

'Is that all they said?' asked Bailey, his eyes narrowing.

'Yes,' said Dave, deciding rightly not to mention that Sally Skinner believed there'd been a rift between Bailey and his wife as a result of Eunice's propensity for flirting.

'I've never heard such a load of crap in all my life,' exclaimed Bailey. 'What d'you propose to do about it?'

'Do about it?' I asked. 'What d'you suggest?'

'This man can't go around spreading lies like that. Surely there's something you can do.'

'It's not a matter for the police,' said Dave. 'It's a matter for the civil courts, but only if you've been defamed in some way. And I wouldn't imagine that a claim to know you and your wife could be construed as slanderous. If you were to take proceedings, Skinner would probably claim that it was a case of mistaken identity. Anyway, such statements to the police are usually regarded as privileged.'

'How the hell would you know, Sergeant?' snapped Bailey angrily. 'Are you a bloody lawyer or something?' I got the impression that he didn't much like either black men or detectives. And that a combination of the two was anathema to him.

'No,' said Dave calmly. 'I'm just saving you the cost of a libel lawyer.'

'Well, don't bother,' said Bailey irritably. 'I'm perfectly capable of obtaining legal advice if I need it. And paying for it.'

'Would you be prepared to make a written statement confirming that you do not know, nor have ever heard of, Nigel and Sally Skinner, Mr Bailey?' I asked.

'No, I bloody well wouldn't. I'm sick to the back teeth with you people bothering me. Now let me say this again, just in case you didn't get it the first time: I don't know where my wife's gone, and I don't care. And now I'd be glad if you left. I've work to do.'

'What d'you think, Dave?' I asked as we drove back to Curtis Green.

'Either Bailey's lying, or Skinner is.' Dave was always very good at getting to the crux of things. 'But it was interesting that Bailey refused to make a statement denying knowing Skinner.'

'Yes, it was, and I only put it to him to see what his response would be.' We didn't need a statement from Bailey, and it would have been of no use to us anyway. But his refusal to make one seemed to indicate that he was the one who was lying, but why? However, Bailey was, to all intents and purposes, an upright citizen at the head of a lucrative business. But it did cross my mind that he might also have been involved in Skinner's porn business. However, his wife had walked out on him and he didn't care. I suppose it was understandable that he was tired of our frequent visits.

Nigel Skinner, on the other hand, was not only a smuggler of obscene DVDs who had told us he owned office blocks, but also a man who condoned his wife's participation in skin flicks. But perhaps he owned office blocks as well. Either that, or he used it as an untraceable cover for his nefarious activities.

It was not until Saturday that anything of interest happened. But do not labour under the illusion that during that time I wasn't doing anything. The bane of a detective's life is paperwork, and Dave and I were fully occupied putting together a report for the Crown Prosecution Service on a murder we'd investigated.

Any CID officer will tell you that it is one thing to solve a case, but quite another to reduce the details to writing. And it doesn't end there. Then comes the collation and indexing of all the relevant witness statements and exhibits, and the completion of the multifarious forms without which the CPS can't possibly do anything. Identifying the murderer in this particular case had been the easy part. Chronicling all we had done in the shape of a comprehensible account upon which Crown counsel's brief could be prepared was quite another.

However, enough of this whingeing. Although DS Madison had told me that he hoped the Skinners would return to Hounslow – and the Staines reservoir – late on Friday, I didn't intend hanging around the office that evening on the off chance of that actually happening. I'd wasted time doing it too often in the past. I went home. Which was just as well, because I heard nothing until seven o'clock on Saturday morning when the ringing of my telephone awoke me.

'Mr Brock? It's Patrick Madison, sir.'

'Have you scored?' I asked.

'We certainly have, sir. Last night, we arrested the Skinners, and the pilot of the Cessna. He was a Dutch national called Piet van de Groote.'

'So what's happening now?' I asked.

'They're being transferred from Hounslow nick to Charing Cross as I speak, sir. We'll kick off by questioning them, then conduct a search of their house in Notting Hill, after which we'll probably admit them to police bail.'

'Right, I'll meet you at Charing Cross.'

I telephoned Dave. The phone was answered by a sleepy Madeleine Poole who, having returned from the Royal Opera House at midnight, was not best pleased. And said so. One of the things to which chief inspectors have to get accustomed is that although sergeants are usually deferential, their wives aren't necessarily so.

'Sorry to disturb you, Madeleine,' I said, 'but I need Dave to meet me at Charing Cross police station as soon as possible.'

'OK, Harry, I'll tell him,' said Madeleine drowsily. I just hoped she'd give Dave my message before she went to sleep again.

Dave, who lived in Kennington, a short distance from Charing Cross, was at the nick when I arrived. And so was DS Madison.

'It was a piece of cake, sir,' Madison said. 'The Skinners left Notting Hill at just after ten o'clock last night and drove to the rendezvous. At spot on eleven thirty, the Cessna landed, taxied across as before, and the pilot delivered another crate.'

'What happened next?'

'We arrested the pilot in the act of handing over the goods, and took him and the Skinners to the warehouse. The Dutch guy claimed that he didn't speak English, and the Skinners said nothing. We conducted a cursory search of the warehouse, satisfied ourselves that the contents were indeed pornographic, sealed it, and placed it under guard. Then we took the prisoners to Hounslow nick and banged them up for the night.'

'They're here at Charing Cross now, I presume.'

'Yes, sir. D'you want to sit in on the interview?'

'No, thanks, but I intend to question them separately about another matter. Namely the disappearance of Eunice Bailey. And I want to be present when you search their Notting Hill address. Give me a ring on my mobile when you're done.'

It all took time, but these things always do. Dave and I returned to Curtis Green, but it was gone three in the afternoon before DS Madison called me.

'We've charged the Skinners with various offences under the Obscene Publications Act, sir,' said Madison, when Dave and I arrived at Charing Cross, 'and the customs element of SOCA have charged van de Groote with smuggling. We had some difficulty finding a Dutch interpreter in a hurry, but when we did, van de Groote trotted out the usual defence, claiming he didn't know that what was in the crates was in any way illegal. In fact, he said he thought they contained Edam cheese.'

'Hard cheese!' commented Dave sarcastically.

'No, it's soft,' said Madison in a nervous aside, still unable to come to grips with Dave's sense of humour. 'Van de Groote said he'd filed a flight plan before leaving Schiphol Airport and, as far as he was concerned, it was the normal run and all above board.'

'And did he happen to mention that it was normal to avoid air-traffic control, and land on a bloody reservoir?' asked Dave. 'I'll bet that wasn't in his flight plan.'

Madison laughed. 'No, he couldn't explain that, but we're in touch with the Netherlands Staatpolitie – the state police – and they're looking into it.'

'Where are the Skinners now?' I asked.

'Still here, sir.'

'Good. Dave and I will have a word with them. Separately. The wife first, I think.'

The custody sergeant had already placed Sally Skinner in the interview room, and she was looking rather sorry for herself. She was tired, obviously, because I shouldn't think she'd had much sleep during the short period she was bed-and-breakfasting in one of Hounslow nick's cells.

'Mrs Skinner, I want to talk to you about something uncon-nected with the offences with which you've been charged.'

'What d'you want to know?' Sally Skinner gave the impres-sion of being completely mystified by our arrival.

'When we spoke to you at Notting Hill on the ninth of July, you stated that your husband had been there for the whole of June. Is that true?'

'Not quite.'

'Where had he been?'

'Amsterdam. He was there from the tenth to the fifteenth of June. We both were.'

If that were true, it meant that Nigel Skinner could not have been in Bermuda during that period. And that meant that it was another man called Nigel Skinner who had been at Driscoll's Hotel and, later, in a bungalow at Elbow Beach.

'For what purpose?'

Sally Skinner smiled. 'There's no harm in telling you now. We were making arrangements for the next consignment of DVDs, of course.' She didn't seem at all concerned that she and her husband had been charged with importing and distrib-uting pornography. But in view of society's prevailing attitudes to such material, she was probably justified in thinking that not much would happen to her. Apart from a fine and a loss of trade. 'And we spent some time seeing the sights.'

'You also said previously that you knew Martin and Eunice Bailey.'

'That's true. We do know them.'

'Would it surprise you to know that Martin Bailey denies knowing you or your husband?'

'I can't think why. I told you before that we used to see quite a lot of each other, but then it stopped. Martin's a rather unpleasant man, rude too.' It didn't sound very convincing, and I wondered if there was some other reason why the two couples ceased seeing each other. 'I always felt sorry for Eunice. She was a vibrant girl, always ready for a party, or some fun and games.'

'Like fun and games at the lido?' suggested Dave.

'What do you mean by that?' asked Sally, raising an eyebrow in Dave's direction.

'It was the title of one of the Dutch DVDs found in your warehouse at Hounslow.' But Dave was careful not to mention that he was the one who'd found it. I think he was still worried about us not leaving a copy of the warrant there.

Sally laughed. 'Yes, they're pretty hackneyed, the titles they give them, aren't they?'

'And do you give hackneyed titles to the ones you appear in, Mrs Skinner?' Dave asked.

It was pure luck that Dave had selected one of probably few DVDs in which Sally Skinner featured. And it was very likely that DS Madison didn't know about it yet. It would be the unfortunate task of another officer to go through all the seized DVDs and assess whether they were sufficiently obscene to be placed before a court. Many years ago, I'd had to do it myself, and very boring it was too. In fact, it was enough to turn you off sex forever. I made a note to tell Madison that Sally Skinner was a participant in some of the recordings.

But Dave's question, coming unexpectedly, clearly caught Sally Skinner unawares, and for the first time since the interview began, she faltered. 'Well, I, er . . . ' But then she made a quick recovery. 'I enjoy doing it. It's great fun,' she said, lifting her chin in defiance. 'And there's nothing wrong in it.'

'It's no concern of mine,' I said. 'My sole interest is investigating Eunice Bailey's disappearance. But can you think of any reason why Martin Bailey should deny knowing you?' I decided to push it one last time.

'No, I can't.' Whether the girl had been embarrassed – unlikely though that was – by our discovery that she was a porn actress, she decided not to answer any more questions. 'I've nothing further to say.' She folded her arms across her ample breasts, broke eye-contact with me, and stared across the room.

Indeed, there was nothing more to ask. If Sally's statement

that she and Nigel Skinner had been in Amsterdam was true, that was the end of the matter.

Nevertheless, I determined that I would interview Nigel Skinner.

'I've just been speaking to your wife, Mr Skinner,' I said.

'Oh, what about?' Skinner smiled, and leaned back in his chair, quite relaxed.

'About Eunice Bailey.'

'I think I've told you all I know about her.' Skinner seemed even less perturbed than his wife by their arrest.

'When I last saw you, you said that you'd been in Notting Hill for the whole of June.'

'Yes, I believe I did.' There was an amused expression on Skinner's face as he answered my question.

'But it's not true, is it?'

'No, it's not. But I wasn't going to tell you I'd been in Amsterdam buying up risqué DVDs, was I?' Skinner smiled at his little deception. 'In fact, Sally and I were there from the tenth to the fifteenth of June. We got our business over with very quickly, and spent the rest of the time sightseeing.'

Which was more or less what Sally had said. If they had colluded – or in copper's language, cooked up an alibi – it was something that the state police in Amsterdam would probably resolve for us. Once they had tracked the pornography business back to source.

'Where did you stay in Amsterdam?' asked Dave.

'At the Metropole,' Skinner answered without hesitation. 'It's close to the city centre, but I can't remember the name of the street, other than to say it was near the red-light district,' he added with a smile.

'I have interviewed Martin Bailey again, Mr Skinner,' I said, 'and he is adamant that he doesn't know you, and further claims that he's never heard of you.'

'Well, he would, wouldn't he?'

'What d'you mean by that, Mr Skinner?'

'Now that I've been charged with this business of the DVDs, it won't hurt to tell you. You obviously know that we don't only import them, we make them as well.'

'I would remind you that you're still under the caution administered by DS Madison, Mr Skinner.'

'So what?' Skinner grinned. It was obvious that he too

thought that he was unlikely to go to prison. 'D'you mind if I smoke?'

'Not at all.' I waited until Skinner had lit a cigarette.

'I don't know if you've seen a photograph of Eunice Bailey . . . '

'Yes, I have.'

'In that case, you'll appreciate that she's a very attractive girl.'

'I wouldn't argue with that,' I said, although I was well aware of the extent to which the camera could lie.

'And she was a terrible flirt.'

'So I've heard.'

'She and I had a brief fling about a year ago.'

'Didn't your wife object?' I asked.

Skinner chuckled. 'Good heavens, no. She was there, watching.'

'And didn't Mrs Bailey mind?'

'No, she suggested it. As a matter of fact, all three of us finished up in bed together.'

I never cease to be amazed at the perversities of some people. 'Go on.'

'So Sally asked her if she'd like to take part in one of our productions.'

'One of your productions?' queried Dave, wanting to be absolutely certain what Skinner was talking about.

'Yes, one of our little adult dramas. Sally explained that she took part, and Eunice was all for it.'

'When was this?'

'About a year ago.'

'And did she take part?' I asked.

'No, although she'd said at the time that she'd love to do it. But a couple of days later, she rang Sally and said that she'd mentioned it to Martin. Apparently he's very open-minded about that sort of thing.'

'Even so, it seems to have been an unwise thing to do.' This beggared belief. Would a woman who's been invited to take part in a skin flick really go home and tell her husband? 'Did she say what his reaction was?'

'She told Sally that Martin was all in favour of her getting involved, but that if she did, he'd divorce her on those grounds and she wouldn't get a penny out of him.'

And that, it would appear, was why Martin Bailey had denied knowing the Skinners. But it was probably because he'd been annoyed at losing the chance of getting rid of his wife at no cost to himself. It did, however, indicate that the differences between Martin and Eunice Bailey, and between Bailey and the Skinners, had existed for some time. At least a year. Maybe.

We accompanied Nigel and Sally Skinner, and Madison's team, to Notting Hill.

A search of the house produced nothing new – as far as my investigation was concerned – and even an examination of the Skinners' passports failed to confirm that they had been in Amsterdam when they said they were. But, as Dave pointed out, now that we're in the European Union, other members of that administrative nightmare don't put stamps in the passports of EU citizens.

Although it had no relevance to my investigation, Madison and his team did find an upstairs room that had been converted into a studio. It was here, no doubt, that Sally Skinner's erotic performances were filmed for her unseen audiences.

Thirteen

The Staatpolitie in Amsterdam had been very thorough in their enquiries into the Skinners' blue-movie import business, and within hours reported that they had tracked down the Dutch supplier of the DVDs. In addition, they were able to tell DS Madison that the pilot, Piet van de Groote, had not filed any sort of flight plan at Schiphol Airport. The assumption was that, on more than one occasion, he'd taken off from an unauthorized airstrip somewhere near Amsterdam, and had succeeded in avoiding detection. In a somewhat sinister footnote to their report, they added that they would interrogate van de Groote in depth about this matter when eventually he was returned to the jurisdiction of the Netherlands.

The Dutch police had also examined the register of the Metropole Hotel, and confirmed that Nigel Skinner and his wife had stayed there between the tenth and fifteenth of June.

And that, as far as I was concerned, meant that Nigel Skinner was now excluded from my enquiries into the disappearance of Eunice Bailey.

I wished DS Madison the best of luck, and turned once again to the problem of finding Martin Bailey's wife.

'How are you getting on with that enquiry, Mr Brock?' asked the commander, as he strolled into the incident room on Monday morning.

'Which enquiry is that, sir?' I found it necessary, from time to time, subtly to remind the commander that I had more than one case on my hands.

'The missing-person enquiry. Mrs Bailey, I believe she's called.'

'Oh, that one, sir. I think we've come to a dead end.' I instantly regretted saying that, and the commander seized on it immediately. Unfairly, I thought, given his abhorrence of slang.

'You mean you think she's been murdered?'

'No, sir. I mean that we seem to have exhausted all possible avenues of enquiry.' And I went on to explain about the Bermuda angle, and the story of the Skinners and their arrest, and their association with Martin and Eunice Bailey. I even mentioned the invitation that Sally Skinner had extended to Eunice Bailey to take part in one of her erotic films.

'Yes, well perhaps you've done all you can, Mr Brock,' said the commander hurriedly. Perhaps he thought that I'd be contaminated if I had any further contact with the Skinners' enterprises. Mind you, in the seventies one or two senior officers had come severely unstuck over pornography.

Nevertheless, the commander's reaction surprised me. Usually, he could never see that there were occasions when further enquiries would be fruitless.

'I think it's possible that Mrs Bailey left her husband, deliberately intending that she wouldn't be found, sir.'

'You're probably right,' conceded the commander. 'I shouldn't waste any more time on it, but if anything does come up, doubtless you'll pursue it.' And with that, the boss wandered off to scale his paper mountain.

'Bloody hell!' said Dave.

For the next week, Dave and I struggled with the same old report for the Crown Prosecution Service. It was developing into what we call a ping-pong report. As usual, the CPS had picked holes in it, had sent it back with observations from counsel, and made requests for further information. And that would mean re-writing the damned thing.

But exactly a week and a day after the commander's surprising direction that we should, more or less, discontinue our search for Eunice Bailey, I received a phone call from a sergeant at New Scotland Yard.

'Mr Brock?'

'Speaking.'

'It's PS Andy Gates, sir, at Missing Persons.'

'And what can I do for you, Skip?'

'I think it's more a case of what I can do for you, sir. I had a couple of callers here at the Yard this morning, a Mr Douglas Finch, and his wife Maxine. She said she was very worried about her friend . . . ' There was a pause while, I imagined, PS

Gates searched for the vital piece of paper bearing his notes. 'Ah, here we are. Her friend is a Mrs Eunice Bailey, sir, with an address in Coburn Street, Holland Park. I did a search of the PNC and saw that she was tagged up for you to be informed.'

'Is Mrs Finch still at the Yard?'

'No, sir. I told her that someone would be in touch very soon.'

'What's her address, Skip?'

'Sixteen Fenestra Avenue, Richmond, Surrey, sir.' And Gates added the telephone number.

'Thanks,' I said, 'we'll get on to it straight away.'

It was interesting, but probably irrelevant, that Gina Nash, Bailey's ex-wife, also lived in Richmond. But frustrated detectives tend to seize upon trivia like that when an enquiry begins to display all the signs of defeating them.

It was almost three in the afternoon by the time Dave and I arrived at the Finches' home at Fenestra Avenue.

We introduced ourselves to the man who answered the door, and he introduced himself as Douglas Finch, Maxine's husband.

'Come in, gentlemen,' he said. 'My wife's in the garden. Do come through.'

We followed Finch through the house and out to a small, sun-trapping patio. Mrs Finch, attired in a T-shirt and white shorts, was relaxing on a recliner, reading a fashion magazine. She was about thirty, I suppose, and had long jet-black hair and a pretty face.

'This is Detective Chief Inspector Brock from the police, darling,' said Finch.

Maxine Finch tossed the magazine aside, and leaned forward to shake hands with Dave and me. 'I must say that you've responded very quickly,' she said. 'We only called at Scotland Yard this morning.'

I was hoping that Dave wouldn't say something trite like, 'If you'd left your car on a double-yellow line, we'd've responded even quicker.'

'We do take these matters very seriously, Mrs Finch,' I said. That she and her husband had gone to the trouble of calling at the Yard in person indicated that they were taking it seriously too. Most people would have made a phone call.

'Would you like a drink?' asked Douglas Finch. 'Tea? I know you chaps don't drink on duty.'

Like hell we don't! 'That's very kind, thank you, Mr Finch.'

'My husband thinks I'm wasting your time, Chief Inspector,' said Maxine, while we were waiting for the tea to arrive, 'but a woman gets a feeling about these things, you know. So I persisted and eventually persuaded Douglas to come with me to Scotland Yard to speak to someone about it.'

'The time of the police is never wasted, Mrs Finch,' Dave said. 'There are many occasions when we wish that people would share their concerns with us much earlier than they do.'

Phew! That was quite a speech from Dave, but then he's a sucker for a good-looking woman. And Maxine Finch was a good-looking woman. It came as no surprise when we later learned that she was a part-time model.

She leaned across and took a packet of cigarettes from a small aluminium patio table, before casting us a guilty glance. 'I know I shouldn't,' she said, 'but I just can't seem to give up.'

'I know the feeling,' I said.

'Oh, d'you smoke too? Have one of these.'

But Dave was quick on the draw, and with all the dexterity of a magician, a packet of Silk Cut appeared in his hand, and was being proffered in Mrs Finch's direction. Just as he'd done when we interviewed Gina Nash.

'Thank you very much.' Maxine beamed at Dave, and he produced his lighter.

'Thank you, Sergeant,' I said pointedly.

'My apologies, sir,' said Dave, and offered me a cigarette.

Douglas Finch returned with a tray of tea, and we were able to get down to business.

'What exactly are your concerns about Eunice Bailey, Mrs Finch?' I asked.

'Douglas and I got back from the South of France last week,' Maxine began. 'We'd spent a month or so on the Riviera.'

'Very nice, too,' remarked Dave.

Maxine rewarded Dave's comment with a smile. 'Well, Chubby can afford it, can't you, darling?' she said to her husband. I don't know why she called him Chubby; he was as thin as a rake. A family joke, perhaps. She looked at me again. 'He's a stockbroker, you see. Licence to print money. Now, where was I? Ah yes. Anyway, I hadn't seen Eunice in all that time, obviously. Nor, in fact, for a week or so before we went away.'

'I take it she's a friend of yours,' I said.

'Absolutely. We've known each other for simply yonks. So last week, I decided to pay her a visit, at her place in Holland Park.'

'And she wasn't there,' I said.

Maxine raised her eyebrows in surprise. 'Oh, you know, do you?'

'We've been looking for her for seven weeks.'

'D'you know where she is?'

'No, Mrs Finch. All I can tell you is that her husband told us that Mrs Bailey had left him – for good – and gone to America. But I'm afraid the trail's gone cold.'

'I don't like Martin Bailey,' said Maxine, 'and I don't know why on earth Eunice married him. He's conceited and rude. An arrogant bastard, in fact. I can't stand the bloody man.'

'Apart from which, he's quite a nice bloke,' put in Douglas Finch.

'This is serious, Chubby,' said Maxine, with a frown. 'I think something's happened to her,' she continued, turning back to me.

'What makes you think that, Mrs Finch?'

'As I was saying, I called at Coburn Street unannounced, and Martin answered the door. But not before he'd gone through all that nonsense with his CCTV camera, of course. He's bloody paranoid about security. However, he invited me in, at the same time making it quite apparent that my arrival wasn't welcome. He didn't ask me if I wanted a drink, and it was as much as he could do to offer me a seat. I started asking him about Eunice and whether she was out shopping, or what, when some child-like blonde trollop came into the room. She was not unlike a younger version of Eunice, actually. But it was obvious that she was living there, because she flounced across the room and flopped in an armchair as though she owned the place.'

'Did Martin Bailey say anything to her?'

'He told her to go back upstairs as he was having a private conversation. He was quite sharp about it.'

'And did she go?'

'Yes, but she didn't hurry. She got up, pouted at Martin,

and strolled out of the room, waggling her arse,' said Maxine. 'If she ever tried for a job on the catwalk, she'd fall flat on her face.' She paused and giggled. 'Mind you, falling flat on her face would be difficult for her with the boobs she's got. Might succeed in Shepherd Market, though. In fact, that might be where he found her.'

I smiled at that; Shepherd Market in Soho was a traditional hunting ground of prostitutes. 'Did he introduce her to you?'

'Not in as many words. But after she'd left the room, I asked who she was, and Martin said that she was his secretary. Secretary, be damned! I'll tell you this much, Chief Inspector, I reckon her IQ is less than her bust measurement. All tits and no brains, that one.'

'If she's who I think she is,' I said, 'she's called Jane Grant, and she's admitted to being Martin Bailey's girlfriend.'

'That was blatantly obvious,' said Maxine. 'She was certainly behaving as though she had the run of the house. But that just indicates that she doesn't know Martin as well as she thinks she does. One false move and she'll get the bum's rush. Unless Martin's changed radically. But I doubt that very much.'

'What did Bailey say when you asked after Eunice?'

'He said what you told me just now, that his wife had left him and gone to America, and he didn't know where she was. What's more, the callous bastard said he didn't care. But I didn't believe him. I might've believed him if he'd said he'd thrown her out and replaced her with little Miss Fanny.'

'Did you ever hear Eunice speak of a man called Nigel Skinner?' asked Dave. Despite having dismissed him from our enquiry, it seemed that Dave still harboured suspicions about him.

Maxine weighed the question carefully before answering. 'Yes, she did mention someone of that name, but it was a while ago. Perhaps a year. I think she had an affair with him.'

'Did that surprise you, Mrs Finch?' I asked.

'Good heavens, no. Eunice was always having a fling with some man or other, but it never lasted long. She was a great girl for one-night stands, but that's the way she was made. She fell in love – and into bed – over and over again.'

'Was Martin aware of these affairs?'

Maxine shrugged. 'He might have been. I don't know. But

he wasn't averse to a bit on the side himself. He even tried it on with me once, but I told him in fairly earthy terms what he could do. Actually, I told him to go and—'

'I think the chief inspector gets the picture, Max darling,' said Douglas Finch, hurriedly interrupting. Facing me, he added, 'Models are all the same, Mr Brock. They swear like troopers.'

'Well, let's just say I told him to fuck off,' said Maxine, probably out of devilment to confirm what her husband had just said about her language. 'I think Martin took a dislike to me from then on.'

This was all a fascinating insight into the relationship between the Baileys, but it did nothing to further our hopes of finding Eunice Bailey. But then Maxine Finch came up with something of real importance.

'What I forgot to mention just now was Eunice's jewellery. It was why Chubby and I went to Scotland Yard.'

'What about it?' I asked, taking a sudden interest.

'Eunice had this magnificent brooch that must have cost a fortune. It was in the shape of a green iris, made up of an emerald on a diamond-studded gold mount. She told me that it had been a birthday present from Martin. Apparently he'd told her that the green was to match her eyes, and the gold to match her hair. But I doubted that a mean sod like Martin would've forked out six or seven thousand pounds, because that's the least it would have cost. I think it was more likely to have been a gift from a rich admirer whose bed she'd shared for a week or so. Anyway when that little whore – Jane Grant, did you say she was called? – came into the room, she was wearing it. Now, you men may not know this, but any woman who decides to leave her husband will take her jewellery. It's the most important thing she owns. She might forget her knickers, but never her jewellery.'

I told Maxine Finch about the abandoned wedding ring that had started this enquiry, but she was dismissive.

'Not the same as jewellery. Anyway, a wedding ring didn't mean much to a girl like Eunice. If you ask me, she wanted it enlarged so that she could have it off whenever it suited her not to have it on.'

'I mentioned Nigel Skinner just now, Mrs Finch. Would it surprise you to know that Skinner's wife, Sally, invited Eunice to take part in a pornographic DVD her husband Nigel was making?'

Maxine didn't react to that at all, and it was almost as if she'd expected it. 'It was heterosexual, I hope, and not some lesbian drama.'

'As far as I know it was a man and woman thing, if the others that were found are anything to go by.'

'Lucky girl,' commented Maxine, and shot a teasing air kiss at her husband.

'But she declined to take part.'

'Doesn't sound like Eunice,' said Maxine. 'I've never known her turn down a good screw.'

'Did Eunice ever mention the names of other men with whom she had affairs?'

'I'm sure she did, but there were so many that I can't remember any of them. She was more interested in describing their sexual prowess, or lack of it. She was quite miserable if a week went by when she hadn't been laid by some passing Lothario. D'you think she's gone off with one of them?'

'I don't know, Mrs Finch. All we have discovered so far is that she spent just over three weeks in Bermuda from late May to mid-June. After that, we've found no trace of her.'

Maxine Finch swung her legs off the recliner, turning towards me, her face registering shock. 'Oh God, you don't think she's been murdered, do you? I tried telling her that she was taking too many risks. I told her, over and over again, that if she didn't get her throat cut one day, she'd probably die of Aids, the silly little bitch.'

'We have to consider the possibility that she's dead,' said Dave gravely. 'But until we have proof of her death, we'll keep on looking. It's possible, I suppose, that she actually has finished up in the United States.'

'Is there no way of finding out? Surely their immigration people would have a record, wouldn't they?'

'Checking with the United States Citizenship and Immigration Services is a long and tortuous business, Mrs Finch,' I said, 'and we have it in hand.' We hadn't, of course, but it was something I supposed we'd have to try. I'd made enquiries of the US authorities in the past, and, helpful though they were, the sheer magnitude of their inbound traffic made it difficult if not impossible to trace a visitor quickly. Their concentration, rightly, was on terrorism, not absconding wives with a penchant for casual sex.

'What are you going to do now, Chief Inspector?'

'Continue our enquiries, Mrs Finch,' I replied enigmatically. And in view of Maxine Finch's information about Eunice Bailey's jewellery, I didn't see that we had much option.

Having learned a little more about Eunice Bailey, and her predilection for brief affairs, there was an increasing likelihood that she'd been murdered. But where? Here? Or in Bermuda? Or even in the United States.

'Have you thought, guv,' said Dave, 'that although we've got confirmation that Skinner was in Amsterdam from the tenth to the fifteenth of June, we don't know where he was after that?'

'What's worrying you, Dave?'

'Just because Eunice Bailey booked out of the bungalow at Elbow Beach on the sixteenth, doesn't mean that she didn't book in somewhere else that we, or Mr Mercer, haven't discovered. And it's always a possibility that Nigel Skinner flew out there on, say, the seventeenth and—'

'Whoa! Hold your horses, Dave. If that's the case, you're talking about two different Nigel Skinners. The guy who was in the bungalow was the same guy who was seen by Darrell Nightingale in the bar on Middle Road. It's too much of a coincidence that two different men, both called Nigel Skinner, were swanning about in Bermuda that close together.'

'I suppose so,' said Dave grudgingly. It was obvious that he was unhappy about Skinner, and was worrying at him like a dog at a bone. But this particular bone had no meat left on it. The real reason, I suspected, was that Dave had an intense dislike of people who exploited women by making pornographic films featuring them.

'I'm still puzzled why Maxine Finch attached so much importance to this business of Eunice Bailey's jewellery,' I said.

'I think she had a point there, guv. If Madeleine ever decided to ditch me, I'm sure that her sparklers would be the first things she packed,' said Dave at his phlegmatic best. 'But more to the point, what are we going to do about it?'

'I think it's time we started rattling a few bars, Dave.'

'Like whose?'

'Well, there's Jane Grant, and there's Martin Bailey himself. That bastard is much too confident for my liking.'

'About bloody time,' muttered Dave. He had taken a great dislike to Martin Bailey, and I could see he was just aching to have a go at him. And so was I. 'Where are you going to interview Jane Grant? At her shop, or at the nick?'

'Neither for the moment, Dave. I think a few more background enquiries are called for. And we'll start with John, our failed private eye.'

Dave rubbed his hands together. 'Now that, I am looking forward to.'

Fourteen

E leven o'clock on Wednesday morning, and time to start putting the pressure on Martin Bailey, but not directly and not immediately. And as I'd decided to start with John, the bent ex-detective sergeant, that's where we went.

Cornelius Street, Putney, is a street of mean terraced dwellings, at least a hundred and fifty years old. I doubted whether anyone now living could tell us why it was called Cornelius Street, but it was probably named after some long-dead town councillor who wanted his name committed to perpetuity when the street was constructed. I don't know why such petty officials bother; most are forgotten the moment they leave office. If they were ever known in the first place.

Number thirty-four was shabbier than most of its neighbours, and that's saying something. Loud music emanated from the house opposite, its rhythmic, heavy beat transcending any melody it might have had. The street was lined with wheeled refuse bins. Today, I supposed, was collection day, but their presence did nothing for the ambience of the area.

The unshaven, ferret-like face of John peered round the edge of the door. 'Oh, it's you, Mr Brock.' He was clearly taken aback by our unheralded arrival.

'Yes, it's me, John,' I said, pushing the door open, 'and I want a word with you.'

'What about?' John, a desperate expression on his face, retreated into the hall. He did not present a pretty sight, dressed as he was in a rugby shirt and the bottom half of a tracksuit.

'Mr and Mrs Bailey, and more particularly Mrs Bailey. They're who we want to talk about.'

'I've told you all I know,' whined John, leading the way into his sitting room. You'll note that I am careful not to describe it as a living room; it defied belief that anyone could actually *live* in such a tip.

'So, this is the centre of your private-investigation business, is it?' I asked, gazing round at the detritus. The furniture, such as it was, was worn, undoubtedly cheap, but definitely not cheerful. Dirty curtains hung forlornly at the equally dirty windows, and there were newspapers spread about on the unswept carpet. Dust lay uniformly on the unpolished floorboards surrounding it. A Formica-topped table bore an overflowing ashtray, and numerous dirty mugs and glasses, all of which vied for space with sheaves of paper upon which were scribbled notes. I presumed they constituted the latest of John's ongoing enquiries. 'Why did you give up your prestigious Tottenham Court Road suite of offices, John?' Pure sarcasm, of course.

'I couldn't afford to keep it on, Mr Brock,' said John, and rapidly changed the subject. 'Would you like a cup of tea? It'll have to be a cup; I haven't got any clean mugs.'

Peasant! I glanced again at the dirty crockery. 'No, thanks, John.'

'Have a seat.'

'No, thanks, John,' I said again. A brief examination of the threadbare and stained armchairs convinced me that they should have displayed a health and safety warning. Dave and I remained standing.

'Here, that's private information.' John became quite animated when he saw that Dave had picked up his notes, and was reading them avidly.

'If we nick you, old son, all this lot'll come with us as prisoner's property,' said Dave, continuing to read. 'And right now, I think my guv'nor has a mind to remove you to Wandsworth nick.'

John did not like the sound of that. 'I've done nothing wrong, Dave, honest,' he pleaded.

'"Honest" is not a word I'd've used in connection with you or your activities, John,' replied Dave. He turned to me. 'Think I ought to caution him, guv?'

'Not yet, Dave. We'll see how forthcoming he is first.' This little conversation was conducted as though John wasn't there.

'I've told you everything I know about Mr Bailey,' John repeated earnestly.

'I don't think you've even started, John. Dave, give John a résumé of what he told us last time.'

Dave fished out his pocketbook, thumbed through a few

pages, and began. 'To summarise, you said you went to Bermuda on the eleventh of June in order to make divorce enquiries on behalf of Martin Bailey.' He looked up, querying.

'That's right.' John licked his lips. 'It's true.'

'And you went on to say that you made a few of those enquiries in and around Hamilton, but couldn't find out anything. You also claimed that there didn't seem much point in trying anywhere else because no one had heard of Eunice Bailey anyway.'

'Yeah, well I never had any contacts over there. Not like in the Smoke. No snouts, see. It was like a foreign country.'

'It is a foreign country,' said Dave. 'Remind me why your enquiries didn't take you further afield.' He knew perfectly well what excuse John had made previously, but was testing his recall of what we both now firmly believed was fiction.

'Well, I reckoned that Hamilton would be where she was if she was anywhere.'

'So you did. And you further said that you reported back to Bailey once a week, on a Friday, but not always in person.'

'Yeah.' John was becoming increasingly nervous as Dave accurately recounted details of our previous conversation.

'You also claimed that you returned from Bermuda two days later. On the thirteenth of June is what you said.'

'Yeah.'

'Which airline did you travel on?'

'Er, let me see . . . ' John made a pretence of giving careful consideration to the question. 'Yeah, it was British Airways.'

'Supposing I was to tell you that we'd checked with BA and they have no record of you travelling to and from Bermuda on the dates you gave us.' Dave had made no such checks, but John wouldn't know that he hadn't.

'I used a duff name. You can't be too careful in this game.'

'How very true, John.' Dave nodded sagely. 'What d'you think, guv?' he asked, turning to me. 'Conspiring to pervert the course of justice? Worth at least four penn'orth at the going rate.'

'Here, what are you on about?' John's white face, coupled with the sudden onset of an ague, indicated that he was severely distressed at this turn of events.

'You didn't go to Bermuda at all, John,' I said, guessing wildly. But it was a guess based on years of experience in dealing with villains, both in the Job and out of it. 'What you told us previously, and what you've just unwisely confirmed, is a complete pack of lies. Now, before I start to get nasty about all this, I think you'd better tell us the true story.'

John sagged visibly, like someone who had just had all the air let out of him. 'If I tell you the truth, will that let me off the hook?'

'Not necessarily. You know better than to try and make deals with me, John.'

John sighed. 'Mr Bailey hired me—'

'How did he find you?' asked Dave. 'Bailey told us he'd looked you up in *Yellow Pages*, but you're not in *Yellow Pages*.'

'I don't know. I suppose he must have spoken to someone who'd hired me before.'

That was probably true, although it must've been a very short list because I couldn't see anyone in his right mind taking on this excuse for a private investigator.

'Go on,' I said.

'It was true about him hiring me on the eighteenth of May, but he said I wasn't to do anything. He said it'd look good if he hired a PI to look into his wife's disappearance. But he said he didn't want her to be found.'

'Don't stop there, John,' I said.

'He paid me a grand and told me to forget about making enquiries, but that if anyone came asking, I was to tell them I was actively seeking evidence for his divorce.'

'And you didn't go to Bermuda at all, did you?'

'No, but he said that I was to say that I'd been over there if anyone asked.'

'Like me?' I suggested.

'I suppose so.' John spoke reluctantly, but it was fairly obvious that it was the police Bailey had had in mind.

'Did Bailey tell you why he thought his wife had gone to Bermuda?'

'Yeah. He said that he'd got a place over there, and that's where she'd likely have gone because she knew it, and had been there before. But he said he wasn't interested in getting her back, and that he'd already got enough evidence for a divorce. He said something about her being a porn actress, and taking part in blue movies.'

'Did he tell you where in Bermuda this place of his was?'

'No. I asked, but he said I didn't need to know, because I wasn't going there anyway. It wasn't important, he said.'

'What exactly did he say about Eunice Bailey being a porn actress?' Dave asked.

'Nothing, really. He just said that he knew she was at it, and that was all the evidence he needed, so I never had to bother.'

'Are you still working for Martin Bailey, John?'

'I suppose so.'

'What about the weekly reports that you make on Fridays?'

'I never made any,' said John miserably.

'So the up and down of it is that you got a grand for doing bugger-all,' I said.

'Yeah. Don't get many jobs coming up like that.' John forced a grin.

'D'you still hear from Bailey?' I asked.

'Haven't done for a few weeks. I suppose it's all over. Pity, that.'

'So what were you doing coming out of Bailey's drum when we saw you on the first of July?' asked Dave.

There was a distinct pause, and then, 'I was going to try and tap him up for a few more quid.'

'What did he say?'

'He wasn't there.'

'More likely he saw you on his CCTV camera and decided not to answer the door,' said Dave, and laughed. We knew that Bailey had been at home.

John looked at me imploringly. 'I really can't help you any more, Mr Brock. You can't charge me with anything on the basis of that, can you?'

'Perhaps not,' I said thoughtfully, 'although I've nicked people for less in the past. But there is one other thing you can do for me . . . '

'Anything, Mr Brock. Just say the word.' Suddenly John was desperate to help.

'I want you to let Martin Bailey know that we forced you into telling us the truth about your fictional trip to Bermuda. But don't tell him that I asked you to tell him. Got that, have you?'

John's brow furrowed for a few moments while he sorted out that instruction. 'Sure. No problem.'

*   *   *

'D'you reckon he will tell Bailey, guv?' asked Dave, as we drove back to Curtis Green.

'He's too scared not to,' I said, 'because he knows we'll come looking for him if he doesn't.'

'But we've no grounds for nicking him, have we?'

'Of course not, Dave, but John was never a good enough detective to know that. He's not a good liar, either. If my memory serves me correctly, if he nicked someone and hadn't got any evidence, he'd make it up. It was a good day's work when the Job got rid of him.'

'What d'you think Bailey will do when he hears that John told us the tale, guv?'

'That's what I'm waiting to find out. Either he'll blow his top and complain, or he'll keep shtum. Whichever way it is, I'll be interested in his reaction.'

'And if he doesn't show out, do we go and see him?'

'Not until we've had another word with Jane Grant. I'm anxious to know how she came into possession of Eunice Bailey's brooch. It's time we put the pressure on Martin Bailey because he knows more than he's telling. And I can't think of a better way than putting the frighteners on his current bit of arm candy.'

I decided not to waste time. With any luck Martin Bailey would have received two very distressing pieces of news before the end of the day.

We crossed Putney Bridge, and stopped for a quick spaghetti bolognese at an Italian restaurant in the King's Road, Chelsea. By half-past two we were entering the boutique where Jane Grant worked.

'Can I help you, sir?' It was Jane herself who glided forward intent on serving me, but then she recognized Dave and me. 'Oh, it's you.' The carapace of the sophisticated Chelsea saleslady vanished in an instant. 'What d'you want? It's not convenient right now,' she whispered. Oh joy! We'd got her rattled before we'd spoken a word.

'I'm afraid you'll have to make it convenient, Miss Grant,' I said. 'Is there somewhere we can talk privately? If not, we'll have to go to Chelsea police station.'

That throwaway line further discomfited Martin Bailey's bedmate. 'There's an office at the back,' she said hurriedly.

She led us behind the counter and through a door that opened on to a small room. There was hardly enough space for the three of us, but it would do.

'We are looking into the theft of a piece of jewellery, Miss Grant,' I began.

'But I told you last time you were here that we only buy from reputable suppliers. There's certainly nothing here that's been stolen.'

'I think this particular piece is more expensive than the sort of stuff you sell, Miss Grant. Apart from which, I'm talking about a brooch that's in your personal possession, not something that's in your shop.'

'I don't know what you're talking about.' Jane started fiddling with a gold chain that hung around her neck. I wondered if that also belonged to Eunice.

'Sergeant, describe the piece of jewellery we wish to trace.'

Dave opened his pocketbook and repeated Maxine Finch's description of the emerald-and-diamond iris brooch that she had seen Jane Grant wearing at Bailey's house in Coburn Street.

Jane Grant went white, and for a moment I thought she was going to faint.

'I see you recognize the piece,' I said.

'It was a present,' mumbled Jane.

'Oh? Who from?'

'Martin. Martin Bailey.'

'Do you know where he got it?'

'Of course not. You don't ask people where they bought a gift. All he said was that he'd had it made especially. But why are you asking about it?'

'Because we have reason to believe it was not Martin Bailey's to give, Miss Grant.'

'But that's ridiculous.'

'Is it? Or did you perhaps appropriate it when you found it at Coburn Street among Mrs Bailey's jewellery.' I didn't for one moment imagine that this girl would have the effrontery to wear the brooch without Bailey's permission.

'Certainly not. I told you, it was a gift from Martin that he'd had made for me,' said Jane, recovering some of her composure.

'Well, I'm sorry to have to tell you that we've received information that the brooch in question belongs to Eunice Bailey.

I may, therefore, have to consider charging you with handling stolen property.'

Jane Grant paled dramatically, and reached out to a filing cabinet for support. 'I didn't know anything about it being stolen. You ask Martin. He'll tell you it was a gift. Martin's got lots of money. He doesn't have to steal things.'

I appeared to give the matter some thought. 'All right,' I said eventually. 'We'll leave it for the time being, and I'll speak to Mr Bailey about it, probably tomorrow some time. Will he be at home, d'you know?'

'Yes, I'm sure he will. He works at home a lot these days, but I'm sure he'll be very angry about your allegations. It's all nonsense.' Jane seemed to have recovered some of her confidence now that she realized she wasn't about to be arrested.

'Where is the brooch now, Miss Grant?' asked Dave.

'At home. It's much too valuable to wear to work. It cost—' Jane broke off, probably realizing that she was about to say too much.

'How much did it cost?' asked Dave.

'I, er, I don't know. You're confusing me. I was going to say it must have cost a lot of money. I just assumed that anything that Martin gave me would be expensive.'

'Thank you for your assistance, Miss Grant,' I said. 'We will, of course, have to speak to you again.'

And with that we left an extremely distressed young woman who was very likely wondering whether Martin Bailey was all that she had believed him to be.

'I reckon that'll put the cat among the pigeons, guv,' said Dave, as we strolled along the King's Road. Given the widespread lawlessness now existing in the capital, we'd considered it advisable to leave our car at the police station in Lucan Place for safekeeping. In the old days, a villain would never think of stealing a police car, but nowadays it was regarded as an achievement attracting street cred. Apart from anything else, this time there hadn't been a parking space right outside the boutique.

'One thing's sure, Dave, Bailey will either go up like a can of petrol the minute Jane Grant tells him the tale and ring the Commissioner, or he'll wait and see what we have to say when we visit him tomorrow. I just hope that John's been on the phone to him already. Nothing like a double whammy to get things going.'

'D'you reckon Bailey knows where Eunice is, guv?'

'I'm bloody sure of it, Dave. I'm just hoping that the tales John and Jane tell him of the nasty police leaning on them will cause him to become more cooperative.'

'If we pull that off, it'll be what I believe the Americans call a slam dunk, guv.'

'What in hell does that mean, Dave?'

'It's a dramatic and unqualified success . . . sir. Apparently it's something to do with basketball.'

'Nice. I must remember to use it when next I talk to the commander.'

Fifteen

I decided that eleven o'clock on the Thursday morning would be as good a time as any to call at Martin Bailey's house in Coburn Street. I rang the doorbell and waited for the CCTV camera to swivel in our direction. It didn't move, and there was no answer.

'The bugger's not here, guv,' said Dave.

I rang the bell again, a long and sustained peal this time. But still nothing.

'We could try his office.' Dave thumbed open his pocket-book. 'It's in Soho.' He glanced at me with a grin on his face. 'Where else?'

I hoped the address was correct. It was the one that Fat Danny had obtained, and published in his newspaper article. And it was certainly the one that Kate Ebdon had obtained from Companies House. But directors have been known to overlook advising the registrar of any changes. Sometimes by design.

However, on this occasion the address proved to be correct. The offices of Bailey's business were on the ground floor of a building in one of the streets off Golden Square. It didn't look impressive enough to house a multimillion-pound empire, but perhaps that's why it was successful . . . or maybe it wasn't successful. There were no security guards, no atrium, and no little pools with fountains that so often feature in the reception areas of prestigious companies these days. And I wouldn't mind betting that Bailey's Rolls-Royce didn't have a person-alized number plate. That, in his view, would be pointless profligacy.

A listless girl was seated behind a computer screen, but she didn't give the appearance of one engaged in high-powered commercial activity. Certainly perusing a copy of the *Sun* news-paper didn't come into that category.

'Help you?' The girl looked up, her expression implying that to assist us was the last thing she had in mind.

'Mr Bailey, please.'

'Not here.' The girl fingered the stud in her nose.

'Any idea where he is?'

'No.'

'*Ab asino lanam,*' murmured Dave, quoting from his abundant stock of Latin tags.

'What's that mean?' I asked.

'Wool from an ass, sir. Or, in the vernacular, "you can't get blood from a stone".'

'Thank you for that, Dave.' I turned to the unhelpful one. 'We're police officers,' I informed her, somewhat belatedly, 'and we need to speak to Mr Bailey.'

'Sorry, love, don't know where he is.' The receptionist opened a drawer and took out a nail file.

'When did he last come into the office?'

'Monday.'

'Does he often come in?'

'Not lately.'

'What does that mean?'

'Well, sometimes he's here, and sometimes he's not.'

That was very useful. 'Is there anyone else here, or someone who might be able to assist me?'

'No, just me,' said the girl, answering both questions in one brief sentence.

'What about Mr Bailey's chauffeur?' asked Dave, just as I was about to ask the same question. I recalled that Gladys Damjuma, the diplomat's wife who lived next door to the Baileys, had mentioned that the entrepreneur's Rolls-Royce had been driven by a chauffeur when it called for him.

'What about him?'

I was expecting Dave to come up with yet another Latin tag, this time about pulling teeth. 'Where does he live?'

'I don't know,' the girl said, 'but I can give you his phone number.' After a certain amount of rummaging in one of the drawers in her desk, she gave us what proved to be a mobile number. But that was better than nothing. Unfortunately, it was unlikely to provide us with his address.

'What's his name?' I asked.

'Tommy Hooper,' said the girl.

'If Mr Bailey does come in, or telephones, will you tell him that Detective Chief Inspector Brock is anxious to have a word with him?' I said, playing my last card.

'Sure. Got a phone number?'

Although Bailey knew my number, I gave the girl one of my cards without much hope of my message ever reaching him.

Before we moved off, Dave rang Colin Wilberforce to ask for a subscriber check on Tommy Hooper's mobile phone.

'Where to now, guv?' he asked, once that was dealt with.

'King's Road, Dave. We'll see if Jane Grant knows where Bailey is.'

We decided against parking the car at Chelsea nick, mainly because Dave had found a space for it on double-yellow lines right outside the boutique where Bailey's girlfriend worked. It's no mean feat to find a parking space in the King's Road – even on double-yellow lines – but if anyone could do it, Dave was the man. An enthusiastic policeman – a rare sight – made a beeline for the car just as Dave put the police logbook in the windscreen. The policeman veered off, disappointed.

'Good morning.' I greeted the saleswoman I'd spoken to on our first visit. 'Is Miss Grant here?'

'I'm afraid not,' said the assistant. 'She called in sick this morning. Some virus, she said.'

'What time was that?'

The assistant glanced at her wristwatch. 'About a quarter past nine, I suppose. Just after we opened.'

'We'll have another go at John,' I said, when we'd returned to the car. 'I want to know if and when he spoke to Bailey.'

Traffic was terrible, despite attempts by the Greater London Authority to persuade its suffering taxpayers to use public transport. Unfortunately, the GLA had overlooked the need to establish a decent public-transport system first. It took nearly forty-five minutes to get from the King's Road, Chelsea, to Cornelius Street, Putney, a distance of three miles.

We'd wasted enough time already, and I didn't intend to waste any more. The moment John answered the door, I pushed it open, almost sending him flying backwards into the hall.

'Did you speak to Bailey yesterday, John?' I asked.

'Yes, of course I did, Mr Brock.'

'On the phone, or in person?'

'On the phone.'

I guessed John would've phoned Bailey, rather than risk any physical violence that might have resulted from a personal confrontation. That would not have appealed to this particular unsavoury ex-copper.

'What time was this, that you phoned him, John?' asked Dave.

'Straight after you left. What was that, about half-past twelve?'

'And what did he say, John?' I asked.

'He sounded a bit upset, Mr Brock.'

'Only a *bit* upset?' I doubted that Bailey would have responded to John's news of police harassment by being 'a bit upset'. Particularly if Jane Grant had telephoned him immediately after our visit to the King's Road boutique, and tearfully poured out her account of our accusations of theft and handling of Eunice's brooch. In fact, I imagined that there had been a blazing row with Bailey lambasting the poor girl for speaking to us at all without a lawyer being present.

'Well, actually, he was bloody annoyed. He said he was going to take it up with his solicitor and complain to the Yard.' John looked gloomy. 'And he said I might find myself in court as well for breach of confidence.'

'What appalling bad luck, John,' said Dave.

Colin Wilberforce rang as we returned to the car.

'That mobile number for the chauffeur we got from the bird in Bailey's office, guv,' Dave said, when he'd finished the call, 'goes out to Bailey's company at the Soho office. So I suppose the company picks up the tab.'

'Damn!' I said. 'Well, next up is to try the neighbours.'

We drove to Coburn Street, and called at the Bailey house again. But there was still no reply.

We went next door.

Gladys Damjuma seemed pleased to see us. Perhaps she didn't have many visitors. I can only imagine that her social life was restricted to diplomatic functions, and there wouldn't be a lot of fun in those.

'We're trying to locate Mr Bailey, Mrs Damjuma,' I said, once we'd been escorted to the sitting room, and tea had been ordered. 'We were supposed to meet him here this morning, but there's no answer, and he's not at his office. We're a bit worried about him.'

'He's gone away, Mr Brock,' said Gladys.

'Gone away? Have you any idea where?' I made a pretence of being surprised, even though I had half suspected that was what had happened.

'Oh yes. Last night I happened to be looking out of my window,' said Gladys, affording us an embarrassed smile, 'and I saw Martin's chauffeur putting suitcases in the boot of the Rolls-Royce. Then a little bit later, Martin came out with that nice young secretary of his, and they drove off.' She paused, and smiled again. 'I suppose she *is* his secretary,' she added, pensively. 'I've never actually spoken to her, but she seems very nice.'

'What time would this have been, Mrs Damjuma?' asked Dave.

Gladys stared out of the window for a second or so. 'It must have been about eight o'clock, I suppose. I was waiting for my husband Bim to get home from the office. It's no fun being a diplomat, you know, and he has to work late sometimes. Yes, it was about eight o'clock, because I remember that Bim got in at about twenty past. I mentioned to him that Martin had gone on holiday.'

'D'you know that for a fact, Mrs Damjuma?' I asked. 'That he was going on holiday, I mean.'

'Well, no, not exactly. I just presumed that's where he was going. He works very hard, you know, and I'm sure he deserves a holiday. I think he was very upset when his wife left him. Of course, I suppose it could've been a business trip of some sort. I remember Martin telling Bim, when we last had dinner with him and Eunice, that he was interested in investing in our country. He said that there were a lot of business opportunities in Africa. He and Bim talked about it for quite a long time. Business was all Martin ever talked about.'

The woman with the flowered apron came in with the tea, and Gladys spent a few minutes serving it.

'I suppose you haven't seen Mrs Bailey since we last spoke, have you, Mrs Damjuma?' Dave asked.

'No, I haven't,' said Gladys. 'I don't know where she's gone. Such a shame. She was very lonely, you know, what with Martin always working.' She sighed and held out a plate of oatcakes.

We drank our tea, and talked of this and that, but learned no more about the Baileys than we knew already. Apart from the fact that Bailey had done a runner. And that interested me greatly.

As we were leaving, I gave Gladys one of my cards. 'If you should happen to see Mr Bailey return, perhaps you'd telephone me, Mrs Damjuma. It is rather urgent that we get in touch with him.'

'Yes, certainly.' Gladys paused at the front door. 'I do hope nothing bad has happened to Eunice, Mr Brock. She was a very good friend. I really don't know why she left.'

We returned to Curtis Green to consider what little we'd learned in what had been a fruitless day.

'There's only one thing for it, Dave,' I said. 'I'm going to have to ring the chauffeur's mobile.'

To my amazement I got an instant reply.

'Hello?' responded a rough voice.

'Mr Hooper?'

'Yeah. Who's that?'

'The police, Mr Hooper.'

'Oh yeah? What d'you want, then?'

'I had an appointment to see Mr Bailey this morning, Mr Hooper, but he's not at home and he's not at his office.'

'Wouldn't be, would he?'

'Why's that?'

'Gone off on his holidays, ain't he?'

'Oh, I didn't realize that. D'you happen to know where?'

'Nah! The guv'nor always plays his cards close to his chest. I'll tell you this much, I wouldn't never play him at poker.'

'But I presume you took him to wherever he was going, Mr Hooper.'

'Yeah, course I did. I drove him down Gatwick Airport about nine o'clock last night. Him and Jane, that fancy bit of skirt he's shacked up with.'

'And you don't know where he went from there?'

'Not a clue, guv'nor. I just dropped him at one of the hotels.

The Sofitel, it's called. Five-star, very swish. Well, it would be, knowing the guv'nor. He don't slum it, I can tell you.'

'Did he arrange for you to meet him when he returned from wherever he was going?'

'Nah,' said Hooper. 'He said as how when he was due back, he'd give me a bell in sufficient time for me to pick him up.'

'Thanks for your help, Mr Hooper. If you should see him before I do, perhaps you'd tell him that Detective Chief Inspector Brock would like a word. He knows how to contact me.'

'No problem, guv'nor.'

'One other thing, Mr Hooper. When did you last see Mrs Bailey?'

'What, Eunice?'

'Yes.'

There was a pause. 'Must've been nigh on three months ago. P'raps a bit less.'

'I might need to see you again, Mr Hooper. Perhaps you'd let me have your address.'

But Hooper had already terminated the call. And I had the distinct feeling that he wouldn't answer any calls again until the name Bailey popped up on the little screen of his mobile phone.

I relayed the details of the conversation to Dave, and within seconds he was telephoning his mate Bob Winston at Heathrow Airport.

Ten minutes later, Winston returned the call.

'Guess what,' said Dave, after a brief conversation.

'Bermuda?'

'Got it in one, guv. If only we'd known earlier, because he flew out on BA 2233 at five past three this afternoon.'

'So, he must've been staying overnight at the Sofitel. He definitely has done a runner, Dave. I reckon he panicked as soon as Jane Grant told him about us, and then, on top of that, John rang him. So he upped sticks and took off. Literally. Although I don't know why.'

'Guilty knowledge,' said Dave, and peeled a banana.

'I think there's some sort of scam going on here, Dave. Bailey hired John, but told him not to do anything about finding Eunice. Suppose that he took out a hefty insurance policy on Eunice's life. She disappears and fakes her own death. Then Bailey claims the money, and he and Eunice split the proceeds.'

'I'm beginning to think that anything could've happened, guv,' said Dave. 'But I certainly don't believe all this malarkey about her not putting up with him any more, and walking out. It doesn't ring kosher.'

I rang through to Colin Wilberforce in the incident room. 'What time is it in Bermuda, Colin?' I should've known, having been there, but I'm not much good at remembering things like that.

'Four hours behind us, sir,' said Colin promptly. 'That means it's half-past one in the afternoon there.'

'Good. Colin, see if you can get Detective Superintendent Mercer on the phone.'

It took Colin about ten minutes to get through, and for the Bermuda Police to locate Don Mercer.

'Harry! What can I do for you? You found this woman yet?'

I gave Mercer a summary of what had occurred since our return from Bermuda, and finished by telling him that Martin Bailey and Jane Grant were on an aircraft that should arrive at Bermuda International at about seventeen-twenty local time.

'What d'you want me to do, Harry?' asked Mercer.

'I assume he's going to Flatt's Village, Don, but I'll be interested to know if he goes on from there, maybe to the States.'

'That's no problem. I can put a tail on him, but what d'you think he's up to?'

'Right now, Don, I don't have a clue. It may be some sort of company fraud, or it may be an insurance scam involving his wife. I'm beginning to think that this story about her leaving him is a load of old moody.' I told him about John, his unsavoury background, and what he'd told us of his arrangement with Martin Bailey to do nothing, and then expanded my theory. 'I'm beginning to think there's a fiddle going on, Don, and I'm about to enquire if he insured Eunice Bailey for a substantial sum. If he has, and he's decided to hide her and then claim on the policy, he might have a hidden agenda to share the payout with her. We're about to take a hard look at his business affairs, and it could well be that he's not as flush as he would like everyone to believe. Certainly his office doesn't look like the hub of a multimillion-pound empire.'

'I'll do what I can, Harry, but I don't suppose you want him pulled in, or alerted to police interest.'

'Not at the moment, Don. I just want to know that he's there, and where he's going when he leaves.'

'Leave it with me, Harry,' said Mercer. 'And the best of luck.'

Sixteen

I received a telephone call from Don Mercer on Friday afternoon. It was two o'clock.

'Good afternoon, Harry.'

'And a very good morning to you, Don,' I said, rather cleverly, I thought. However, the truth of the matter was that Colin Wilberforce had produced a little chart from which I was able to deduce that the time in Bermuda was ten a.m.

'My surveillance team followed Martin Bailey and Jane Grant from the airport when they arrived yesterday, Harry, and they went straight to Bailey's cottage in Flatt's Village.'

'Thanks, Don. Difficult though it is for a cynical old copper like me to accept, I suppose it's possible that they could be there on holiday.'

'Maybe,' said Mercer cautiously. 'But there's been an incident here that you ought to know about.'

'I don't like the sound of that, Don. What sort of incident?'

'The beach-squad constable on Shelley Bay Beach came on duty at eight o'clock this morning,' Mercer continued, getting straight to the point of his call, 'and he found a small pile of clothing on the seashore.'

'Where's Shelley Bay Beach, Don?'

'Less than a mile from Flatt's Village.'

'Should this interest me?' I knew damned well it would, otherwise Mercer wouldn't be ringing to tell me about it. I was starting to get an apprehensive feeling that what was to come next might further complicate an already complicated enquiry.

'Oh, it'll interest you all right, Harry. The clothing consisted of a woman's G-string, a pair of white shorts, a T-shirt, a pair of flip-flops, a towel, and a pair of sunglasses. In the pocket of the shorts was a small wallet containing a few dollars and a credit card in the name of Eunice Bailey. But of Eunice herself there was no trace.'

'Oh, bloody terrific,' I said. 'Any sign of a body being washed up, Don?'

'No. Immediately after this gear was found I ordered the police helicopter up, and alerted one of our Marine Section launches to begin searching the immediate offshore area of Shelley Bay, but so far nothing.'

'It's got to be something to do with Martin Bailey,' I suggested.

'Well, that's possible, I suppose,' said Mercer, his thoughtfulness apparent even over the telephone. 'But not directly.'

'How so?'

'We've had him and Jane Grant under constant observation ever since they arrived in Bermuda, and I'm satisfied that neither of them left the cottage, let alone went anywhere near Shelley Bay Beach. Of course, we don't know how long the clothing had been there, but it's a popular venue for swimming, and I don't think it would've been there long without someone noticing. The previous day's beach-squad constable swears it wasn't there when he went off duty at eight last night. My guess is that Eunice Bailey went for a dip early this morning, sometime before either the beach-squad constable or the lifeguard came on duty. Most of the beaches around Bermuda are prone to undertow and dangerous rip tides, and for someone not familiar with them, they can be fatal.'

I couldn't see that any purpose would be served in Dave and me flying out to Bermuda a second time, at least not until a body was found. But Mercer's information led me to wonder whether my theory about an insurance scam involving Eunice Bailey might be right. It would be a classic: indications of a drowning, but no trace of a body. And that, the locals would probably tell us, would not be unusual. Especially as Mercer had mentioned undertow and rip tides.

Furthermore, if Martin Bailey was somehow involved, he must have an accomplice in Bermuda. The police surveillance of Bailey and Jane Grant ruled out any direct participation on their part.

'What was the number of the credit card, Don?' I opened my action book and found the requisite page.

Mercer read out the details. It was the credit card that Tom Nelson had given Eunice when he and she were in Bermuda together.

'Keep me posted, Don, and thanks for all your help.'

'No problem. Incidentally, I was thinking of bringing Bailey in and questioning him to see if he knows anything about this affair. Have you any objection to that?'

'Not at all, Don. I'll be interested in what he's got to say. But if it turns out that Eunice has been murdered in Bermuda – rather than dying in a drowning accident – I'm afraid it's fairly and squarely on your plate.'

'Yeah, thanks a bundle, pal.'

'Mind you, Don, I'll be surprised if you find a body,' I said, and expanded on the theory I had mentioned in my previous phone call. 'It's possible that Eunice Bailey's been in Bermuda ever since the last reported sighting of her. After all, there's no evidence that she ever left there.'

'It's a possibility,' said Mercer, 'and in the waters around here, it could be ages before we find a body, if ever. I'll let you know how we get on.'

I sent for Dave and told him of the latest development in the saga of the missing Eunice Bailey.

'Martin Bailey's got to have had something to do with it, guv,' said Dave, unwilling to concede that the entrepreneur was an innocent party. 'It's too much of a coincidence that he arrives in Bermuda, and within twelve hours his wife has drowned. Assuming she has, of course.'

I rang through to Kate Ebdon's office and asked her to join us.

'Kate, I want you to have a good look into Martin Bailey's business affairs.' I explained my theory that he had, perhaps, insured Eunice's life for a substantial sum, and that he and Eunice had planned her 'drowning' in order to claim on the policy.

'But why would he wait until he's back in Bermuda, sir?' asked Kate. 'Much better if her apparent death had occurred while he was in this country.'

'I agree, but if he has an accomplice, or even if it was Eunice herself who left her gear on the beach, it might be that neither of them knew that Martin Bailey was back in Bermuda. On the other hand, the date for this "drowning" might have been arranged some time ago.' I chuckled at the thought that the smug Bailey might have erred, and that such a simple mistake could have scuppered an otherwise elaborate plan. But I had to admit that I was working very much on a hypothesis that might ultimately prove to be without foundation.

'Yeah, that's a possibility, I suppose,' said Kate. 'It'd certainly be crazy to cast suspicion on himself deliberately.'

It was about half-past eight when Don Mercer telephoned again.

'I've interviewed Martin Bailey, Harry.'

'What did he have to say?'

'Apart from giving a masterful performance of being utterly distraught at his wife's apparent death, he claims to be at a loss to explain the abandoned clothing on Shelley Bay Beach. He said Eunice wasn't keen on swimming, and he didn't even know she was in Bermuda. He told me that he sent a private detective over here in the middle of June, looking for her, but this guy found nothing. I remembered what you'd told me about this ex-cop John not having come here at all, Harry, but I didn't show out. I thought you'd want to keep that card up your sleeve for the time being.'

'Bailey already knows, Don. I got the PI to tell him that he'd told us. I think that's why Bailey did a runner. Perhaps we forced him into bringing his plans forward.'

'None of this surprises me,' said Mercer. 'I don't reckon Bailey much. Too fond of playing both ends against the middle. He might've got away with it in business, but I reckon he's out of his league with this scam. If it is a scam.'

'Did Bailey say why he was in Bermuda?'

'He said he was on holiday, but was doing some business as well. That's why he'd brought his secretary, he said. I'll tell you this much, Harry, I wish I could find a secretary who looked like her.'

'Did you talk to her, Don?'

'Yes, I managed to have a word with her separately. That girl was a bundle of nerves. She confirmed that she was Bailey's secretary, but that she hadn't been with him long.'

'She's a cunning little liar, Don. She's his girlfriend, lives with him, and sleeps with him. She admitted that much when I interviewed her. She's the manageress of a boutique in Chelsea, and she phoned in sick the day she left for Bermuda.'

'I thought they were a dodgy pair, Harry, but I didn't get anything substantial out of them. Either they're for real, or they're putting forward a cover story that they haven't prepared very carefully.'

'And still no sign of Eunice Bailey's body, I suppose.'

'No, nothing,' said Mercer. 'We've called off the search. I suppose she might turn up, but as I said this morning, it could be days, or even weeks. Or not at all.'

I related the details of Mercer's call to Dave, and sent him home for the weekend. There was nothing to be done before Monday, and it would be no bad thing to wait for any further information that might come from Bermuda.

'Hello, stranger!' said Gail, when I arrived at her front door on Saturday evening. 'I haven't seen you for ages.'

'Sorry, but I've been extremely busy,' I said, handing over a large bunch of flowers and a bottle of wine. I know how to smooth my girlfriend's ruffled feathers.

'Oh, you poor thing. Come in and let me pour you a large Scotch.' I wasn't quite sure whether there was an element of sarcasm in Gail's apparent sympathy, but I think she's slowly coming to terms with what's involved in going out with a copper. Or, more to the point, *not* going out with one.

I'd telephoned her that morning and suggested dinner out, but she said she'd cook for me. That was a double bonus: Gail is a brilliant cook, and I'd had enough of eating out just lately.

The meal that Gail prepared was a culinary delight, but her meals always were, and afterwards we relaxed in her sitting room on the first floor of her town house. The French windows were open to the evening air, but the atmosphere was marred by the odour of someone's barbecue. It is a feature of the British that on any warm night they have an overwhelming desire to drag their food into the garden and set fire to it. The food, I mean, although sometimes they actually do set fire to the garden. And on occasion even themselves.

'So what onerous tasks have kept you from seeing me, darling?' asked Gail, handing me a glass of cognac.

'Among other things, I've interviewed a porn actress, and I've been to Bermuda.'

'Bermuda!' Curiously, Gail seemed more envious of my Bermuda trip than annoyed about the porn actress. But I remembered her telling me that some members of her profession had made blue movies when they couldn't get regular work. And on one occasion, Gail had even suggested that she might have to take up doing strippergrams if she couldn't get an engagement. But I think she was joking. I hope she was, having seen the behaviour of some of my lascivious colleagues when striptease artistes had appeared at various police functions. Of course, it doesn't happen any more, not now we're a politically correct, sea-green incorruptible police force. Sorry, police *service*.

'All in the course of duty, darling,' I said. 'Honest.'

Perhaps it was mentioning my conversation with a sexy porn actress that did it, but Gail stood up and walked from the room. Five minutes later, she returned, wearing nothing but a feather boa. 'Well, don't just sit there,' she said. 'Do something.'

'An email came in during the night from Superintendent Mercer in Bermuda, sir,' said Colin Wilberforce, when I arrived at Curtis Green on the Monday morning. 'When I took over from Gavin Creasey, he said he'd taken a chance on not disturbing you with it.'

'What's Mr Mercer have to say, Colin?'

'He reports that Martin Bailey and Jane Grant left Bermuda International Airport on flight BA 2232 last night at twenty-ten hours Bermuda time, sir. Due to arrive Gatwick at oh-six-four-five BST this morning. It also said that Mr Mercer would telephone you this afternoon. He actually said "this morning", but as they're four hours behind, he probably means this afternoon, as far as we're concerned. Gavin told me that he'd alerted Special Branch at Gatwick to report the arrival of Bailey and Grant.'

'And did they arrive?'

'Yes, sir. SB picked them up at immigration, and followed them out of North Terminal building, where they departed in a Rolls-Royce. SB sent us the index mark of the vehicle, but it's the one we've already got on record.'

'Good. Thanks, Colin. So Bailey and Jane Grant were only there for three days,' I said. 'I wonder what that was all about.'

'It's got to be connected to that business of Eunice's clothing on the beach, guv,' said Dave.

'Don Mercer said that neither Bailey nor Jane Grant left the cottage before the clothing was found.'

'Wouldn't necessarily have had to, guv. Bailey could've

told his contact – whoever that is – to put the gear on the beach. He wouldn't have had to leave his cottage. One of the things I noticed when we were over there is that they have telephones . . . sir.'

But at noon all my theorizing was set at naught when Colin rang through to say that Tom Nelson was on the phone.

'Put him through, Colin.'

There was a short delay and then Tom Nelson was on the line.

'Hi, Detective Brock, it's Tom Nelson here.'

'I understand you have some information for me, Mr Nelson.'

'Yes, *sir*. It's about Eunice.'

'What about her?'

'You remember that I told you I'd given her a credit card, so she could spend what she liked in Bermuda . . . ?'

'Yes, I do. And you gave me the last account you'd received.'

'Sure thing. Well, Detective, I just got another one.'

'What, another account?'

'Yep. Looks like the card was used on the sixth, seventh, and eighth of July. In Bermuda.'

'When did you get this account, Mr Nelson?'

'I only found it this morning, but it's dated the fifteenth of July, the usual accounting day.'

I was about to protest that Nelson should have told us about this as soon as he received the account, but he answered that question before I could ask it.

'I've been on vacation in the States, Detective. I only got back this morning, and it was on the mat waiting for me.'

So, Nelson was in the States, eh? Or had he perhaps been in Bermuda? Something else to be checked out.

'D'you think you could get your secretary to fax this account to me, Mr Nelson?' I said that tongue in cheek. I was still unconvinced that Trudy was a secretary.

'Sure thing. But I don't have a fax machine. Not any more. I'll get Trudy to send it by email with the account as an attachment. What's your email address?'

This was all too much for me. I handed Nelson over to Dave, who provided him with the necessary information. *Bloody computers.*

The American playboy was as good as his word. Fifteen

minutes later, Colin Wilberforce brought a computer printout into my office.

'Well, Dave, this throws everything back into the melting pot. According to this, Eunice dined at restaurants between the sixth and eighth of July, and made yet another purchase at Swimsuit Extravaganza on the seventh. And Bailey told Don Mercer that Eunice didn't like swimming.'

'Doesn't have to, guv. A lot of women buy bikinis just to lounge about on the beach. I'm married to one. But it does mean that Eunice was out and about in Bermuda when we were there.' Dave tossed that comment across the desk like it was a hand grenade.

'Bloody hell, so she was. For God's sake don't tell the commander, Dave.' I was sure that the great detective would firmly believe that because we were in Bermuda it would have been a matter of simplicity for us to find the damned woman.

'What do we do now, guv?' asked Dave.

'We go and see Bailey again, I suppose. See if we can get something out of him about Eunice's abandoned clothing that Don Mercer didn't.'

Mercer rang again at about four o'clock. 'You got the message saying that Bailey and Jane Grant had left, did you, Harry?'

'Yes, we did, thanks, Don. And we had our people check that they actually arrived. I'm going to see him this evening to see if we can get any more out of him. I suppose you haven't found a body yet?'

'No, there's no sign, Harry, and I'm beginning to wonder if we ever will.'

I told Mercer about the credit-card account that Tom Nelson had received, and gave him details of where it had been used.

'Have you still got the copies of the photographs we left with you, Don?' I asked.

'They're right here on my desk, Harry.'

'If it's not too much trouble, perhaps you could get someone to show them around.' I mentioned Swimsuit Extravaganza, and gave Don the names of the restaurants. 'Just to see if anyone can confirm seeing Eunice Bailey.'

'Leave it with me, Harry, I'll get one of my sergeants on to it straight away.'

* * *

'I didn't think it'd be very long before you turned up again,' said Martin Bailey, but there wasn't the usual hostility in his voice. 'Please come in.'

This time, Jane Grant was in the sitting room, and Bailey made no attempt to dismiss her. Although she wasn't wearing Eunice's distinctive brooch, I noticed that she seemed a little disconcerted by our arrival. But perhaps Bailey unnerved her more than we did.

'We've received information from the Bermuda Police about some clothing found on Shelley Bay Beach on Friday last, Mr Bailey. Items found in the clothing appear to point to it having been left there by your wife.' I said this as though I was unaware that Bailey had been in Bermuda at the time, or that Don Mercer had spoken to him about the mystery.

'I know that Eunice walked out on me, Chief Inspector, but I didn't want it to end like this. I'm sure we could've patched things up, given time.' Bailey shook his head gloomily.

It was a curious statement for Bailey to have made. Apparently oblivious to Jane Grant's presence, he was now talking of having wanted to 'patch things up' with Eunice, and that would have meant Jane's rapid departure. Unless this tale was part of the scam and Jane Grant was in on it.

'It's a terrible thing,' Bailey continued, 'and to think that I was there – in Bermuda, I mean – when it happened. But I dare say the police over there told you that.'

'You were *there*?' I asked, feigning surprise.

'Oh yes, but only for three days. I had some business to attend to. In fact, I was interviewed by a very sympathetic detective after Eunice's things had been found on the beach. We both were.' Bailey waved a hand in Jane Grant's direction. 'Have the police over there said whether they've found her body?'

'I spoke to the officer in charge of enquiries this afternoon, Mr Bailey, and there's no news as yet.'

'Are you likely to be speaking to him again?'

'Almost certainly, I should think.'

'You see, I'd like to have her body brought back here for burial. D'you think you could mention that, and ask them how I go about it?'

'A much better idea would be to get in touch with one of

the big London funeral directors, Mr Bailey,' said Dave. 'They'll know the procedure, and make all the necessary arrangements.'

'Thank you, that's very kind.' It was amazing how conciliatory Bailey had become. The brash, hard-nosed entrepreneur had given way to a man clearly distressed at the news of his estranged wife's demise. He glanced at Jane Grant. 'Jane, be a good girl and get that tray of whisky from next door. I'm sure that these gentlemen will join me in a drink.' He raised an enquiring eyebrow in our direction.

'Thank you,' I said, 'but my sergeant's driving. He'll have something non-alcoholic.'

Jane Grant, a suitably funereal expression on her face, rose from her chair and silently left the room.

'I have to apologize for my earlier behaviour, Chief Inspector,' said Bailey wearily. 'When you first started enquiring into Eunice's disappearance, I thought you were being unnecessarily intrusive, but I realize now that you were only doing your job. I'm just sorry you weren't able to find her before this terrible tragedy occurred.'

I was saved from making a reply by the return of Jane Grant. She put a salver of drinks on a side table and poured three stiff whiskies, and a Coca-Cola for Dave.

'I don't suppose I'll be seeing you again, but I'd like to thank you for your efforts,' said Bailey, raising his glass in salute, 'even though they proved to be unsuccessful.'

'May I remind you that Mrs Bailey's wedding ring is still with the jeweller's where she took it for enlargement, Mr Bailey,' said Dave.

'Ah, so it is. Yes, I must remember to pop in and collect it some time. I think she should be wearing it when she's buried.'

'Assuming that Eunice Bailey has drowned, guv, it looks as though that's the end of our enquiry,' said Dave, as we drove back to Curtis Green.

'I'll believe that when I see the body, Dave. I'm afraid the change that's come over Bailey only makes me more suspicious. He didn't say a word about John, or about our accusations of handling against Jane Grant.'

'But what else can we do?'

'Wait,' I said.

*   *   *

We didn't have long to wait.

At two o'clock on the following day, Tuesday, Don Mercer telephoned with a piece of information that turned the whole enquiry on its head.

'My sergeant took the photographs round the restaurants where Eunice Bailey's credit card was used, Harry, and to Swimsuit Extravaganza. Staff at two of the restaurants, and the swimwear shop, immediately identified the woman who paid with that credit card.'

'And presumably they confirmed that it *was* Eunice Bailey.'

'No, Harry, it was Jane Grant.'

Seventeen

I was now presented with a tricky legal situation. Jane Grant had been caught out using a credit card that she was not entitled to use. But the venue of the offence was outside the jurisdiction of the English courts, even though the head office of the credit-card company was in the United Kingdom. Not that any of that mattered because I didn't see the credit-card company stirring itself to launch a prosecution. In the general scheme of things, the sums involved were paltry, and the cost of taking Jane Grant to court – even if they could – would far outweigh the loss sustained.

That, however, wasn't going to stop me from having her arrested. When she was by herself. I sent for Detective Inspector Ebdon, and explained the situation to her.

'No probs, guv. I'll put a tail on her, and the minute we catch her on her own, we'll nick her. Incidentally, as far as I can tell, Bailey's clean. We did a lot of in-depth enquiries, and tapped a few sources, and he's reckoned to be worth eight or nine millions.'

'So what the hell's he playing at?' I mused, for what must've been the hundredth time.

'I think we're about to find out, guv,' said Dave.

'And we'll start right now in the King's Road,' I responded.

'I don't suppose Jane Grant will be there, guv. Probably still back at Coburn Street helping Bailey to mourn.'

'I'm hoping she won't be, Dave, but that's not why we're going anyway. I want to talk to one of her colleagues.'

'I'm afraid Miss Grant's not here, Chief Inspector,' said one of the two remaining blondes at the Chelsea boutique.

I affected disappointment at this statement. 'Really? When *will* she be here?'

'I don't know. She telephoned this morning to say that she

was still unwell, and would probably be off for the rest of the week.'

'Does that make you the acting manageress, then?'

'Manager, actually, but yes. What can I do to help you?'

Funny how women – even attractive ones – like to use the masculine version of their job titles.

'You can tell me if Miss Grant was here during the week beginning the first of July.' In view of what Mercer had told us, it was obvious that she wasn't, but it's good to get confirmation. Apart from which, prosecuting counsel like to have everything buttoned up. Two or three times over, if possible.

The woman took a diary from under the counter. 'No, she was on holiday. From the first of July to the fourteenth.'

'Did she happen to mention where she was going?' asked Dave.

'Apparently she has a sister in Cornwall. I seem to remember her mentioning something about spending the fortnight with her.'

'I'd like you to make a statement to that effect, then,' I said.

'A statement? Is this serious?'

'Very,' I responded.

Dave produced the necessary stationery and began writing.

DI Ebdon arrived in my office at ten o'clock the next morning with more good news.

'I arrested Jane Grant early this morning, guv. She was coming out of Bailey's house in Coburn Street, on her way to do some shopping, so she said. She's now locked up in Charing Cross nick.'

'Excellent, Kate. Well done. You and I will go and talk to her. Like now.' It is always advisable to take a woman officer when interviewing a female in custody; it prevents any nasty allegations.

Before we left, I asked DS Tom Challis to organize a search team and put it on standby. I had a feeling that before the day was out, we'd be closely examining the contents of Martin Bailey's house.

As we had prima-facie evidence that Jane Grant had committed a crime, albeit in Bermuda, I decided that the interview with her should be on a formal footing. Consequently, once the

custody sergeant had brought her in to the interview room,
Kate Ebdon switched on the tape recorder, and informed it
that DCI Brock and DI Ebdon were questioning Miss Jane
Grant. I'd left Dave outside purposely; we didn't want to be
accused of duress by having *three* police officers interviewing
our suspect. Believe me, defence counsel can come up with
all sorts of convoluted reasons for a jury not to convict their
clients.

'Why on earth have I been brought here?' demanded the
girl spiritedly. But even though she'd gone immediately on
the offensive, she was clearly unnerved by her arrest. She was
as taut as a coiled spring, her legs crossed and her arms tightly
folded across her breasts.

But I've dealt with far tougher suspects than the twenty-
five-year-old callow blonde sitting opposite me. 'Did you
enjoy your fortnight's holiday in Cornwall with your sister?'
I asked for starters.

'What? What are you talking about?'

My question had clearly caught Jane wrong-footed, as I'd
intended it should. It's always a good idea to lead off with a
question that's totally unexpected.

'You took leave from your boutique from the first to the
fourteenth of last month, and told your colleagues you were
going to Cornwall.'

'Oh, that. Yes, that's right.' And making a quick recovery,
she added 'The Cornish coast is very beautiful in July.'

'I imagine it is. Perhaps you'll give my inspector the address
so that we can confirm that you were there.'

'I don't see why I should. It's not a crime to go to Cornwall,
is it?'

'No, but using someone else's credit card is a crime, Miss
Grant,' said Kate. 'And you weren't in Cornwall at all during
that period. You were in Bermuda.'

'I don't know what you're talking about. What credit card?
What d'you mean?'

'Eunice Bailey's credit card,' I said, as Kate passed me the
copy of the account that Tom Nelson had emailed to me earlier
today. 'And it was used at several restaurants, and a shop
called Swimsuit Extravaganza, all of which are in Bermuda.
Do a lot of swimming, do you?'

'I don't know what you're talking about,' said Jane again,

but her denial was negated by the ashen expression her face had suddenly assumed. She interlinked her fingers tightly, presumably to stop them shaking. 'I want to see a solicitor. I'm entitled to have one. And I want Martin to be told I'm here. I shan't say anything else until that happens.'

Damn the woman! I didn't think she knew that much about the Police and Criminal Evidence Act, but I did. And so would her defence counsel if she eventually stood trial.

I terminated the interview and raced upstairs to the superintendent's office.

Having introduced myself, I explained about Jane Grant's arrest and her possible involvement, together with Martin Bailey, in the disappearance, or abduction, or even murder, of Eunice Bailey.

'I have yet to interview Martin Bailey in connection with this matter, sir,' I continued, 'and as he may be arrested as a co-conspirator, if not a principal in a case of murder, I fear that he may interfere with any evidence that police may seize at a later date if he is alerted to Miss Grant's arrest.'

The superintendent appeared slightly bemused at this rapid-fire legal psychobabble. 'What d'you want of me, Mr Brock?' he asked.

'A written order authorizing a delay in permitting my prisoner access to either a friend or to legal advice. You see, sir, as a chief inspector, I can't give that authority. It's all in PACE, sir,' I added helpfully.

'Ah!' The superintendent reached for a copy of the legislation, and spent a few minutes studying it. 'Yes, all right,' he said. 'I'll authorize it. I'll send the written authority down to you once my clerk's prepared it.'

Thank God! A Uniform Branch superintendent with bottle. I returned to the interview room, and told the tape recorder that I had done so.

'The superintendent at this police station has refused your request for access to legal advice, or for Mr Bailey to be informed, Miss Grant,' I said. 'At least, for the time being.'

'That's outrageous,' exclaimed Jane. 'It's my right.'

I wasn't going to get involved in an argument about the law. 'Now, do you deny having used Eunice Bailey's credit card in Bermuda?'

'Of course I do.'

'The staff at three separate establishments in Bermuda have been shown a photograph of you,' said Kate, 'and they positively identified you as the woman concerned.'

'What were you doing with a photograph of me? Where did you get it from?'

'Miss Grant . . . ' I was getting a little tired of Jane's constant denials in the face of incontrovertible evidence. 'I don't think you realize what this is all about. Your use of this credit card could be only the tip of an iceberg in what might be a serious conspiracy. What we have learned so far about Eunice Bailey's disappearance seems to indicate that Martin Bailey has known all along where she is.'

'But she drowned. While Martin and I were in Bermuda.' But Jane's response lacked conviction, and it was clear that she was having doubts.

'Her body has not been found, Miss Grant. Furthermore, I'm obliged to tell you that Martin Bailey will shortly be arrested in connection with the disappearance of his wife.' I hadn't a clue what I was going to arrest him for, but I was hoping that Jane Grant would give me a reason. 'But that apart, papers will be submitted to the Crown Prosecution Service, and you are likely to be charged with fraud.' I knew that there wasn't a cat's chance in hell of that happening, but I was interested to see what her reaction would be.

'It was all Martin's idea,' blurted out Jane.

'What was?'

'Me using Eunice's credit card.'

I glanced at Kate. 'Caution her,' I said.

'Jane Grant, you are not obliged to say anything, but . . . ' Kate began, and recited the caution from memory, clever woman.

The administration of the caution can have one of several effects. Either the prisoner will clam up completely, or they'll make a clean breast of their crimes. Hardened criminals will usually go shtum, if they haven't been shtum from the very start, that is. But inexperienced first-time offenders will often tell all. I hoped that Jane fell within the latter category. And she did.

'Martin's running out of money. He told me he'd made one or two bad investments, and it's hit him hard. He said that if he couldn't inject some capital into his business soon, he'd go bankrupt.'

'Go on, Miss Grant.' Although I didn't believe any of this, I'd no doubt that it was the tale Bailey had told this naive girl. And I'd no doubt that she'd believed him.

'He took out a heavy insurance policy on Eunice's life, and told me that together they'd planned to fake her death, and then claim on the policy. The plan was that Eunice would go to Bermuda, and eventually be found apparently drowned. She and Martin really were sick of each other, and Eunice agreed to disappear, probably to America, and then stay out of Martin's life forever provided she received half of the insurance money when the policy was paid out. And then Martin and I would be married.'

Oh, you poor naive kid. If that were true, the marriage would be bigamous.

'So the Bermuda Police are wasting their time searching for Eunice Bailey's body off Shelley Bay Beach.'

'Yes.'

'Where is Eunice Bailey now, Miss Grant?' asked Kate.

'I don't know. I suppose she's gone to the States. That was the plan, so Martin told me.'

'And you and Martin went to Bermuda to oversee Eunice Bailey's supposed drowning, was that the idea?'

'Yes.'

'And how was that arranged?' I asked.

'Martin told me that he had a contact in Bermuda who would put the clothes on the beach the morning they were found. He telephoned whoever it was the night before.'

'And who was this person?'

'I've no idea. I didn't overhear the conversation, and he said it was better that I knew as little as possible about it.'

'Did he explain why you should use the credit card on the sixth, seventh, and eighth of July, Miss Grant?' I asked. 'If Eunice was in Bermuda, why didn't she use it herself? That would have saved you from being identified using it fraudulently, and thus becoming a co-conspirator.'

'It was Martin's idea,' responded Jane lamely, presumably because there was no logical reason for her to have been dragooned into doing it.

'And did Martin tell you where he got the credit card from?'

'No.'

'Would it surprise you to know that it was taken out by a

man named Tom Nelson specifically for Eunice to use when she was in Bermuda with Mr Nelson between the twenty-fifth of May and the sixth of June?'

'I don't know anything about that.'

'When did you last see Eunice Bailey, Miss Grant?'

'I've never met her. Martin told me that she'd left on the eighteenth of May to start the deception.'

'And it was the very next evening that Martin picked you up at a nightclub.'

Jane bridled at that. 'He didn't pick me up, as you put it. He asked me for a dance and we got talking. But I told you that before.'

There were several inconsistencies in what Jane Grant had told us, statements that didn't chime. I was now certain that Martin Bailey had gone out on the evening of the nineteenth of May solely for the purpose of finding a girl whom he could use as a cat's-paw. And Jane Grant had the misfortune to be that girl. No doubt Bailey's blandishments, his generosity, and the ride in his Rolls-Royce, had won her over. She probably couldn't believe her luck when he'd invited her to move in with him. And for him, there was the added bonus of her willingness to sleep with him. It was but a short step from there for him to use her in furtherance of his plans.

'It might interest you to know that, far from being nearly bankrupt, Miss Grant, Martin Bailey is worth between eight and nine million pounds. I'm afraid you've been made use of. And I've no doubt he would have cast you aside once you'd served your purpose. He certainly wouldn't have married you, as you claim.'

'I don't believe it,' Jane whispered, but from the expression on her face, it was obvious that she did believe, albeit belatedly, that she'd been a mere tool in Bailey's scheme. It was then that the tears came.

'I should like you to make a written statement, Miss Grant, detailing all you have just told us,' I said.

'What will happen then?'

'You'll be released on police bail to return here one month hence. If, on the other hand, we find that we don't need to see you again, we'll let you know.' But her release wasn't going to happen until I'd got Martin Bailey under lock and key.

We left Kate to record Jane Grant's statement, by which time it was half-past two. As good a time as any to arrest Bailey. I just hoped that he was at home, but gut instinct told me that he would be. I was wrong.

We drove straight to Coburn Street.

There was no reply to repeated knockings, as policemen tend to say.

We went next door to our faithful informant, Gladys Damjuma.

'Oh, Mr Brock, do come in and have a cup of tea.'

'Thank you, but I'm afraid we don't have the time right now. I was wondering if you'd seen Mr Bailey since we spoke last.'

'I'm sorry, but I haven't seen Martin since yesterday.'

'He appears to be out,' I said, and paused. 'I suppose you've still not seen Mrs Bailey?' It was a formal question to which I was expecting a negative reply, but I was still working on the theory that Eunice's supposed drowning was a put-up job. However, she might have been crazy enough to return to Coburn Street to collect her jewellery.

'No, not at all. Not since she left Martin.' Gladys held on to the edge of the door. 'And I'm still puzzling why she went. Perhaps the building works were getting on her nerves. We had to have some work done in this house when we first moved in. Oh, the noise of the banging and all that really got me down. I said to Bim that we ought to move into a hotel for a few weeks.'

'Building works, Mrs Damjuma?' This was the first I'd heard of any building works at Bailey's house, and it suddenly interested me.

'I don't know. I might be wrong, but Martin had some cement delivered one day. In one of those lorries with a big revolving barrel on the back.'

'When was this?' asked Dave.

'I can't remember exactly, but it must've been about six weeks ago. Perhaps he's doing up his house to sell it. He is in the property business, isn't he?' Gladys laughed. 'If he does, I hope we get a neighbour who's as nice as Eunice.'

'So do I, Mrs Damjuma,' I said. 'However, if you do see Mr Bailey, perhaps you'd let me know. It is rather urgent.'

'I've still got your card, Mr Brock. If I see him, I'll tele-phone you.'

'That would be most helpful, Mrs Damjuma. Thank you.'

Gladys closed the door reluctantly. I got the feeling that she was disappointed that we weren't staying for tea.

'Building works, Dave,' I said pensively. 'I wonder what that's all about. Time to speak to some of the other neigh-bours, I think.'

We went straight to the house on the other side of the Bailey residence from that of the Damjumas.

We introduced ourselves, and the couple that lived there told us they were called James and Renate Grainger.

I explained that we were investigating the disappearance of Eunice Bailey, and needed urgently to speak to Mr Bailey. But I decided against mentioning that Eunice might have drowned in Bermuda.

'I'm afraid I haven't seen anything of him lately,' said Mrs Grainger.

'We saw something in the newspapers about her running off, but I've no idea where he is,' said James Grainger, and then, without any prompting from me, added, 'Frankly, I can't stand that bloody man Bailey. He's arrogant and rude. A jumped-up middle-aged yob who's made a lot of money out of property deals, so I understand. And from what Renate's told me, Chief Inspector, I don't think anyone would blame Eunice for leaving him.'

'I felt sorry for Eunice,' said Renate Grainger. She spoke with a slight German accent.

'Did you know her well?' I asked.

'Not particularly, but if we met in the street, or at the shops, we'd stop and talk. Oh, and there was a time when we bumped into each other in a coffee shop and had a chat over a latte.'

'And did she complain about her husband?'

'Not in as many words,' said Renate, 'but it was obvious she was unhappy. She often mentioned that she and her husband never went out anywhere together, like to a restau-rant for a decent meal, or to a club to dance. She said she was very fond of dancing, but that Martin was so busy he could never find the time to take her. A terrible shame, that he had all that money, but never wanted to spend it, at least not on Eunice. She wasn't really complaining about Martin;

it was more a case of her feeling sorry for him, having to work so hard.'

'From what you've said, Mr Grainger,' said Dave, 'I assume you never met the Baileys socially. Like having dinner with them, or they with you?'

Grainger scoffed at the very idea. 'Definitely not. I wouldn't give the man houseroom. And if you want my opinion, I think that Eunice got to the point where she'd had more than enough and walked out. And who could blame her? I think she probably put up with more than any woman should have to put up with.'

'D'you think that Martin and Eunice argued a lot, Mrs Grainger?'

'Oh, I don't think so,' said Renate. 'She never said anything about having rows, and women do, you know. To other women.'

'Did Mrs Bailey ever mention going to Bermuda?' I asked.

Renate Grainger smiled condescendingly, almost as if I'd asked a ridiculous question. 'Good heavens no. I think she did go on holiday by herself a few times, but she often told me that she'd really like to go somewhere with her husband.'

'We've been told that Mr Bailey had some building work done about six weeks ago, Mr Grainger,' Dave said. 'D'you know anything about that?'

'It's news to me. But I'm usually out all day. You're lucky to have caught me this afternoon.'

'Out at work, presumably?'

'Yes, I'm in the wine trade. Imports from France, Spain, and Italy mainly. Bring in a bit of stuff from Chile and South Africa, but Europe's my main area of supply. It entails going across the Channel at frequent intervals, but Renate always comes with me.'

'But he never goes to Germany,' complained Renate with a smile. 'I keep telling him there are some very good wines in Germany. Moselles and Rhinehessens, for example.'

'You come from Germany, do you, Mrs Grainger?'

'Yes, from Paderborn. We met when James was in the army there.'

'I gave up soldiering after about seven years,' Grainger volunteered. 'More money in wine, believe me, Chief Inspector.'

All of which was very interesting, but actually got me no further forward in terms of solving the mystery of Eunice Bailey.

Mrs Grainger recalled my question. 'Now you mention it, I do remember seeing a lorry delivering cement to Martin's house one afternoon, and some workmen were standing about with shovels.'

'Did these workmen have a truck, Mrs Grainger?' asked Dave. 'Apart from the lorry delivering the cement.'

'I think so. I noticed two men there, talking to the driver of the cement lorry. Rough-looking fellows they were.'

'Did you happen to see a name on the workmen's truck?' Dave had his pocketbook out, ready to record this information, but he was disappointed.

'No, I'm sorry. I didn't think it was important. I know there were three letters, like ABC Builders, except that it wasn't ABC. Oh, and there was a phone number, but I don't remember what it was.'

It was worth a try, but if Renate Grainger had come up with the information we wanted it would've been a first. I've never known an adult who was able to recall what was written on the side of a van. Children are best at it; they notice everything.

We thanked the Graingers, and left, no better informed than when we'd arrived. Well, almost.

Suddenly, enquiring into Martin Bailey's building works had assumed a priority.

Eighteen

'We'll try that house opposite, Dave,' I said, leading the way across Coburn Street. 'With any luck we'll find a nosey neighbour, and God knows we need one.'

'Are we getting anywhere with this, guv?' asked Dave. 'All we've found out so far is that Bailey's a nasty bastard who had a wife everyone felt sorry for. No one's had a good word to say about him. But we knew that already.'

'Trust me,' I said, as I knocked on the door of number twelve.

'Yes, sir,' said Dave.

A girl of about twenty-two answered the door, and the moment we mentioned that we were police officers, she adopted the worried look of someone who regularly smoked pot.

I explained that we were making enquiries about Eunice Bailey.

'Who?' queried the girl.

I told her that the Baileys lived opposite, and the girl said that I should speak to her father.

The man invited us in, and introduced himself as Geoffrey Parsons, but spoke with a mid-European accent. Oh well.

'Yes, I remember builders being at Mr Bailey's house,' said Parsons. 'As a matter of fact, I went over one weekend and asked him who they were, and if he could recommend them. You see, we want some work done here.' He waved a hand at a wall in the sitting room. 'I want some double glass doors put in there, so that we can walk straight into the dining room without having to go into the hall. It would be much more convenient, when we're having dinner parties, if our guests could go through a door there.'

'Yes, I can see that,' said Dave, expressing a false interest, but I think he was getting fed up with the whole business. 'That would be very useful. French windows would look nice, with little bevelled plate-glass panes in them, don't you think?'

Parsons appeared to give this suggestion careful consideration. 'Yes, that would look good, but my wife is rather keen
on having all-glass doors so that you only see the hinges.
Discreet hinges, of course.'

'What did Mr Bailey say about the builders, Mr Parsons?'
I asked, interrupting this cosy chat about French windows.

'He was quite rude, as a matter of fact. He said they were
no good and he wouldn't recommend them to anyone. He
didn't really want to talk about them.'

'So you've had to look elsewhere.'

'No . . . well . . . yes. As it happened, I saw their lorry the
very next day, driving down Holland Park Avenue, so I took
down the number and rang them. But they said they couldn't
do what I wanted. Apparently they could knock the hole in
the wall, and talked knowledgeably about RSJs, whatever they
are. But they said I would need to get a specialist glazier to
fit the doors. Well, that was no good. I wanted someone who
could do the whole job. I rather suspected that they were
cowboys anyway.'

'D'you still have their telephone number, sir?' asked Dave.

'Yes. Just a moment.' Parsons left the room, returning
moments later with the details on a piece of paper. 'There you
are,' he said.

Once back in our car, Dave rang Colin Wilberforce for an
urgent subscriber check on the telephone number Geoffrey
Parsons had given us. Within minutes, we had an address in
Hammersmith.

It was an old house in one of the streets off Talgarth Road.
And, on the paved-over front garden, there was a truck with
that very phone number on it. Hooray! The system works.

'We're looking for Mr Callaghan,' I said to the woman who
answered the door.

'Are you now, and what would that be all about?' The
woman spoke with a Southern Irish accent.

'We're police officers.'

'Glory be,' said the woman, and disappeared down the hallway.
'Sean,' she shouted, 'there's a couple of constables here for you.'
Somewhere in the background, a child was screaming its head
off.

'I'm Callaghan.' The man who eventually appeared was wearing jeans and a coloured shirt, and had a piece of toast in his hand. Standing beside him was a small boy with his thumb in his mouth. He too was clutching a piece of toast. 'Away and find your ma,' he said to the boy, before facing me again. 'And what is it the police would be wanting with me?' He too was Irish, both by accent and appearance.

'I want to talk to you about Martin Bailey of Coburn Street in Holland Park, Mr Callaghan.'

'Is that a fact? You'd better be coming in, then.'

We followed Sean Callaghan into a small room that had been converted into a sort of office. But God alone knows how he ever found anything among the piles of paper that covered a small desk and overflowed on to the floor. To his credit, there was no sign of a computer. I don't like computers.

'I understand that you recently did some work for Mr Bailey.'

'Might've done,' said Callaghan cautiously.

'This is not the time to pussyfoot about, Mr Callaghan,' said Dave, and indicated me. 'This is Detective Chief Inspector Brock of Homicide and Serious Crime Command at Scotland Yard, and I'm Detective Sergeant Poole.'

'Homicide, is it?' Callaghan was taken aback by this pronouncement. 'I never had nothing to do with no homicide, and I'll not have no truck with the IRA, if that's what you're on about.' He finished eating his toast, took a partly smoked cigarette from behind his ear, and lit it with a shaking hand.

Dave wrinkled his nose at Callaghan's inappropriate use of multiple negatives, but Dave's an English-language purist. When it suits him.

'No one suggested you did, Mr Callaghan,' I said, wondering why the mention of homicide had so disturbed him. Perhaps he knew something, or maybe had had something to do with someone else's death. 'But tell me about this work you did.'

'There was nothing to it, really. Mr Bailey wanted his cellar concreting over. It was a hard packed-earth floor, but he said he wanted to make a wine cellar out of it, and was fed up with all the dust flying about the place. We ordered up some ready-mix, and did the job for him in about eight hours.'

'How did he pay you?'

'Cash.' Callaghan waved a hand at the jungle of paper on the desk. 'But all the VAT and that sort of business is paid up, if that's what you're worried about.' He was obviously more worried about it than we were.

'We're police officers, not tax collectors, Mr Callaghan,' I said. I don't know why, but I frequently find myself explaining that the police are not interested in people's tax returns. Unless it becomes a useful stick to beat them with.

'How thick a coating of concrete did you lay?' asked Dave.

'Now look here, officer, we did a good job there,' protested Callaghan. 'Has Bailey been complaining? Is that what this is all about?'

'I don't care if you sprayed the floor with emulsion and charged for six inches of concrete,' said Dave. 'Just tell me how thick.'

'About two inches. I recommended at least four, better still six, but Mr Bailey said that two inches would do. And I told him that it ought to be laid in sections – what we in the trade call bays – otherwise it'd break up once it dried out and started to contract. And to be honest with you, I think it'll have started to break up already, and I told him it would. But he said he didn't want to spend too much.' Callaghan shook his head. 'I'll tell you this much: despite all his money, that Bailey was a mean man, so he was.'

I was now concerned that Martin Bailey had somehow discovered that Jane Grant had been arrested, and as a consequence had decided to desert both the girl and Coburn Street. Back at Curtis Green, I had Colin Wilberforce send an all-ports warning to every seaport and airport in the country, and to the Eurostar terminal at London's Waterloo Station. In addition, I told Colin to send an email to Don Mercer in Bermuda, asking him to keep a lookout for the man.

But it was all in vain. Fifteen minutes after Colin had completed all the necessary paperwork, I received a telephone call from Gladys Damjuma.

'I thought you'd like to know that Martin's just come home, Mr Brock,' she told me.

'I was just going to telephone you, Mr Brock,' said Bailey, when he'd admitted us to his house in Coburn Street.

'Why was that?'

'Jane's gone missing.' Bailey shot a lingering glance in Kate Ebdon's direction, clearly impressed by her tight-fitting jeans and the man's shirt that emphasized her figure. *Forget it, squire. She'd have you for breakfast.* 'She went out to buy a news-paper first thing this morning, and I haven't seen her since. I tried her mobile, but it was switched off.'

And that, my friend, is because it's in the prisoners' property store at the nick.

'She's not missing, Mr Bailey. She's in custody at Charing Cross police station.'

'In *custody*?' It was a marvellous combination of surprise and outrage. 'Whatever for?'

'Fraudulent use of a credit card on several occasions while in Bermuda in July.'

'Good God, surely not.' Bailey was trying hard to conjure up an expression of shock, but wasn't making a very good job of it. Furthermore, it was interesting that he didn't claim that Jane Grant had been with him in London at that time.

'She has also made a full confession of her part in conspiring with you to defraud an insurance company.'

'I've never heard such nonsense. The girl's lost her reason. Why on earth should you – or she, for that matter – imagine that I'd want to defraud an insurance company?'

I wasn't about to explain the ins-and-outs of Jane Grant's statement. Time enough for that at the police station, where he would be provided with his very own copy.

I turned to Dave. 'Carry on, Sergeant.'

'Martin Bailey, I'm arresting you on suspicion of attempting to defraud an insurance company,' said Dave, and cautioned him before laying a hand on his arm as a token of his detention.

'This is absolutely preposterous,' yelled Bailey, directing his anger at me as he shook off Dave's hand. 'You wait until my solicitor gets to grips with you, mate. Your fucking feet won't touch. I'll sue you for every bleedin' penny you've got, mister.'

Ah, Martin Bailey had at last returned to his East End roots. He was rattled.

Kate stepped very close to Bailey. 'Just watch your language, cobber, unless you want my knee in your crotch,' she said, her Australian accent suddenly becoming quite marked.

Bailey moved away slightly, doubtless fearing that Kate meant what she said. And knowing her as I do, I knew that she meant it.

'Call in the team, sir?' Just before we'd arrived at Coburn Street, Tom Challis had phoned Kate to say that the search team was in position.

'Yes, please, Miss Ebdon.'

'What's that all about?' demanded Bailey.

'We are going to search these premises, Mr Bailey,' said Kate.

'Are you indeed? Got a warrant, have you?' Bailey demanded sneeringly.

'Don't need one,' said Kate. 'You've been nicked and we're entitled to search the place where you were nicked. Got it?'

Challis and four other members of Kate Ebdon's legwork team had been parked in Gospel Street, and arrived within minutes of her call. I took them into another room. 'You're looking for an insurance-policy document, Tom,' I said, 'that shows that Eunice Bailey's life was insured for a large sum of money. Plus anything else that might indicate what's happened to her.'

'Right, guv,' said Challis, and he and his team spread out through the house.

'What about the cellar, guv?' asked Dave.

'We'll have a look down there now,' I said.

We found the door that led to the cellar, and took Bailey with us.

'I understand that you've recently had this area concreted, Mr Bailey,' I said.

'Yes.'

'Why was that?'

Bailey shrugged. 'It was untidy, just having a packed-earth floor,' he said. 'No good for a storeroom as it was.'

I examined the cement surface of the cellar and noticed that it was already beginning to break up, in precisely the way that Sean Callaghan had predicted.

'Your builder doesn't seem to have done a very good job,' Dave observed. But we both knew it wasn't the builder's fault.

Bailey shrugged again, but said nothing.

We returned to the ground floor.

'I'm taking Mr Bailey to the police station now, Miss Ebdon. Give me a ring if you find what we're looking for.'

'Yes, sir. I think it would be a good idea to get the SOCOs in now.' Kate, like me, had yet to come to terms with the new title of 'forensic practitioners' that had been visited on the scientific support teams. God knows why the Metropolitan Police has to keep changing the names of everything. You'd've thought that they had their hands full trying to curb the capital's increasing criminal mayhem.

Just before leaving, I rang the custody sergeant at Charing Cross nick. 'You can release Miss Grant to police bail now, skipper. The usual conditions.' I didn't want any collusion between her and Bailey until I'd questioned him. I told Kate that the girl might be returning to Coburn Street, although I wasn't sure, but that she was to be kept out of the house while the search of the premises was in progress.

Dave put handcuffs on Bailey before escorting him to our car.

'Is that really necessary?' protested Bailey.

'My guv'nor wouldn't be at all happy if you did a runner,' said Dave. But I suspect that he was really hoping that the neighbours would witness this little scene from behind the twitching curtains of Holland Park.

Nineteen

'You are entitled to a copy of a statement made earlier today by Miss Jane Grant,' I said to Bailey, once we were ensconced in the very same room where we'd interviewed his paramour and co-conspirator that morning.

Bailey took the document, glanced briefly at it, and tossed it to one side. 'I'm not interested in anything that girl told you,' he said dismissively. 'She's a born liar. And before you ask any of your damn-fool questions, I want my solicitor here.'

Unfortunately, I had no reason to refuse Bailey's request, and I suspended the interview while the necessary arrangements were made to get his lawyer to the station.

It took an hour, and it was almost half-past nine by the time Bailey's legal representative arrived from Stratford. I could only assume that Wednesday evenings must be a particularly testing time for the average East London lawyer.

The solicitor placed a bulging briefcase on the floor, and donned a pair of rimless spectacles that he took from the top pocket of his sharp suit. The first thing he did was to demand a private conference with Bailey, a request to which police were legally bound to accede. I gave him a copy of Jane Grant's statement.

Thirty minutes later, the jousting commenced.

'What exactly is this piece of fiction supposed to prove, Inspector?' asked Bailey's legal representative, throwing the statement carelessly on to the table. 'It seems to be nothing more than the outpourings of some poor demented young woman. Knowing my client as I do, I suspect that there's not a shred of truth in anything she says.'

'The rank is *chief* inspector,' I said, before Bailey's mouthpiece could go on. I could only assume that he'd been watching too many cop shows on television; the sort of trash where the fictional chief inspector calls himself an inspector, and allows others to do the same, as though there was no difference. But there is a difference, and it's about eight grand a year. So nobody calls me 'inspector' and gets away with it.

'Yes, well, *Chief* Inspector,' the solicitor continued, only slightly abashed.

'Regardless of your view of the statement's contents, I intend to question your client about it.'

'As you wish.' The solicitor shrugged. 'But I suggest that you're wasting your time. Mr Bailey is a very wealthy man, *and* a man of probity. He has no need to defraud an insurance company. I really can't think why you're taking that seriously.' He waved a disparaging hand at Jane's statement. 'I presume that police have the policy document.'

'No, we haven't,' I said.

'And you won't find one, either,' put in Bailey.

The solicitor placed a restraining hand on Bailey's arm. 'Leave this to me, Martin,' he said.

'But there are inconsistencies in Miss Grant's statement that require closer examination,' I said, ignoring Bailey's intervention.

'Such as, *Chief* Inspector?' Having again placed sarcastic emphasis on my rank, the solicitor sat back in his chair and folded his arms. Late-evening sun shone through the interview-room window, and glinted on his spectacles.

'Where, for example, did Miss Grant obtain Eunice Bailey's credit card if it wasn't from you, Mr Bailey?'

'I suggest you ask Miss Grant.' But that was Bailey's final utterance on the matter.

And so it went on. I queried why Jane Grant should have gone to Bermuda in July, unless it was at Martin Bailey's behest. And why did she say she was going to Cornwall? I drew attention to her statement that Bailey had told her of the plan he had devised to fake Eunice Bailey's death, and claim on the insurance. I mentioned that, according to Jane Grant, Bailey had told her that he'd arranged with a third party to leave Eunice's belongings on Shelley Bay Beach to imply that she'd drowned. And I mentioned Jane Grant's claim that Bailey had proposed to her.

But it was all to no avail. Throughout my attempts to impli-cate Martin Bailey in this plot to defraud, he remained silent, and so did his solicitor. They both just sat there with smiles on their faces. When I'd finished, the solicitor leaned forward, linking his hands on the table.

'I would remind you, Chief Inspector, that the accusations of one alleged co-conspirator against another alleged co-conspirator have little or no evidential value. But setting that aside, Miss Grant's statement is merely an admission on her part that she fraudulently used a credit card outside the jurisdiction of the English courts. And I can tell you that the CPS will have no truck with it. There is no credible evidence, and no corroboration, to implicate my client in any sort of conspiracy. I put it to you that this is merely a case of a woman who, perceiving herself to be wronged, is attempting to wreak revenge. Mr Bailey has told me that his affair with Miss Grant is over, and that he had asked her to leave his house. It surely comes as no surprise to you that, in the circumstances, she would behave like a woman scorned.'

'If that's the case, why was he so worried about what had happened to her, when we called at his house to arrest him earlier today?'

The solicitor smiled again. 'My client is not heartless, Chief Inspector. Even though he had requested Miss Grant to leave – amicably, I may say – he was not going to throw her out on the street. He was actively seeking alternative accommodation for her, for which he was prepared to pay, and he was naturally concerned about her welfare when she didn't return home this morning.'

The trouble was that Bailey's solicitor was right on every count. I didn't believe a word about Bailey having terminated his affair with Jane Grant, and I was convinced that the girl had told the truth when we interviewed her. She was too scared not to. But belief and proof are poles apart where the law is concerned, and the solicitor knew it.

'I have to tell you, Chief Inspector, that my client will be seeking redress for wrongful arrest and false imprisonment. I suggest that you now arrange for his immediate release in order not to exacerbate your torts.' The solicitor stood up, put Jane Grant's statement in his already full briefcase, and looked expectant.

It was not the first time I'd been threatened with a civil action for wrongful arrest, and I doubted it would be the last.

But if it was Bailey's intention to launch such an action, I might just as well give him something really to bitch about.

'Your client will remain in police custody overnight,' I said. 'And certainly until my enquiries are complete.'

The solicitor contrived outrage, probably for Bailey's benefit. 'You seem ill disposed to see common sense, Chief Inspector,' he spluttered. 'I shall seek bail from a judge in chambers.'

'You'll have to wait until tomorrow morning,' I replied.

The solicitor departed, no doubt to start writing up his bill, and Bailey was lodged in a cell.

Dave and I returned to Bailey's house at Coburn Street.

'Any joy, Kate?' I asked.

'We've searched every nook and cranny where there might be papers, guv. We found a credit-card account in Eunice Bailey's name that showed she stayed in a West End hotel from the eighteenth to the twenty-third of May, for what that's worth. But there's no indication as to whether it's been paid.'

'That would have been the time she was seeing Tom Nelson on a nightly basis,' I said. 'So much for a flat in Marble Arch. What a waste of money. I'll bet she didn't spend many nights there. But what about an insurance policy, Kate?'

'There's no sign of one anywhere, guv,' Kate said. 'I reckon that if it does exist, it's tucked away in Bailey's cottage in Bermuda.'

'It certainly wasn't there when we searched it,' I said.

This was not good news. I knew that if we didn't find any documents that would support Jane Grant's allegations, Martin Bailey would be walking out of Charing Cross nick tomorrow morning with a spring in his step, and a smile on his face.

'However,' continued Kate, 'we have found some other interesting evidence.'

'Such as?'

'There's a separate closet off the main bedroom that's been converted into a dressing room for Eunice Bailey. It contains all her clothes, nearly as many shoes as Imelda Marcos owned, and enough underwear to sink a battleship. In a separate cabinet there are expensive cosmetics, and perfume that any girl would die for. But more to the point, all Eunice's jewellery is there. A woman splitting from her husband might leave clothes and shoes behind, but she'd never, ever forget to take her jewellery. Believe me, guv, I'm a woman. I know.'

And that was exactly what Maxine Finch had said when she told us she'd seen Jane Grant wearing Eunice's distinctive brooch.

'Frankly, guv,' observed Dave mildly, 'I don't think that Eunice Bailey went anywhere further than the cellar.'

'Crippen?' I said.

'It's a possibility, guv,' said Dave.

Back in 1910, Hawley Harvey Crippen had murdered his wife, a failed music-hall artiste called Belle Elmore, and buried her in his basement at 39 Hilldrop Crescent, North London. He too had told friends and neighbours that she'd gone to America. But friends of Belle had seen Ethel le Neve, Crippen's new girlfriend, wearing Belle's jewellery. Police were alerted and eventually one of my predecessors, DCI Walter Dew, pursued them by ship and arrested them in Halifax, Nova Scotia.

I was beginning to think that history was about to repeat itself.

'Anyone been down to the cellar since Dave and I had a look down there, Kate?'

'Not yet, guv.'

'Right, in that case, we'll have another look. Where's Linda?'

'I'm here, Mr Brock.' Linda Mitchell, attired in her sexy white coveralls, appeared in the doorway.

'Linda, d'you have anything like a pickaxe or a shovel among your vast array of kit?'

'Yes, we do. I'll get one of the lads to get it.'

'Tell him to bring it down to the cellar, will you?'

One of Linda's assistants was despatched to find the pickaxe, and a few moments later, he joined us.

For several seconds we stood there, surveying the cracked surface of Bailey's concreted cellar.

'Want me to have a go at it, Mr Brock?' asked the forensic practitioner called Trevor.

'It's only two inches thick, Trev,' said Dave, 'but I should try the cracks first. Probably find that you can lever large pieces of it away. There's only packed earth underneath it. Apparently Bailey was a stingy sod, and wouldn't lash out on having it done properly.'

It was a comparatively easy task. Those pieces that couldn't be lifted, broke up easily under the onslaught of Trevor's professional wielding of the pickaxe. Within half an hour, he had cleared a large space in the centre of the floor.

'We won't find disturbed earth under that lot, not with the naked eye,' said Dave pessimistically. 'Have you got that gear with you that might point us in the right direction, Trev?'

'Not in the van, but we can get it from Lambeth.'

It was yet another hour's delay, but we couldn't stop now.

The machine was brought down into the cellar, not without a struggle on the part of the technicians. But it took them only minutes to locate an area where the earth had been disturbed.

By now, we'd been joined by Linda, plus another of her forensic practitioners, and a photographer.

'OK,' I said, 'get digging, lads.'

'I've come across something, Mr Brock,' said Trevor, five minutes later.

'Right, just use your hands now.'

'Start photographing, Mr Brock?' asked the girl with the camera.

'Yes, every stage from now on.'

Two of the FPs began carefully to remove the earth until they found plastic. More earth was removed until it was apparent that the plastic formed part of a makeshift shroud containing a body.

'Bring it out, Mr Brock?' asked Trevor.

'No,' said Linda, before I had a chance to answer. She turned to me. 'Pathologist next, I think, Mr Brock. We may harm the evidence if we do any more before he gets here.'

And so we encountered yet another delay while the pathologist was called out. We retired to don white coveralls, overshoes, and masks. This was now undeniably a murder scene. I know we'd heard that Martin Bailey was tight with his money, but I doubted that even he would bury his wife here if she'd died of natural causes. Assuming, of course, that this was Eunice Bailey.

I appointed Tom Challis as exhibits officer, and sent for a laboratory liaison officer. The LLO, a detective sergeant called 'Shiner' Wright, would be responsible for the body from now until all the scientific tests on it had been concluded.

At midnight, Henry Mortlock appeared on the scene.

'D'you have to dig up dead bodies at this time of night, Harry?' he asked gloomily. 'I'd much prefer it if you did it at about ten in the morning. Upsets my schedule, and plays merry hell with my eating habits.' He set down his bag of ghoulish instruments and began humming a few bars from Strauss's *Blue Danube* as he bent to examine our find. 'Probably dead,' he said. 'Where d'you find it?'

'Where it is now, Henry. What did you think, that we found it in the street and dumped it in that hole to keep it out of the rain?'

'It's not raining, dear boy,' said Mortlock. 'And I hope it stays that way. I was supposed to be playing golf tomorrow. Before you went about digging up bodies.'

'All right to lift it out?'

'Yes, fetch it up, and let's have a look at it.'

I should explain that the aptly named Henry Mortlock has a macabre sense of humour, but that, I imagine, is to be expected of a man who's dealt with more dead bodies than most people have had hot dinners. He was also an opera buff, and I was a little surprised at his choice of a Strauss waltz for this particular occasion. Maybe he had an arcane repertoire of music for different situations.

'Perhaps you'd be so good as to cut away this plastic covering, Miss Mitchell,' said Henry, once the body had been brought out and laid on the floor beside its shallow grave. 'But be very careful.'

That was a dangerous thing to say to Linda Mitchell. 'I have dealt with dead bodies before, Dr Mortlock,' she said curtly, as she began to strip the covering from the human remains.

Mortlock looked at me and grinned.

There was a certain amount of deterioration to the body – especially to the face – which was only to be expected. It did, however, prevent us from positively identifying the remains, beyond the fact that it was female, as those of Eunice Bailey, although I was in no doubt it was she. And that meant that we'd have to rely on DNA and fingerprints.

Linda Mitchell arrived at the same conclusion at the same time. 'Looks as though identification's going to be a problem, Mr Brock. I'll get the house searched for fingerprints. And we might be lucky enough to find a hairbrush that has a hair with a root, but don't bank on it.'

'I don't suppose you'd be prepared to hazard a guess at time of death, Henry, would you?' I asked.

Mortlock laughed. '*Date* of death would be difficult, dear boy, never mind time. But I can say this with a reasonable measure of confidence: judging by its condition, that cadaver has been there less than one year. I'll probably be able to narrow it even further after the post-mortem.'

Splendid. We knew that Martin Bailey had occupied this house for at least five years – that had been on the certificate of his second marriage – so he couldn't blame the human remains on a previous occupier.

'There's something else down here, Mr Brock,' said Trevor, who was peering into the depression from which the body had just been disinterred.

'Fetch it out, then.'

Lying flat on protective boarding, Trevor removed a small plastic-covered package, and handed it to me. 'It's a knife,' he said.

'Oh, that we should be so lucky,' I commented, handing the package to Linda. 'Your department, I think.'

Linda examined the package. 'It appears to be bloodstained, Mr Brock, and with any luck there'll be fingerprints on it,' she said, placing it in an evidence bag, and handing it to me. 'We'll let the lab unwrap it.'

I gave the evidence bag to Tom Challis. 'Get that up to the lab straight away, Tom, and they'll send it on to Fingerprint Bureau when they've done with it. If I'm right, it'll be Bailey's fingerprints on that knife.'

Having dealt with that, a belated thought occurred to me. 'Kate,' I said, 'did Jane Grant turn up here, by any chance? She was released on bail from Charing Cross at about the time we arrested Bailey.'

Kate shook her head. 'She hasn't been back here, guv.'

'Guilty knowledge,' commented Dave. But he always said that.

Nevertheless, I began to wonder whether Dave might be right, and it had been a mistake to admit Bailey's lover to bail. Perhaps she was possessed of greater cunning than I'd given her credit for, and maybe she knew more – much more – than she had told us. And she might've taken a bigger part in all this than she'd confessed to. However, we had other more pressing matters to deal with right now.

Linda Mitchell began a search throughout the house for fingerprints. She also found a hairbrush with some hairs on it that she had hopes of using for a DNA comparison. But it would take time, despite the fact that Linda and her team had promised to work through what remained of the night.

The body was removed to Henry Mortlock's favourite carvery – Horseferry Road in Westminster – and the house was secured as a crime scene.

'What's the drill for tomorrow, guv?' asked Dave.

I glanced at my watch. It was now two o'clock in the morning. 'I'll see you at Curtis Green just before eleven, Dave,' I said. 'And we'll go straight to Charing Cross nick. I'm looking forward to having another word with Martin Bailey to see what explanation he has for the body in his basement.'

My final word was with one of the local PCs who'd been assigned to guard the property. 'If a Miss Jane Grant turns up here, she's not to be admitted for any reason. Tell her to put up at a local hotel. The Job will pick up the tab,' I added, trying not to think what the commander's reaction would be to such profligate use of the Police Fund. 'And if Miss Grant gives you any hassle, speak to Detective Inspector Ebdon, who's inside.'

'What does this Jane Grant look like, sir?' asked the constable.

'She's a gorgeous blonde, twenty-five, and with an hour-glass figure.'

'Cor!' said the policeman, licking his lips.

'Don't go getting any ideas,' I said. 'I might yet charge her with conspiracy to murder.'

The policeman was suitably impressed, and I could visualize him regaling his mates in the canteen with the story of how he'd played a major part in a murder investigation.

Twenty

D ave and I arrived at Charing Cross police station on the stroke of eleven o'clock, and it was just as well that we'd left it no later.

Martin Bailey and his solicitor were coming down the steps, chatting animatedly to each other. Each had a triumphant smile on his face, a smile that broadened when they caught sight of Dave and me.

'My client was granted bail by a judge in chambers this morning, *Chief* Inspector,' said Bailey's solicitor smugly. He was still emphasizing my rank. 'And His Honour expressed the opinion that the statement you obtained from Miss Grant in no way justified keeping Mr Bailey in custody. The judge therefore directed that he should be released forthwith.'

'I think the judge was probably right,' I said.

'You agree?' The solicitor seemed astonished, and at once pleased, that such an admission should have come so easily from a policeman whom he'd probably believed was none too good at his job. 'Furthermore, I previously warned you that proceedings would be commenced for wrongful arrest and false imprisonment. Well, Chief Inspector, that's going to happen. My client's reputation as an upstanding member of the business community has been besmirched by this whole ridiculous affair, and he will be seeking substantial financial redress.'

'Yes,' I said, having let Bailey's brief go on unchecked, 'but that's all in the future, isn't it? In the meantime,' I continued, stepping closer to his client and seizing his arm, 'Martin Bailey, I'm arresting you on suspicion of the murder of Eunice Bailey.' I turned to Dave. 'Sergeant.'

And off went Dave again, reciting the caution word-perfect.

Bailey was visibly stunned, and so, to a lesser extent, was his solicitor. But it was the latter who spoke.

'This is preposterous. An outrage. It's quite clear to me, Chief Inspector, that for some reason best known to yourself, you are conducting a vendetta against my client. I shall lodge a formal complaint to the Commissioner and to the Independent Police Complaints Commission. And this time you won't talk your way out of it as you did on the previous occasion.' Bailey's solicitor obviously hadn't forgotten the exchange we'd had when he'd complained previously. 'I assure you that you've not heard the last of this, not by a long chalk.'

'Are you coming in?' I asked the solicitor, as Dave steered Bailey back into the police station.

'I most certainly am, and I insist on being present when you question Mr Bailey. I warn you, Chief Inspector, that I shall take this matter to the House of Lords if necessary.'

'That's your right, of course, although I'm only going to take it as far as the Old Bailey,' I said. 'But you're wasting your time. I don't intend to question your client at this stage.'

The solicitor stopped abruptly, and turned to face me. 'I presume by that remark,' he said acidly, 'that you still don't have any evidence against my client.'

'I have plenty of evidence, believe me,' I said, 'and it will be disclosed to you when I'm ready to do so. Now, if you'll excuse me, I have work to do.'

But the solicitor didn't give up that easily, and insisted on being present while the custody sergeant filled out all the forms that are a necessary prerequisite to detaining a person at a police station. Presumably the lawyer had to justify the exorbitant fee he would later charge Martin Bailey.

'Didn't expect to see you again so soon, Mr Bailey,' said the custody sergeant, with a broad grin.

It was a comment that pleased neither Bailey nor his solicitor.

Linda Mitchell and the rest of the forensic-science people, working all out, had done a superb job. By four o'clock that afternoon, I was in possession of all I needed to make a case against Martin Bailey.

The body had been positively identified as that of Eunice Bailey, and the knife found beneath it bore fingerprints which tallied with the set I'd had taken from Bailey. And the blood on the knife matched Eunice's. Gotcha!

Henry Mortlock's preliminary findings were that Eunice Bailey had died as a result of the knife penetrating the neck beneath the floor of the skull. In almost unfathomable medico-legal jargon, he had mentioned, in great detail, how the jugular vein and the medulla had played a part in her death, but the conclusion was that Eunice Bailey had been murdered. But then I'd guessed that.

'Have Bailey brought up to an interview room, Skip,' I said to the custody sergeant.

'Right away, sir.'

A few minutes later, Dave and I were face to face with Martin Bailey once more.

'What the hell's all this about murder?' demanded Bailey, maintaining his usual aggressive stance.

'I suggest you sit quietly and listen,' I said, once Dave had cautioned the arrogant entrepreneur. 'Late last night, we searched your house at Coburn Street, in the course of which we found the body of your wife, Eunice Bailey, buried in the cellar beneath a covering of concrete. We also found a blood-stained knife bearing fingerprints that have been matched to those we took from you when you were arrested. The forensic pathologist has determined the cause of death as stabbing with that knife. And now, I suppose, you want me to send for your solicitor.'

'Do I hell!' exclaimed Bailey. 'He's a useless bastard. All he does is make soothing noises, attacks the police, and then sends me a hefty bill.'

'Martin Bailey, I shall shortly charge you with murder. But is there anything you wish to say before I do so? I must warn you, again, that you're not obliged to say anything, and you're under no obligation to answer any questions we may put to you.'

'Looks like you've got me bang to rights.' It was a rare admission for a man like Bailey to make. But there was no doubt that he'd been badly shocked by the discovery we'd made, and the other evidence we'd gathered.

'Is that all you wish to say?'

'What's going to happen to Jane?'

'That rather depends on anything else you may wish to add. But at the moment, I have it in mind to charge her with conspiracy to murder.'

'That poor innocent kid didn't know a thing about the murder. I told her it was a scam to claim money on an insurance policy I'd taken out on Eunice's life, and that Eunice would disappear after we'd shared the proceeds. But there *was* no insurance policy. And if it hadn't been for Eunice's bloody wedding ring, I might've got away with it. I didn't know anything about her having it enlarged until you people came knocking on my door.'

He was certainly right about that. If it hadn't been for the ring, Bailey almost certainly would have got away with murder.

'By which time, I imagine, you'd already murdered Eunice.'

'Yes. On Tuesday the eighteenth of June, two days after we'd got back from Bermuda. The day you people turned up on my doorstep.' Bailey laughed, a macabre sort of laugh. 'You didn't know it, but Eunice's body was already lying in the cellar when you called.'

'It was you who was masquerading as Nigel Skinner in Bermuda, was it?'

'Yes.' Bailey laughed again. 'Serve the bastard right. D'you know he tried to recruit Eunice to take part in some porn film? So I thought I'd make him squirm a bit, because I knew you people would make enquiries in Bermuda, and that you'd give him a hard time.'

'Skinner actually finished up being arrested,' I said.

'Yeah, I saw something about it in the paper.' That seemed to afford Bailey some amusement.

'D'you want to tell us why you murdered your wife, Mr Bailey?' asked Dave.

'She was threatening to divorce me for adultery and mental cruelty. She'd hired some bloody private detective and he'd got all the evidence. One evening, she waltzed into the sitting room, sat down opposite me, and calmly told me she intended to take me for at least four million quid, plus two hundred and fifty grand a year for life.'

'And did she have the evidence?'

'Too right. She threw a load of photographs on the table that her miserable little gumshoe had taken of me with women in nightclubs, and one of a woman he'd claimed was a prostitute. Unfortunately, he was right; she was, and he'd got a statement from her. There was even a photo of me coming out of some woman's house in the small hours. Would you believe that? Well, I'd seen some of the settlements those bewigged bastards in the High Court had handed out, and I was going to make bloody sure they weren't going to do it to me. A few years ago, I made the mistake of going over the side with Eunice while I was still married to Gina, and Gina saw me off for two million, the bitch, and I wasn't going to let it happen again.'

'So you saw murder as the answer.'

'It was a last resort, Chief Inspector. I couldn't see any other way. Mind you, I thought that I was in the clear when Eunice laughingly told me that Skinner wanted her to make a blue movie, and I told her to go ahead. I knew that if she did, she'd have no chance of fleecing me in the divorce courts. But she obviously saw that coming, and turned down the offer. Frankly, I don't think she had any intention of becoming a porn actress; I reckon she was just winding me up. A crafty cow, was Eunice.'

'I take it you knew about Eunice and Tom Nelson,' I suggested.

'I didn't know anything about him, not until you told me about this anonymous guy who'd taken Eunice to Bermuda. When I found the credit card, I knew I hadn't given it to her. I suspected she was having it off with someone, and I had her followed by a private detective, but he didn't come up with anything. And I'm not talking about that idiot ex-copper, John somebody, either. I only took him on for the sake of appearances, so that it would look as though I was looking for Eunice. But he grassed me up to you lot.'

'So you went to Bermuda, pretending to be Skinner, and somehow persuaded Eunice to return to England with you. How did you manage that?'

'Rapprochement,' said Bailey.

I don't know where Bailey discovered a word like that, but Dave nodded approvingly.

'Really?'

'Yes, I buttered her up. Apologized for all my past sins, and promised that things would be different in future. That we'd hit the high life, and spend, spend, spend.'

'And she swallowed that, did she?' I asked.

'Of course she did. There were times when she could be quite naive, but she was cunning when it came to money. And that made her bright enough to realize that being the wife of a millionaire was not something to be given up lightly, and although she thought she could take me for four mill, I knew better. But divorces can go either way, and I wasn't prepared to take the chance. So I persuaded her to come back home. It was time to kiss and make up, I told her.'

'There was no record of you flying out of Bermuda,' observed Dave.

'Of course there wasn't. I knew you'd check that, so I chartered a private plane to take us from Bermuda to North Carolina, and we took a scheduled flight from Charlotte to Gatwick. I think you know the rest. I went out in search of some blonde airhead to help me with the insurance story, and was lucky enough to find Jane Grant in a nightclub. Well, I spent a few quid on her, and gave her twenty grand up front to play along with my fictional scam. Eunice still had the credit card that you say Nelson had given her, so I got Jane to pop over to Bermuda and spread it around.'

'And the clothing on the beach?'

'I remember reading about some Member of Parliament who'd done that many years ago, and I thought that you lot would come to the conclusion that she'd drowned. End of story.'

'We know it wasn't you who put the clothing there, so who did?'

Bailey laughed. 'That's something you'll have to find out for yourself, isn't it? I'm not a grass. Anyway, he got well paid for his trouble. And he's not committed any crime. Just left a few bits of clothing on a beach without knowing why he was doing it. What are you going to nick him for, leaving litter? Forty dollars, top whack. If he's unlucky.'

And that was that.

Bailey's trial ran its inevitable course, as all good murder trials should. When he was arraigned at the Central Criminal Court at the Old Bailey, he pleaded not guilty. Why not? But, despite the forensic skills of his learned counsel, the jury was having none of it.

Once evidence of his chicanery had been adduced, the twelve wise men and women concluded that he had committed a cunning and premeditated murder. But he'd not been quite cunning enough to fool them, and they found him guilty.

Like so many killers who had gone before him, he'd slipped up on minor points. One of those points had been ordering only two inches of concrete to be spread on his cellar floor. Had it been six inches, we might've accepted that he wanted to use the cellar to store wine. There again, perhaps not. Another was to have Jane Grant use the credit card that Tom Nelson had given Eunice. It would have been far better if he'd not done so, because all he'd achieved was to draw attention to the girl. Inevitably, at the end of it all, he was sentenced to life imprisonment.

'At least we won't be subpoenaed to give evidence in Bailey's divorce case,' said Dave, peeling a banana. 'I don't like the civil courts.'

Almost the first person we met on our return to Curtis Green was the commander on his way to his office.

'I knew there was something in that missing-person report, Mr Brock,' he said, without breaking step.

Doesn't it just make you sick?

There was, however, a sad and uncanny corollary that concerned Jane Grant.

Bailey's girlfriend and accomplice never returned to Coburn Street, even on the night we found Eunice Bailey's body. Neither did she answer to bail at Charing Cross police station. Not that it mattered; the Crown Prosecution Service had decided that she had no case to answer.

But six months after Martin Bailey began his sentence, I received a phone call from Don Mercer in Bermuda.

'We had occasion to search Martin Bailey's cottage at Flatt's Village this morning, Harry. It looks as though Jane Grant had been living there for the past six months. Among her property, we found bank statements that showed she was worth about fifteen grand sterling.'

'What the hell did you search the cottage for in the first place, Don?' I asked.

'You're going to find this hard to believe, Harry,' Mercer

said, 'but this morning some clothing was found on Shelley Bay Beach. It turned out to belong to Jane Grant. It looks very much as though she'd gone for an early morning swim and got caught by a rip tide. Her body was washed up several hours later. No suspicion of foul play.'